ONE NIGHT OF PASSION

Desire spread through her. She wanted him. All of him. Inside her.

"My lady," he murmured.

Sighing, she threaded her fingers into his hair, enjoying the crisp, prickly texture against her palms.

She could love a man such as him. The thought gave her pause, but he leaned forward and swirled his tongue around one of her nipples before she could entertain it.

"James," she murmured, closing her eyes.

Raising his head, he gazed at her. His eyes glowed with blue fire. In several skilled motions, he made quick work of the dress. The hard metal was cold against her skin and the garment fell away in slices . . .

Books by Jessica Trapp

MASTER OF DESIRE

MASTER OF PLEASURE

THE PLEASURES OF SIN

Published by Kensington Publishing Corporation

The Pleasures of Sin

JESSICA TRAPP

ZEBRA BOOKS
Kensington Publishing Corp.
http://www.kensingtonbooks.com

ZEBRA BOOKS are published by

Kensington Publishing Corp.
119 West 40th Street
New York, NY 10018

All Kensington titles, imprints, and distributed lines are
available at special quantity discounts for bulk purchases
for sales promotion, premiums, fund-raising, educational, or
institutional use.

Special book excerpts or customized printings can also be cre-
ated to fit specific needs. For details, write or phone the office
of the Kensington Special Sales Manager: Attn. Special Sales
Department. Kensington Publishing Corp., 119 West 40th
Street, New York, NY 10018. Phone: 1-800-221-2647.

Zebra and the Z logo Reg. U.S. Pat. & TM Off.

ISBN-13: 978-1-4201-0094-5
ISBN-10: 1-4201-0094-7

First Zebra Printing: May 2009
10 9 8 7 6 5 4 3 2 1

Printed in the United States of America

To my son
You are an amazing creative soul.
My life has been enriched because you are in it.
Thank you for your patience, your support, and your love.
And don't read this book until you're older.
Because I said so, that's why.
grin
I love you.

Acknowledgments

I am grateful for the many, many people who have encouraged me—I have been blessed beyond my wildest dreams. This is a very incomplete list.

Thank you, Joe, for your love and care. The research *wink* was pretty good too.

Thank you, Mom, for being a sounding board.

Thank you, Betty Pichardo, for your friendship and prayers. And the shoe shopping.

Thank you, Terri Richardson, for your support and help.

Thank you, Ann Peake, for your imagination.

Thank you, Sara King, for your critique.

Thank you, Suzy Kasper, for your keen eye and soft heart.

Thank you, 100 group, for your support and tough love.

Thank you, Romance Unleashed Authors, for being there.

Thank you, Artist Wayers, for your uplifting spirits.

Thank you, Sha-Shana Crichton, for your help and belief.

Thank you, John Scognamiglio, for all you do.

Chapter One

Lady Brenna enjoyed her banishment to the musty north tower.

Shivering with the thrill of rebellion, she tossed her kirtle onto the floor planks, perched naked on a three-legged stool, and lifted one of her many paintbrushes to capture what she saw in the looking glass.

Alone, isolated from the rest of the castlefolk, she reveled that she could shun the very garments that defined her lot as a pawn in men's war. Her refusal to marry and insistence on entering a convent had not set well with Papa.

The scent of spike lavender oil curled into the air as she stroked her brush across parchment, transforming her chamber from prison to sanctuary. Here she could paint. Here she could dream. Here she was free from society's demands and duties.

A crimson trail unfurled from the tip of her paintbrush: the tongue of passion that drew a spread-legged view of a young noblewoman with springy copper-colored hair on both her head and nether lips. A nude of herself, painted as she gazed into the looking glass.

So much more lush and naughty than the many proper paintings of saints and angels propped haphazardly about the chamber.

The crossbar scraped against the bedchamber door, and she jumped, smearing a brushstroke.

"Devil take it!" she cursed, launching into a mad rush to cover the parchment and snatch her kirtle over her body before the intruder discovered the subject matter of this painting.

Her skirt swirled around her ankles just as the door banged open. The three-legged stool clattered and tipped over.

"Brenna, you must help us!" Her sister Gwyneth rushed inside, wearing a disheveled silver-blue wedding houpelande. An enormous butterfly headdress covered with a rich veil propped precariously on her head. Curly strands of her golden hair bounced around her like a flailing mop, and tufts of ermine trim floated into the air.

Heart pounding, Brenna shielded her miniature like a mother protecting a child. She'd been banished to this tower a year ago because she wanted a life of her own, a chance to make her own way in the world.

She'd defied her father—refused to marry and had boldly told him she would run away and join a convent. If Papa found her erotic works, he'd burn her painting supplies. If the town's head churchman, Bishop Humphrey, found them *she* would be burned.

"My bridegroom—James—the wedding—" Gwyneth's words tumbled over one another, each one rising in pitch. Tendrils of golden hair escaped from her curled and coifed arrangement as if she'd been tearing at the strands in panicked worry. The butterfly headdress slid to one side, and her veil hung haphazardly in her hair, clinging halfway down the length by one hairpin.

Thrusting her brush into a jar of spike lavender oil, Brenna composed her features as her sister closed in on her. "The wedding took place this morn, did it not?" She'd listened for the shouts of jubilation that should have filled the great hall hours ago, then decided perhaps the guests had been too few for the sound to carry to her tower.

"Papa—the woods—sunrise—" Hands shaking, Gwyneth rattled across the floor planks like a skeleton quivering in the breeze. She nearly tripped over a large board painting of the birth of Christ that lay drying. "The men—the weapons—"

Brenna pursed her lips; her worry about the erotic paintings evaporated. Gwyneth was too wrapped in her own issues to notice the nature of artwork.

"Take a deep breath, sister."

Sucking in several gulps of air, Gwyneth tugged the sleeve of Brenna's simple kirtle. Her soft fingers looked out of place against the paint-splotched and threadbare garment.

"Papa's been captured!" Gwyneth finally gasped out.

Fear iced Brenna's stomach. "Dear stars! What happened?"

"Papa ambushed the wedding party as they traveled here, and The Enforcer took him hostage."

The Enforcer.

James Vaughn, Earl of Montgomery. A privateer commanded by the king to annihilate smugglers and rebels.

Her sister's fiancé.

"Bloody hell," Brenna cursed, then winced remembering the beating Papa had given her last time she'd spoken bad language aloud.

She squeezed her sister's shoulders. The Enforcer punished any who dared question King Edward's ultimate authority. It was said he killed whole crews of ships' men and confiscated honest cargo, murdering and stealing all in the name of the crown.

She and her father had issues, but he was still her papa. And she did not want him destroyed at the hand of some monster.

"Papa tried to stop the wedding."

Ice turned to fury. Brenna felt a wave of frustration that she'd been locked in her chamber and knew so little of the comings and goings of the household. "Of all the idiotic—Papa's a dunderhead, I tell you! Why the devil did he ambush the earl? I thought he wanted you to marry him." *And you always do as you are told.*

"He did. But I–I–I–" Tears leaked down Gwyneth's pale heart-shaped face and dripped off her pert little chin.

Brenna resisted the urge to shake her sister. "Tell me."

"James of Montgomery is a b–beast! He killed his last wife in cold blood." Gwyneth covered her eyes with her hands and began to cry loud, moaning wails. "I didn't want to marry him—and I told Father—and—"

"Tsk, tsk." Turning her sister by the shoulders, Brenna led her toward the large four-poster bed, sat and hugged her while Gwyneth blubbered incoherently. Her brows had been freshly plucked, and she smelled of wedding scents—fresh lavender, silk, and wildflowers.

A sting of jealousy catapulted into Brenna's heart. Both of them had refused marriage. But her father had declared imprisonment for her and a war party to defend Gwyneth!

She shoved her envy aside and stared at the vase of purple foxglove on her painting desk. Where others had forgotten her, Gwyneth brought her flowers.

'Twas not her sister's fault that their father loved her more.

Gwyneth sniveled into her hands, sniffing and wiping at her eyes.

From her seat on the bed, Brenna peered out the open door and wrapped her arms tighter around her sister. Now would be a good time to escape. She was ready: gold and food were packed in a small parcel beneath her bed along with pots of pigment and her favorite paintbrush, the tiny hog's hair one. She had a letter from Mother Isabella, the abbess of La Signora del Lago, a nunnery in Italy along the coast.

Brother Giffard, the traveling monk, had arranged for her passage on a ship leaving for Italy at week's end. 'Twas a voyage fraught with danger, but an escort was set to meet her and she had plans to take shelter at her brother's home until she could make it to La Signora del Lago. If Nathan knew she was coming, he would try to stop her, but he would not turn her away if she showed up on his doorstep. For months she'd been practicing with a knife to be able to protect herself if need be.

Snatching her pack and leaving while the door was unbolted and the castle was in chaos would make her getaway easy. Her sister would marry Montgomery, her father would be set free, and she would be gone afore anyone realized what had happened.

After a few moments of hysteria, Gwyneth lifted her tear-stained face toward Brenna and began fumbling with the mother-of-pearl buttons on her houpelande. Around her, the bed curtains shivered.

"Gwyneth! What are you doing?"

"Montgomery plans to hang Father at sunset unless I agree to marry him. But I cannot. You have to help me."

Oh, for heaven's sake. Pulling Gwyneth's fingers from her buttons, Brenna stroked the back of her hand. "Peace, sister. Montgomery is an earl, a wealthy one at that. 'Tis no sacrifice to marry him."

"Brenna," Gwyneth choked out through tears, "I–I saw him at the faire. He's the spawn of Satan. He nigh beat a man to death with his bare hands. He's huge and strong. It took three large men to pull him off of the wretch."

"Surely he had reason—"

"Nay, sister, he did not. 'Twas because the man spilt a few drops of ale on his new paltock. Adele and I followed him from the tournament field to see him without his armor and helm. He's a hideous scarred monster—his face full of white, puckered skin instead of a man's features. Children ran from his pathway."

With a hearty tug, Gwyneth yanked a wicked-looking dagger from the bodice of her voluptuous gown. The blade was short, only as long as a woman's palm, but it gleamed sharply. It had a small pommel and a red ruby winked in its hilt.

"Our family will ne'er be safe if I marry him. He must die!"

Her sister had gone mad! "Cease, Gwyneth. This is daftness. You cannot murder anyone."

"Nay, sister, not me—you!"

"Me?"

Gwyneth waved the blade in the air, pointing to a painted wooden target that was half-hidden behind an enormous canvas containing a scene with a glowing risen Christ and his worshipful followers gazing into the heavens. Using canvas, a gift from Brother Giffard, instead of boards or parchment was new to her, so Brenna was especially pleased with the piece.

"I know of your skill with a knife," Gwyneth said pointedly, not even noticing the new painting. "Of your practice with a blade."

Brenna blinked at the charge, and tamped down the small disappointment that her sister did not notice the canvas. 'Twas true she'd spent hours plunging daggers into that scrap of wood in preparation for her trip to Italy, but she was no murderess. "My knives are for protection!"

"Then protect us." Gwyneth held the dagger high in the air. The sharp blade shook in her fingers as if 'twas possessed by Lucifer himself. "Kill The Enforcer. This is a special blade—*l'occhio del diavolo.*"

Italian, the language Brenna had been studying. *L'occhio del diavolo:* The Devil's Eye. What an odd name for a dagger.

Brenna lurched to her feet; her paint-splattered kirtle swirled about her ankles. Best to get this situation under control afore her sister cut herself.

"Give me that, you ninny! No one is going to kill anyone." She grabbed the weapon, stalked to her table, swiped back the mortars she used to mix her paints, and set *l'occhio del diavolo* on the far side of the cluttered surface. Brushes scattered onto the floor. The scent of turpentine and oil of spike lavender floated around them.

In a quick slight of hand, she covered the nude self-portrait with a rag.

At Gwyneth's downtrodden look, Brenna quickly added, "You will mar your lovely hands, sister."

"Devil rot my hands."

At that moment Duncan, a scrappy black-and-tan terrier, and the slight figure of Adele, Brenna's younger sister, burst into the room. She, too, wore wedding finery: a heavy blue velvet gown with fanciful dagged sleeves and a steepled hennin on her head. She held St. Paul, her gray cat, in one hand and her staff in the other. Her frothy black hair fluffed around her shoulders and down her back past an embroidered gold girdle at her hips. Panthos, her large mastiff, flanked her, panting his retched breath into the chamber.

Leaning heavily on her cane, Adele wended through the scattered maze of painted boards as heedless of her artwork as Gwyneth had been. "Montgomery has reached the castle! Father is tied and being dragged across the courtyard on his knees. Make haste! You must stand in Gwyneth's stead for the marriage ceremony and kill Montgomery tonight."

Brenna looked from one of her sisters to the other. How could they ask this of her, after all she'd gone through without asking help from either of them? She glanced around at the paintings of saints and angels that had been her companions these past months during her confinement.

"I am not going to kill anyone."

"You must," Gwyneth insisted. "You are the only one who stands a chance."

The mastiff barked, and Adele held her hand out to calm him. Her oval face looked pensive. "Victory starts with Montgomery's death. We will inform Father Peter of the bride change. You must slay The Enforcer in the bridal chamber when you see the snuffing of the candle in the chamber across the bailey. That will be the signal that the men are in place and ready to retake the castle and free our father."

And then your father would love you, a dark voice whispered inside her mind. *You would be a heroine instead of a burden.*

"This is lunacy." Out of habit, Brenna reached for the fat, wooden cross that usually hung around her neck. When she realized it wasn't there, she picked up a paintbrush and turned it over and over in her fingers. "I am to be a bride of Christ. I cannot harm anyone."

Gwyneth rolled her eyes. "As Father says, you are ill suited for a nunnery."

"Ne'ertheless, I intend to give my life to God." She indicated the myriad of religious paintings strewn about the chamber, hoping to further her claim. She would be damned if she was going to end up like her mother, waiting hand and foot on an inattentive man with a passel of brats to care for until she collapsed from sheer exhaustion. Better to live in a convent.

The fact that Bishop Humphrey refused to consider hanging her art even in one of the cathedral's privies was one more proof why she needed to leave England and head to Italy where she could join a nunnery and become powerful in her own right.

"I have seen your targets. You wield a dagger and paintbrush with equal aplomb," Adele insisted. "You can do this deed."

"A few months of practice hardly equals master—"

"You *can* do it!" Gwyneth swirled toward her, ermine trim flying. "You defended me against Lord Brice. And set Sir Edward's breeches on fire. And shot Thomas in the arse with an arr—"

"Zwounds, sister, hush your babble." Brenna clapped her hands over her ears, not wanting to hear any more of her supposed sins listed. Her father railed at her enough. "Those men deserved it. And"—she glanced around at her prison of a bedchamber—"I'm still paying penance."

Gwyneth slid next to her, touching her on the arm. "I know of your plans to go to Italy. That you have been exchanging letters with the abbess of La Signora del Lago."

Brenna winced at the discovery. But of course, Gwyneth would know. Adored by the servants and brightly sociable, her sister knew all the workings of the castle. She'd probably crafted some damn needlework to mark the event.

"Just do this one last deed, and we will help you on your journey. For certes, Father would grant you permission to enter the convent."

Permission. The one thing she needed to be accepted into the holy order.

Adele rapped her cane on the planks, causing her raven hair to bounce. Duncan barked and scurried atop a trunk. "We will have men ready to whisk you away as soon as Montgomery is dead. They will be outside this door when we give the signal, and Panthos will lead you out the back tunnel to a safe cottage by the river."

"Panthos?" The mastiff. "I'm to commit murder, then be led by a *dog* to escape the wrath of The Enforcer's men?" Both of her sisters had turned lunatic.

"Aye," Adele said calmly. Her intense, dark eyes shone with intelligence, not fever. St. Paul stretched languidly in her arms and let out a loud purr. "I have told Panthos of your danger, and he has agreed to protect you. Duncan will go with you as well; he is good at catching rabbits."

Brenna perused her dark-haired sister who was composed and serene, floating as always in her secret ethereal haze above the pain of her deformed leg and the chaos of the earth. Of a truth, she had uncanny kindred with the beasts of nature, but—to be led by one dog and fed by the other?

"You are both daft."

Panthos sat on his haunches and cocked his head at her.

"You too," she told him.

"Prithee, Brenna." Gwyneth shuddered, and the stiff silvery-blue houpelande rustled with the motion.

Gwyneth's silky skirt contrasted with Brenna's own shabby, faded wool one. More proof of their father's love toward his favored daughter. She tamped down the ache in her chest. If only she could have won even half as much of his love. Her father had taken all of her beautiful clothing away years ago. As a nun, she would have to give them up anyway, but her chest still ached from the memory.

Gwyneth plucked the falling headdress and veil from her blond hair and set it on Brenna's head. The veil was a thick material sewed with tiny pearls. The heavy frame that fashioned the hat into a butterfly shape felt awkward and foreign.

"We are nigh the same height, and if we cover your red hair, he will not suspect," Gwyneth said.

Brenna snorted. The elaborate hat looked bizarre against her simple clothing. Save for the height, she and Gwyneth looked naught alike. Especially not since she'd hacked off her thigh length curls. Gwyneth's hair, when loose, was a mass of shimmering gold that hung past her hips; her own was a close cropped mess.

Reaching up, Brenna touched the scar on her cheek that ran from her ear to the bridge of her nose

and lifted a strand of her copper hair. 'Twas shorter
than *l'occhio del diavolo* and not nearly as symmetrical.

"Surely Montgomery has heard you are the fairest
lady in all of England," Brenna said to Gwyneth.

Gwyneth shot her a sympathetic look, but did not
deny the charge. Both of them knew Gwyneth's beauty
was a possession most prized by their father—'twas the
thing that would catch the eye of a wealthy man so
he would have more gold to pump into his cause of
ridding England's throne of its king.

"I am sorry about your hair," Gwyneth said gently.
"I truly appreciate your sacrifice to save me from Lord
Brice. It was so brave of you to shear it and pretend
you were me so I could be rid of him."

Brave? Bloody hell. All she'd had to do was introduce
herself as Gwyneth. Without her long beauteous locks
to soften her features, her face had frightened him into
running like the very devil chased him. As if she was
plagued. No man wanted a scarred, ugly, shorn woman
as wife. Another reason her father should have allowed
her to enter the convent. Silently, she cursed his stubbornness. Why did he have to be so obstinate?

"What's done is done," Brenna said, refusing to
allow herself to dwell on her missing locks. What need
did an artist and a nun have for vanity?

Gwyneth reached up and patted Brenna's short
curls. "But I know you miss your hair. I've seen you tug
at the strands."

Adele rapped her cane again, causing the terrier to
run around in tight circles. "There is no time to talk of
hair! Get dressed, Brenna. Use the veil to cover your
scar—there is enough fabric to obscure your face. I
swear, I'd kill Montgomery myself, but for this lame
foot of mine. I do not look enough like Gwyneth to

pass, and only a bride will be able to get close enough to slay him."

Before Brenna could open her mouth to insist that she did not look like the beauteous Gwyneth either, Gwyneth scrambled from her wedding gown and held it out. "You have pretended to be me before; you can do it again."

Clad only in her shift, Gwyneth reminded Brenna of a specter. A specter of her *past*.

Brenna had a new life awaiting her in Italy. Glancing at the open door, she thought of her satchel beneath the bed.

"Oh, curse it all to the devil. This battle is not my concern," she said. She needed to leave. She could not spend her life rescuing her sister from one suitor or the next. "Marry the man and he'll set Father free. With your looks, you'll be able to bend him to your will."

At that moment, thunderous footsteps clamored up the stairs of the tower.

The chamber door banged open.

The three sisters gasped. The dogs barked, and St. Paul bolted beneath the bed.

The largest pair of men Brenna had ever seen stepped inside the room. They were fully clad in chain mail and armor and seemed to be at least seven feet in height.

One had eyes so blue they glowed like the coals of hell beneath his full-face helm. He carried a large broadsword. The other held a crossbow at the ready. They seemed to scrutinize the bed, the trunks, the table-desk, and the paintings before gazing intently at Brenna and her sisters.

Gwyneth, still in her shift, tried to hide behind Brenna and Adele.

The mastiff barked wildly, rearing upward. Adele held him by the collar, bracing her booted feet against the floor. Her hennin bobbed. The terrier leapt into the window embrasure seat and growled low.

"Call him off," the crossbow-man commanded, swinging his weapon around to the mastiff. He was a tall, dangerous looking brute with a missing finger.

Gwyneth grasped Brenna's hand in a clammy grip.

With a few whispered words, Adele calmed Panthos. Duncan tucked his tail and bolted beneath the bed with St. Paul.

"I am here to collect my bride. Which of you is she?" the man with the wicked blue eyes asked. He swung around to Gwyneth, seeming to take in her sunshine-like beauty.

Chain mail clinked as he reached for her, more beast than man. Huge hands. Brawny shoulders. An arrogant masculine presence. *Bloody hell.*

He was worse even than Lord Brice.

He'd eat her sister alive.

Gwyneth gave Brenna a look of pleading desperation as the man's brutish hand touched the pristine linen of her shift. Her pulse fluttered in her neck.

With one last glance at the satchel under the bed, Brenna stepped forward, pushed Gwyneth firmly behind herself, and faced off the monster. She could not leave her sister to be raped and ravished by this fiend. Her skill with a knife would have to be enough.

She said a silent prayer of thanksgiving that Gwyneth had shoved the veil on her head so that her scar was partially hidden and the man would not see her unevenly chopped locks.

"I am your bride, my lord. Just give me a moment to change into my wedding gown." *And hide the dagger.*

Chapter Two

He *would* have revenge.

Through the eye slits in his helmet, James of Montgomery glowered at the hostile crowd gathered near the steps of the chapel for the wedding. Lecrow, the lord of this keep and the bastard who had ambushed him this morn, knelt between two guards, tied in place by ropes. He was a squirrelly, gray-bearded man with fanatical eyes. James vowed silently to see the man beaten and made a public example of in the streets of London.

"Easier to keep guard inside," he said to his men as he flung open the church doors and led them into the darkened sanctuary. His position as an earl allowed him to be married near the altar instead of on the outer steps. He latched his hand firmly around his wife-to-be's wrist and dragged her in his wake.

"Bring her father to the front to witness the ceremony," he barked at the two men holding Lecrow.

His duty was to bring peace to the region and he intended to crush the fight out of the old man by showing him that despite his little ambush, the wedding would go on. Just as the king had commanded. The town's prized port—currently under the command of the Baron of Windrose, but spelled out in the wedding contract to be turned over to James—would be a huge boon to his shipping trade.

He paced past the rows of pews. The others followed. They prodded Lecrow with the point of a sword, and he shuffled forward on his knees.

"You won't get awa—" Baron Lecrow started.

One of James's men drew a dagger and held it to Lecrow's throat, effectively silencing him.

James nodded approval and turned to the woman he was to marry.

Thankfully, his new wife was the strong, stubborn one instead of the weepy, teary-eyed blonde, as he had feared. This one may not enjoy being married to him, but at least he doubted he'd have to listen to tedious pleas for mercy on the wedding night. He had no use for the sniveling cries of women. And he had no intention of granting mercy.

Three of his men lay dead from this morn's attack. Jacob, Robert, and Collin. Good men all.

Guilt ate at him that he had led them to their deaths like defenseless sheep.

'Twas his duty to enforce the king's law and bring to heel the rebels who threatened the peace of England. The port was being used to smuggle in wine and weapons and needed tighter control. The wedding was arranged to bring stability to the region: both this woman and the prized port would be his.

The king had warned him of possible treachery, but he had not expected an outright attack.

Anger curled through him like a living demon as he thought of the price his men had paid.

The ambush had been a betrayal of the lowest kind. Her father had beguiled him to come here to Wind-rose, rather than his grander castle at Montgomery. His bride-to-be had sent him a sweet perfumed message.

And it all had been a ruse to kill him.

He could scarcely imagine this warrior-like queen standing beside him would write something so flowery and delicate.

Tightening his grip on his bride-to-be's wrist, he vowed by all that was holy that both she and her family would learn what it meant to bow to his rule. To live under The Enforcer.

Every step down the chapel's aisle sent another shot of fury pulsating through him.

"Slow down," the woman beside him whispered. Her enormous silver-blue gown rustled. "My slipper—oh, drat it all to hell—" She stumbled slightly, kicked off one of her pointed velvet slippers and righted herself.

The bride-to-be's father glared at him with narrowed eyes. He strained against the ropes.

The urge to take the man by the tunic and hang him from the large oak just on the other side of the sanctuary door snaked fiercely through James. But, nay. The man was a political prisoner, and the king himself must deal with his treason.

His hand tarried to the hilt of his sword, in case her tripping was a ruse to get him off guard so her father could attack. He would *not* be caught unaware again.

A heavy veil obscured her features, but he could feel her glowering at him. "I am coming. There is no need to drag me."

"Mind your tongue, wife."

She propped one hand on her hip, causing her

enormous butterfly headdress to tilt and ruin the serene loveliness of the silver-blue gown. "I am not your wife yet."

He bared his teeth at her, vowing both the stubborn old man *and* his rebellious daughter would be cowed afore this was over.

"You will be, wench." Squeezing her wrist, he pulled her the last few feet down the aisle. Did none in this family know when they had been squarely defeated and have the sense to submit?

A harpist and violist played an off-key wedding song, as if they hadn't had adequate time to tune their instruments.

The priest standing in front of the altar cleared his throat. He had a huge nose and watery eyes, which he rubbed from time to time on the sleeve of his robe. "Ready to begin, my lord?"

James nodded. "Make haste, priest. This helmet itches my neck."

The clergyman opened his Bible. "Dearly beloved . . ."

Not releasing her wrist, James peered down at the woman standing beside him. She stood as straight as any warrior, proud and sturdy. She was covered from head to toe in fabric just as he was clad in armor. Mother-of-pearl buttons lined her sleeves like tiny shields.

She didn't try to pull away from his grip, but she didn't stand any closer than she had to either. Her bones felt small within his grasp, and yet, strength of will radiated from her.

Yes, this marriage was a battlefield. And it would be true justice to bend her will to his. King Edward had demanded this union to bring peace to this turbulent region, and he would definitely start by conquering his own wife.

* * *

As Father Peter droned on with the wedding ceremony, Brenna seethed with anger that her new husband had hauled her here like a prized sow. Coldness from the floor tiles seeped into her one bare foot. Damned barbarian.

She twisted slightly to peer up at him.

He was the largest man she had ever seen—nearly seven feet in height with shoulders as wide as a bull's.

Huge. Enormous. Utterly grotesque. He reminded her of one of the fearsome warriors from her paintings. Only he was fully clad in battle gear, not naked as most of the figures in her artwork were.

He smelled of leather, blood, and the heady scent of male musk. Blood splattered across his blue surcoat, right at eye level.

A tiny bit of relief flowed through her that he didn't flinch when Father Peter mumbled her name. Thank the stars he did not realize he had been duped into marrying the wrong sister. Their union had been arranged by that bastard King Edward so mayhap he did not know the name of his future bride. Or mayhap he could not hear well with the helm on.

"I worship thee with my body," she gritted out when prompted, wishing she could grasp the dagger hidden in the bodice of the wedding gown to bolster her nerve.

Standing beside him here at the altar made her feel tiny, even shorter than usual.

She averted her eyes from the bloodstains on his surcoat and tilted her head back, wishing she could see beneath the shiny silver helm that concealed his features. She swallowed, thinking of her sister's assessment of his scarred face. Bloody hell. Was there nothing about the man that wasn't daunting? 'Twas no wonder children ran from him.

Hail Mary, full of grace, she began silently, unsure if she was saying a prayer or her last rites. Gwyneth said he'd murdered his last wife . . .

She'd have one chance with the dagger. And if she failed, only God knew what her punishment would be. With luck, he'd have her hung. But The Enforcer was not reputed to be a man who merely hung those who crossed him.

She squelched the shudder that threatened to quake her shoulders. Mayhap he was enormous and forbidding, but at the plunge of her dagger, he *would* bleed like any other beast.

"Kiss your bride," Father Peter said, squinting up at the man's covered face. He rubbed his watery eyes and gave Brenna a sympathetic look.

"My lady," her new husband taunted, his voice muffled because of the helmet.

Her heart pounded against the steel blade betwixt her breasts and gooseflesh popped up on her arms. By force of will, she remained stock-still in front of the altar, fighting the urge to flee. Nay, not kiss the beast!

"This is no love match," she sneered, fighting for a measure of control. "We have no need to kiss."

The warrior's palm covered hers, rough and large. Claiming. "The kiss seals our bargain."

Her stomach cramped. He'd been holding her wrist all through the ceremony like a manacle. She glanced down and, for an instant, was surprised to realize he had man-hands, not paws like a bear. He had long, blunt fingers with thick calluses. He was a privateer; no doubt his hands had been roughened from pulling the rigging on a ship. His grip was firm and strong, but not biting or painful.

Fresh from battle, his hands should have been filthy, but instead were clean as if freshly washed for the wedding. She wondered at that small measure of respect.

He pulled her closer and she checked the urge to withdraw her hand. Best to make him think she was cowed and submissive.

Damn beast. Loathsome, unholy barbarian. Brenna ducked her head to keep him from noticing her glower.

"As you wish, my lord," she said through clenched teeth. Tonight, she vowed, 'twould be his life that would be spilt, not her virgin blood.

His chain mail clinked as he released her to remove his helmet.

Patience, girl, patience, she coaxed herself. *Soon he will be without his guard and you can use the dagger.*

Out of the corner of her eye, she saw his warriors grip their sword hilts tighter. They stood around the perimeter of the sanctuary, also still in full armor.

Unbuckling the lower strap, her husband slowly lifted the helm.

Husband. The word sent a new shot of fury through her. Being a wife was akin to death for an artist. A passel of brats. A household to attend. Duties. Duties. More duties.

But, by the rood, she wouldn't be married very long. She would be a widow by the first cock's crow. She allowed herself a small smile at that thought. Widows had freedoms that maidens did not.

Montgomery's helmet rose. Her first impression was a strong jawline chiseled with cold precision. She widened her eyes and leaned her head back so she could peer directly at the monster she would soon slay. Nary a stray whisker protruded from his close-shaven cheeks.

She gulped.

He was not a beast.

He was perfect.

Too perfect.

Like a beautiful painting with no passion. As if he had no tolerance for human flaws.

His black hair was thick and as close-cropped as a Roman warlord's. Cobalt-blue eyes gazed down at her, shining with hard resolve. He had a broad aquiline nose, angular cheekbones, and a severe mouth that could have been carved from stone. Even his eyelashes were blunted into perfect midnight crescents, as black as his soul.

A shiver raced down her spine. Gwyneth had told her wrong information: no scars marred this man's perfection.

He was breathtaking. Magnificent. The handiwork of an arrogant artist, too prideful to show a blemish that would make the work a true masterpiece.

She'd ne'er seen a man like him afore.

Kill him? How could she destroy such beauty?

Biting the inside of her cheek, she hardened her resolve. Beautiful or no, she would not become the chattel of a man to be raped and beaten at will. Nor would she leave her family at his mercy.

Even with her back turned, she felt her father's intense, expectant glare from the front bench in the chapel. This was her chance to finally redeem herself in his eyes—to put to rights the rift that had formed betwixt them. Then she could leave for Italy with his blessing.

Gwyneth sat beside her father on the pew, wringing her hands. She wore a loose blue wool surcoat with a deep red underdress. 'Twas obvious she was trying to look as plain as possible—in place of one of her elaborate headdresses, she wore a wimple—but her beauty was like the sun, too brilliant to hide.

Adele, with her uncanny ways, had managed to escape from the ceremony.

Tension pulled across Brenna's shoulders.

At once she found herself glad of the severity of her new husband's perfection. If he had even some tiny flaw that caused him to seem more human and less cold, she might have found the task of destroying him impossible.

"Wife," he said, reaching for the hem of the silver veil covering her face. "You are mine." A touch of harshness laced his voice.

Her knees knocked when he lifted the pearl-sewn fabric away, but the hidden dagger pressed her flesh again, steeling her. Unless he had fangs, she could surely survive his kiss.

He cupped her chin and tilted her face up to his.

She scowled at him and shifted her feet restlessly when he did not move closer to kiss her.

His gaze roved her face, lingering on the scar that ran across her cheek.

She *thought* he'd seen her scar earlier, but perhaps his helm had blocked his view and now he was having second thoughts about forcing such an ugly woman to marry him. Ha. Served him right.

"Hasten and be done with it, *husband*," she sneered. Mayhap she should snatch the veil from her head, and give him a look at what he'd married. Mayhap he'd run like Lord Brice.

But, as satisfying as that would be, she still needed to get him alone and unarmed if she was to kill him.

"They said you were comely," he stated.

His words stung. There was no reason for them to sting, but they did.

"Well. I'm not." She glared at him. Of course such a handsome man would expect a comely wife.

He thumbed her scar and she hardened her resolve. Yay, she'd kill him and take delight in the act. 'Twas no secret she was unsightly, but for him to stand there in his perfection and inspect her scarred cheek like damaged goods was excruciating.

"As I said," she ground out, jerking her face from his grip, "there is no reason to kiss."

He caught her chin betwixt his fingers and brought her face back to his. Interest lit in his eyes.

A curl of heat formed low in her groin. She'd seen that look a thousand times bestowed on Gwyneth. And on serving maids. And even on Adele.

But ne'er had she herself been the recipient of such a gaze. The intensity nearly took her breath. So this was what it felt like to be desired. Wanted. 'Twas exhilarating.

He continued to stare at her, a deep crevice forming betwixt his brows. "Beg me to kiss you, captive wife," he said, his voice husky and compelling.

Caught in his spell, she opened her mouth to obey, then gasped, suddenly understanding. 'Twas not desire for her that had caught his interest, but the need to conquer, to cow her, to bend her to his will.

The demon! She glowered at him. However this day ended, ne'er would she be a witless slave for him to command. "I'll beg you for naught, barbarian. Now or ever."

The interest in his eyes burned into a blue inferno. His lips touched hers, hot and soft—neither cold nor stone as she had expected. His breath was sweet, clean as if he'd been chewing mint leaves, and the masculine musk of his skin was heady as fine wine.

Her stomach flipped. She stiffened, wanting to pull away. The act was done. The bargain sealed.

His lips lingered on hers.

She tried to step back, but his arms around her shoulders and lower back prevented her from moving from the cage of his embrace.

"Open your lips for me, captive wife," he murmured against her mouth. "I want to taste what is mine."

Her breath quickened, and heat flooded her cheeks. Ne'er had a man wanted to kiss her.

The sensation was as intoxicating as a well-made brushstroke after a series of mishaps while she was painting.

Her father growled, and shame spun through her, hot and prickly. His rage bore into her back.

She pressed her lips closed.

"Ah," her husband said, pulling slightly away, "not as compliant as I was led to believe then. Mayhap we should go straight to the wedding chamber and see to your taming. You respond well enough to my kisses."

Of all the vile things to say! She nearly choked at his words, then drew back her hand and slapped him. The sound cracked across the sanctuary's air. "I'm no pet to be tamed, knave."

Her father snorted.

Montgomery pressed his palm to his cheek. The gleam in his eyes turned from amused captor to merciless conqueror.

Her heart caught in her throat. No wonder children

ran from his pathway. Whirling, she lifted the hem of her skirt to flee.

Like a flash of lightning, his hand lashed out and grasped her wrist. He spun, dragging her in his wake down the chapel's aisle.

A few of his warriors guffawed.

Damnation! He was going to kill her! No husband of worth would take such insolence from his wife.

And this man was a conqueror.

"I—uh—that is—I did not mean—" she began, trying to buy herself time. She needed to appease him so she could get him alone to use the dagger.

"Silence, wife. I will deal with you in our chamber. By the time I am finished, you will wish you had agreed to amuse me by begging for kisses." Armor clanking, he paced toward the church's exit. "Soon, you will beg for much, much more."

Wincing, she dug her toes into the carpet to slow his pace. Unlike her own simple kirtle, the voluptuous houpelande entangled her legs and hindered her movement. He kept walking and she stumbled forward. Her headdress wobbled and the pins smarted against her scalp as they strained to hold the enormous contraption on her head.

He slowed just before she fell to her knees.

"Bastard," she muttered, righting herself.

"What was that?" he asked. His tone was mild, but a feral gleam shone in his cobalt eyes.

She licked her lips, trying to reconcile the soft warmth of his kiss with the harsh, severe man before her. She hadn't intended to slap him, but 'twas too late for regrets. She opened her mouth to repeat the curse, but thought better of it.

"Naught," she bit out.

Scowling, he pulled her forward until she bumped against his torso. He was as solid as the boards she painted. With his free hand, he ran his thumb up her collarbone, then curled his palm around the back of her neck.

Her heart threatened to beat its way out of her chest, and she nearly made a desperate attempt for her dagger. But, nay. She was not so addle-headed to give away her one tiny advantage whilst he wore armor and was surrounded by his men.

She twisted aside, wanting to run. She knew he would follow, but mayhap if she could get him alone, she could salvage some element of surprise and use *l'occhio del diavolo.*

"Cease struggling, captive, ere I turn you o'er my knee here in the chapel."

One of his men laughed.

"Nay! Do not manhandle my daughter!" Her father lurched to his feet, throwing off the men who guarded him. He stepped forward, defiant despite the ropes. His short beard and gray hair looked disheveled, and his nose twitched as if he'd smelled rotten eggs. He wore a simple tunic and hose in colors that would have blended with the forest. Dirt crusted his knees.

"My patience is thin with you too, old man." Montgomery paced forward, and Brenna's heart sank into her stomach.

At that moment, Gwyneth stood up, wailing in a loud cry. "Please, sir, I beg of you, do not hurt her." She raced forward and threw her arms around Brenna, breaking Montgomery's hold and nearly toppling her off-balance. Her wimple slid aside and her long blond hair came unwound and spilled around them.

Oh, for heaven's sake. Brenna felt as if she was enclosed

in a spider's web. She struggled to unwrap herself from her sister's tentacles so she could breathe.

"I'll kill you for this!" her father threatened, fighting against his wrist bonds.

Montgomery went into a fighting crouch. He still wore armor whilst her father was bound, unarmed, unprotected, and not nearly as large as his opponent.

"Do not be daft, Papa!" Freeing herself from her sister, she snagged hold of her husband's armored forearm.

The guards contained her father.

Montgomery whirled, and their gazes locked.

Gulping, Brenna gathered her courage. Gwyneth may have been wrong about his looks, but, verily, he *was* a savage. "Please leave my family be. I'll go with you. Punish me as you will."

With his thumb, he touched the soft place at the front of her neck. The dress was much lower cut than her own clothes, and his fingers looked frightening against her bare skin.

He stared down at her, and she squirmed under the intensity of his gaze. "And you will submit willingly to whatever punishment I design?"

She blinked, her heart pounding faster. What would he require of her? She'd affronted his honor in front of his men. If he beat her, she would be lucky to survive.

His thumb did not hurt her neck, but she could feel every motion either of them made. Feel her heartbeat. Feel herself swallow.

His touch made her want to wrap her arms around herself to keep from shivering.

Straightening her spine, she shook off her alarm. "I'm not afraid of you."

"Little liar."

Arrogant pig. Of a truth, she would have no remorse at all when she could finally stick him with the dagger.

"Bah!" her father said, spittle spewing from his mouth. He glared at her. "You little whore. You want him, don't you?"

Stunned, she stared at her father. It felt as though he'd kicked her in the stomach. How could she tell him about the knife? About Gwyneth?

"Fath—"

He cut her off with a jerk of his head. "You were more than willing to marry my enemy."

Her cheeks prickled. No matter what was between them, how could her father think that she would simply marry the enemy? Why was he so hot and cold to her? He had just defended her a moment ago . . . at once, she hated Montgomery for his part in making her father turn further against her.

"I did not want to marry at all, Father," she said quietly.

Montgomery's lips turned downward in a nearly imperceptible frown, and she found herself amazed that stone could show any emotion at all.

"Enough, old man." He motioned toward the man holding the crossbow. "Gabriel, find a tower to lock him in."

Gritting her teeth, Brenna forced herself to be patient.

She gasped as her new husband clamped her wrist and yanked her forward.

The monster!

Anger flared inside her. She glared at his back as he stalked out of the chapel into the damp spring air, irritated that she was forced to either follow or be dragged.

Dark clouds gathered in the east and the scent of

rain hung heavily in the sky. She contemplated yanking the dagger out of her bodice and stabbing him in the back. No doubt, his men would cut her down afore she could even blink. And slay her family asides.

Nay, she must wait until Adele gave the signal.

The castlefolk lingered nearby watching, but no one stepped forward to help her.

"Paulin," she called to a servant.

He shrank back, hiding partially behind the cistern and pulling his hat over his face. Others averted their eyes.

Damnation! *Do they all think I am a traitor?*

Glowering at her devil of a husband, she vowed that by day's end all here would know where her loyalties lay, and his life would be forfeit. She would go to Italy as a heroine instead of a shamed woman.

Chapter Three

She'd slapped him! In front of his men, no less. The little wench.

Years ago, the first lesson he had learned as The King's Enforcer was that without respect, one could not lead. Faded scars crisscrossed his back—tokens of the mutiny from the one smuggler he'd been merciful with.

He would not make that mistake with his own wife.

If he hadn't seen the look on her face when her father had called her a whore, he'd be tempted to bend her straight over his knee and give her the spanking she so soundly deserved.

But even in his anger, he hadn't missed the stung, hurt look in her eyes.

Ne'ertheless, she *would* learn who was master here. His tunic needed washing, his body needed bathing, and his boots needed polishing. Acts she could perform. Furthermore, he was hungry; *she* would feed him.

Tallow candle smoke stung James's eyes as he stalked down the hallway towing his hellcat wife in his wake. Her silver-blue wedding dress swished along the rushes as she scurried to keep up with him.

They reached her chamber in the north tower, and, barking a command for one of his men to bring a bathing tub and heated water, he pushed the door open and drew her inside. The door slammed with a loud, shutter-rattling bang.

He released his wife, and she scampered away to the window seat embrasure as if her dress were on fire. She sat there staring at him, willfulness in her emerald eyes. The butterfly headdress and trailing veil covered her head, allowing him only the barest glimpse of her copper colored locks, which curled out the sides.

Yards and yards of dazzling blue material trimmed in ermine surrounded her slight body—but the wedding gown looked too delicate for her strong spirit. It might have *fit* her, but it did not *suit* her at all. The thin scar across her face reddened slightly in color as if blood coursed through her in an angry rush.

Dragging her off to her chamber hadn't diminished her insolence one bit.

Scrutinizing her chamber, he debated where to start her training.

Three windows were built into the stone wall: two small ones and a large one with a window seat that his new wife sat upon. The room contained minimal furnishings for a noblewoman: it had a bed, a rough trestle table with two drawers, a three-legged stool, and a dressing screen.

Oddly, a maze of religious paintings were scattered all around the floor and walls. Boards and parchments leaned around the perimeter of the room with depictions of religious scenes of the Annunciation and baptism of Christ. His gaze went back to the trestle.

Pots of color pigment, oils, eggs, rags, and an artist

palette crowded the desktop and five or six paintbrushes spotted the floor beneath it.

Paintings. He had been so focused on collecting his new bride when he'd burst into the room before, he had not even noticed that she was an artist.

For an instant, he thought of the small, exquisite miniatures that the king wanted him to look for. If his new wife was the artist of those, then there was no reason to even attempt at creating a marriage or establishing his place as her lord—his duty would require him to haul her to London and deliver her to his liege. Surely the painting was only a coincidence—she was a noble daughter from a good family, a virgin with no carnal knowledge. Still—

Taking her by the upper arm, he lugged her off the window embrasure and pointed around the room. "Who painted these?"

She straightened her spine. "I did."

He scrutinized her for a moment, then picked through the artistic rubble on the desk. Every brush he turned over made her twitch as if barely contained outrage jumped beneath her skin.

Tough.

She may as well get used to him. And used to him touching her things. And touching her as well.

The desk was made in the fashion of a rough-hewn trestle table with two crude drawers beneath the surface.

Keeping his hand wrapped around her upper arm, he opened a drawer and searched inside. It was unlikely that the artist the king wanted to hang was a woman, and even more unlikely that it was his new wife. But he had learned to be thorough. She flinched as he opened the second drawer and slipped his hand inside.

Several smaller paintings, done on parchment, lay among the supplies. All of them contained figures with golden halos above their heads.

Leaving her standing in the midst of the chamber, he methodically made his way around the room searching for hidden paintings or any clues. More religious art. More depictions of the birth of Christ, of angels, of the Virgin Mary. Nothing of a sexual nature. No pictures of the king and his court in poses of compromise.

"Only religious work? No other paintings?"

Lifting her chin, she managed to look down on him even though she was at least a head and a half shorter. "I was supposed to be a nun."

He lifted the bedskirt and peered under the bed. A small satchel lay amidst the cobwebs. He fished it out and scrutinized Brenna who glared at him as he opened it. A wedge of cheese, a loaf of bread, and other meager supplies lay within. Confused, he held up the sack. "What is this?"

"Naught," she said, swallowing.

"Were you going somewhere?"

"To a convent."

"You will not be a nun. You are my *wife*," he said flatly.

She jerked her head to one side and set her jaw. "Only because it was forced upon us."

"There would have been no force if you and your family would have done their God-given duty to the king."

"Men make their own rules and claim God's authority."

"Mayhap. But 'tis God's law that a woman obey her husband."

"I am sure God makes allowance for women married to cruel demons." With a huff, she sat on the three-legged stool and tinkered with one of the paint-brushes sticking out of a pot of liquid. "In the Bible, Jael was praised for nailing her husband's head to the ground."

His neck prickled at her words, and he determined to keep a close rein on her. 'Twas obvious by the way she had twitched and flinched as he touched her brushes that her artwork meant something to her. Until she learned deference, she would do no more painting.

Walking to the door, he called to the guards in the hallway to bring him an empty trunk. He would tame her piece by piece: reward compliance but discipline uppityness.

The men returned shortly carrying a medium-sized trunk. It was plain, but functional.

When they had left, he set the chest on the floor in front of her desk and nudged it open with his boot. He took the foodstuffs out of the pack then dumped the rest of its contents, including her tiny hog's hair brush and a couple of gold coins, into the gaping space. "Package up the art supplies in the desk."

"What?" Her eyes widened, and she looked like he'd slap her.

"You will have no more time for such dalliances. You now have a household to run, a husband to care for, and heirs to bear."

Brenna cringed as sheer loathing shot through her and it was all she could do to remain still.

She hated him!

His fingers on her painting supplies made her feel violated, and now he wanted to dismiss her life's work like a piece of garbage. Her heart beat rapidly against the dagger, and she wondered the best way to divest him of his weapons and armor so she could use it.

He paced toward her. His movements, like himself, were precise and efficient with no time wasted on leisure.

She wondered if the act of intimacy with him would be as calculated.

Bloody hell. What was she thinking? She was not going to swive him. She was going to kill him.

He came to stand directly in front of her until his armored codpiece was right in her face, and he crowded out the space around her.

She glanced out the window to avert her gaze from the molded steel plate covering his member. It was so . . . large.

"My lady," he said, "do not make this difficult for yourself. Pack your supplies."

The foul beast! Outrage curled in the pit of her stomach. She wished her sister would hurry and give the signal that it was safe to slay the monster.

But it was not even dusk yet.

Angrily, she scooped up her precious brushes. She could not best him by sheer strength—she would force herself to wait for good opportunity. She set the brushes in the trunk, lining them up in neat rows. Likely if she did not do this deed herself, Montgomery would scoop up her supplies and toss them unsorted into the box. The colors would be ruined, the brushes splayed by his thick, brutish hands.

He picked up a pot of blue pigment and rolled it between his fingers. "It was unwise to challenge me in front of my men."

She wanted to snatch the pot out of his hand and

dash its contents in his face. "And it was unwise to kiss me in front of my family."

"We've just been married. I am your family now." Seething, she picked up her palette and spatula and placed them near the brushes. She would *not* let him rile her temper or make her do something stupid. She would wait until the appointed time. And that was that.

"Peace, wife," he said. "This marriage can work in your favor, or it can work against you. 'Tis your choice."

"*My* choice?" Outraged, Brenna sucked in a breath and set two pots of color pigment in the chest. The clay jars clanked together. She grabbed two more and then started tossing half-finished parchments on top of them.

He stalked around the room, looking in corners and crevices and behind the bed. Even though he wore armor, his movements were fluid and panther-like, a testimony of his strength and fortitude as well as the precision and quality of his battle gear.

Mud from his boots flaked onto her cleanly swept floor. The clinking of his chain mail grated on her ears.

He pulled up a corner of the mattress and peered beneath it. "Where are your hidden paintings?"

Her pulse quickened and her hand squeezed. Did he know about the erotic work? She nearly jumped as slime dripped through her fingers. Bloody hell. She'd crushed one of the eggs she used to make her tempera.

Shaking the egg goo from her hand, she snatched a rag from the desktop and began wiping off the now ruined painting at the top of the pile in the trunk. Blasted man.

"I have no hidden paintings," she gritted out.

"All artists have hidden work—things they are

ashamed to let the world judge, but too dear to their heart to toss aside."

She glanced up and realized he was watching her. His blue gaze was as fierce as a stormy ocean. Gooseflesh popped on her arms.

"Why do you care what I paint?" she asked fiercely.

He stepped toward her, looming over her. "I do not. I care about your respect and obedience to me."

She checked the urge to damn the consequence of yanking the dagger out now. But she must be patient if she intended to live. And she *did* intend to live.

"Respect must be earned," she countered. Her voice came out much softer than she had intended. Almost squeaky.

"True enough, my lady. But I'll not have you slapping me in front of my men."

She ducked her head, so she would not have to look at him. Smoothing the gigantic blue skirt over her knees, she composed herself. Acting the hellion would not accomplish her goal.

When she lifted her face again to his, she forced herself to soften her tone. "Fair enough. I will not do that again." *You'll be dead.*

"And I'll have your apology."

Gritting her teeth, she sucked in a deep breath. *Patience*, she told her seething emotions. *Wait for the signal. Wait until your sisters have men in place.*

He lifted one dark brow, his blue eyes watching her intently as if trying to conquer her with his gaze. He stood much too close. "Now, wife."

"Forgive me."

He gave her a small smile that looked more like a grimace. How had she thought he was perfect? He was irritating, irksome. Too large. Too controlling. Likely he'd be fingering all her painting brushes and oils again in a minute, smudging the work surface and muddling the pigments. She silently vowed she'd scour down all her supplies once she got rid of him.

Turning, he marched to the edge of the mattress, ripped back the bed curtains and sat down. 'Twas a relief to not have him so near.

Her bed linens did not have lace and bows as Gwyneth's did. They were neither frilly nor overly feminine, yet he still looked very out of place against the pillows and cushions. The bed sagged against the weight of his armor and the red curtains fluttered.

She turned her gaze to the large painting of the battle between the archangel Michael and the devil. She was fighting the devil too.

The sound of Montgomery slapping his thigh in slow, calculated strokes cracked through the room. "Cross me again, and I'll turn you over my knee and give you the spanking you deserve."

Drawing on her inner strength, she gazed at him disdainfully, giving him her best you-are-beneath-me glare. "I'm no child to be spanked, sirrah."

"Nay, but you *are* a wife who needs to learn to behave."

Turning back to her task, she scrubbed harder at the slimy egg stuff, squeezing her rag so tightly her knuckles whitened. Two of her dress's mother-of-pearl buttons snagged on the trunk and nearly popped loose. "I am packaging my art supplies as you demanded, am I not?"

"You said you would submit to any punishment I set forth as retribution." Brushing the curtains aside, he leaned against one of the bedposts.

"I did not mean I would calmly allow you to spank me."

He glanced at the closed wooden door. "Do you break our bargain already? Shall I fetch your father and finish what we began downstairs?"

The anger in her stomach gelled into a cold knot of fear. He could still have her father and sisters murdered. Her hand paused above the parchments she'd sat in the chest. "Nay."

"You said, 'punish me as you will,' did you not?"

That *was* what she had said. She raised her chin, wanting to deny it, and knew she could not.

A blue flame sparked in his cobalt eyes—rich and warm and intense. For a second, his face was so breathtakingly masculine and flawless, she longed to be able to pick up one of her brushes and capture the blue of his eyes, the length of his lashes. She squelched the wayward thought.

Crooking his finger, he beckoned her toward him. "Come here, captive wife."

Chapter Four

Her fascination evaporated, and she fought the urge to take the dagger and defend herself. Was he really planning to turn her over his knee? She glanced at his hands; they were huge and thick. No doubt they would sting like the devil. If only her sisters and father's lives were not at stake. If only the men were ready and the signal given.

Gathering her courage, she stepped toward Montgomery. Her heart thumped against her ribcage and she feared the worst.

When she reached him, he took her chin between his fingers and turned her face this way and that. She forced herself to remain compliant. Fighting him physically would not win her victory. She had one chance—and that was to throw her knife—something she could not do at this close range and with him fully clothed and in armor.

Icy fear gripped her gut.

After what seemed like hours, he released her chin. "Very good. Your compliance serves you better than your insolence. Help me out of this armor. 'Tis bloody hot."

Releasing a breath of relief that he was not planning to carry through with spanking her, she fought the urge to smile. Getting him out of his protective coverings would definitely make killing him easier.

But, 'twas best not to appear too eager or he would suspect something was afoot.

She silently vowed not to let her tongue or her irritation get the best of her. She would wait until Adele's signal and follow Panthos through the woods as they had planned.

Montgomery held an arm out so she could unfasten the buckles of his vambrace and pauldron. As the plates fell away, she found herself marveling at the size of his limb, which was still encased in chain mail. His thickly muscled arm flexed, and the mail made a tiny metallic sound.

Standing this close to him, she could hear him breathe, a soft whispering that seemed fragile in contrast to the hard, sturdy man before her. Life was like that: frail and uncertain, even for a man of his size. 'Twas why she found capturing fleeting moments in oils and tempera so appealing.

She removed his other arm's armor then moved to unbuckle his cuirass. Her fingers slid across fasteners on his side, and she felt entranced by the thickness of his chest. Slowly she removed the metal plates piece by piece. As she worked, she grew more and more awestruck by the artistry of his body. With each layer more and more of his masculinity was revealed.

She'd helped her father and brother plenty of times with their armor—'twas part of a noblewoman's duty.

But always before it had seemed a dull chore, a drudgery disguised as duty. This man enthralled her like a deadly viper. Both beautiful and lethal.

She finished with the cuirass and helped him out of his chain mail shirt and gambeson until his chest was bare, save for a crucifix of springy hair and a silver heart-shaped locket that dangled on a plain leather cord. The fancy, filigreed piece of jewelry looked out of place against the masculine contours of his torso.

Curious, she reached for it.

"Nay." His hand closed around the locket hiding it from her view before she could touch it. Power seemed to pulse through him like a tangible thing. Fearsome, loathsome even. Marvelous in its intensity as he protected the piece of jewelry from her eyes.

Was the locket a family heirloom? A gift from a lover? She could not fathom why a hardened warrior would wear something so delicate.

Without a word, he removed the locket, wrapped it in a cloth, and set it aside before she was able to inspect it. The warning look in his eyes disallowed question or comment.

She blinked and forced her attention back to the task of inspecting him. If she was to slay him, she did not want to think of him as anything other than a beast, and small silver lockets made him all too human.

She traced a finger along his shoulder. Ne'er in her life had she seen a man such as he. He was wider even than she had imagined. While other men might enhance the width and thickness of their arms and shoulders with pads and fabric, he had no need.

The sheer manliness of his body made her want to run her hands along the sinewy texture of his muscles, just to verify that he was, indeed, human, and could be killed. Dueling thoughts of repulsion and fascination ripped through her.

She counted the thin scars on his biceps. Four

crisscrossed the muscle on one side and seven on the other. Proof of the many battles he'd fought.

And likely won.

Biting the inside of her cheek, she realized she would have to be very, very cautious. His fingers likely could snap her spine in half like a brittle twig. She'd only have one chance with *l'occhio del diavolo* and she prayed its aim would indeed have the eye of the devil.

A thin layer of perspiration covered his tan skin making his shoulders look glossy, as if they had been highly polished with a cloth.

Standing in front of him, she tried to imagine where his heart was. No movement on his chest indicated its beating. Mayhap he had no heart at all.

His face was stony and unreadable, but his eyes were like glittering waves on the blue ocean as he gazed at her. "Kneel and remove my boots."

She smarted at his tone, and sank to her knees.

Hate swelled in her heart. He was the most vile, loathsome blackheart she'd ever known. For certes, undressing him was part of her punishment for slapping him in the chapel. *Get your enjoyment from this, devil. Tonight will be the last time you command me.* She narrowed her eyes at him, but held her tongue.

Mentally, she counted the hours until sunset when the signal would be sent. When that time came, she wanted him as vulnerable as possible. Even wearing only half a suit of armor, he looked capable of killing a man in cold blood.

Or a woman.

She suppressed a shudder, remembering what her sister had told her about the lad who spilled ale on his paltock.

From her position on the floor, he looked even

taller than before. Grasping his large black boots by the heels, she pulled off one then the other.

The muscles in his legs were enormous—like Grecian pillars. The chain mail gave little clinks and the mattress creaked as he stood and indicated for her to remove his chausses and the metal codpiece that protected his privates.

"I do not think I should," she started. Her mouth felt dry as sand and her heart raced as she speculated what he looked like beneath the metal protector. She had some knowledge of the shape of a man's sex— she'd bathed with her twin brother Nathan when they were children: 'twas like a stubby sausage.

She stood abruptly, not wanting to let on about her curiosity. Her inquisitiveness was something her father oft railed about. And it was evil itself to even want to look at a man she hated so much.

"You should remove the rest yourself. You have no need for my assistance."

"'Tis part of what I require of you, wife. I have called for water, next you will bathe me. As a proper wife would."

Bathe him?

She swallowed. Was it her imagination or did the codpiece move slightly of its own accord?

Spellbound, she stared at it to see if it would move again.

It did!

Of all the devilish things!

Mayhap her paintings had not been accurate at all if a man's member was thick enough to move a piece of metal with its swelling. She'd based her miniatures on what she could remember of her brother when they had been mere children.

But this . . . this was interesting. Perhaps she could paint it when she safely reached Italy.

Her gaze flicked to her art supplies stacked neatly in the trunk. In a safe cleft beneath the floor planks under her desk, a half-finished work depicting a naked gladiator was hidden along with a number of other unfinished or inferior paintings. Montgomery had been correct that artists sometimes hid their work.

That gladiator piece was the first one she'd been so bold as to do a complete frontal view of a male figure. Unsure of the exact size and color of a man's member, she had not finished it. It did not seem right to paint a vague sausage-shape as she had done with her other erotic art.

At once the thought of having Montgomery unclad was more than simply making him easier to kill. Doing so would allow her to finish the painting with an edge of realism. That would, for certes, allow her to study with her brother's tutors when she reached Italy.

Emboldened by the thought, she untied the strings holding the codpiece and lifted it away. A large bulge lay beneath it, straining against the chain mail chausses. Eager now, she slid these down his legs until he was clad only in his hose.

She skimmed her hands over the ties, slowly undid the stays and peeled them down his long, long legs. The crisp hair on his thighs prickled against her palms. She felt hot, dizzy. And completely curious.

Without allowing herself time to think, she pulled the strings on his brais and let them slide to the floor.

She gasped as his member sprang loose. 'Twas so much *larger* than she'd expected. *Much* different than the ones she'd painted. It bobbed in the air seeming to defy the laws of nature that pulled things downward. Not like a flabby sausage a'tall!

Amazed, she stared at it and as she did, it seemed to grow even longer.

Hell's fires. All her paintings had been wrong! She'd painted men's members afore, but they looked nothing like this. She'd gotten the color wrong. And it had a slight purplish tint at the end and a very interesting vein that bulged down the length.

Reaching out, she touched it with one finger.

Her new husband hissed and she lurched. Straightening, she looked up at him.

She'd been so entranced by the size and sturdiness of his body, she'd ignored Montgomery the man.

He gazed down on her, his intense cobalt eyes blazing. His dark brows drew together in an enigmatic scowl that made her wonder what he was thinking.

Shivers raced down her spine. The dagger felt hard and steely betwixt her breasts.

"I've never had a woman inspect me like a prized stallion."

She stepped back to put some distance between them, and composed her face. "I was not."

Montgomery chuckled, the sound throaty and warm.

She felt her cheeks heat, and tore her gaze away from his to glance around at the bare walls of her room.

Of a truth, she *had* been looking over him that way. *But only for the sake of her art*, she told her seared conscience.

Reaching out, he grasped her hand and drew her forward.

A frisson of heat skipped through her, seeming to land right in her woman's core. She scowled, wondering what she should do.

Turning her face to one side, she peered into the bailey and hoped for the signal.

Naught but men and horses and servants were in the field.

Catching her glancing out the open window, James marched over and drew the curtain closed.

Devil take it! She'd have to find a way to open them a crack if she was going to see the candle in Adele's window.

Night was still hours away though. She had time.

Montgomery's male member bobbed in the air, pointing the way as he walked back to her. It had lost some of its size and stiffness but was still rather impressive. Brenna found it impossible not to watch, wanting to memorize the look of it for her paintings.

"You are very curious for a virgin."

Her gaze snapped to his face. His lips lifted in a smug, half-smile. Arrogant. He's beautiful and he knows it. Absolutely flawless and exquisite.

Like Gwyneth.

Unlike herself.

Swallowing, she raised her hand self-consciously to the scar on her cheek and was glad she still wore her headdress and wedding veil to cover up her hacked off hair. Between her fascination and her anger, she'd forgotten how most men reacted to her looks—or lack thereof.

He stepped toward her and touched the scar, running his index finger along the bumpy ridge from her nose to her ear.

She shivered and ducked her head.

Catching her chin between his fingers, he turned her face back up to his. "What happened?" He appeared more interested than put off by her disfigurement.

"I've had it since I was a child. My curiosity has oft gotten me into trouble," she said, sidestepping the question.

He smiled. "I like your curiosity, and you are a child no longer. We have all the day and night for you to examine me all you wish."

She blinked. Her heart sped and she wondered at the game he played. It had been her expectation that he would jump on her straightaway and force her to his will, not calmly play the part of a suitor by allowing her to explore his body to her satisfaction.

A knock sounded, interrupting the awkward moment between them. Thank heavens.

A man carrying a wooden tub entered along with a line of servants with buckets of steaming water.

Heedless of his nakedness, Montgomery indicated for them to place the bathing tub beside the bed. He propped one hip against the mattress and crossed his arms, watching dispassionately as the men poured the water into it. His mannerism was so casual that if he hadn't been bare arse naked in front of her, she would have thought he was dressed and ready for a parley with the queen.

She felt her cheeks prickle. Having been used to dealing with the erotic subject of her own paintings, it had been years since anyone had truly disconcerted her. If the servants thought it odd that he was naked, no one said anything or gave any indication by wink or look. Did their master often parade about unclad?

After the men left, Montgomery stepped forward and slowly lowered himself into the steaming tub. He had to bend his knees a great deal to fit.

Silver swirls climbed into the air and drops of water slithered down his large body as he splashed some on himself. Droplets caught in the crisp black hair on his chest. His member had softened and it bobbed gently on the surface of the water.

She found herself wishing she could paint him here like this.

"Do you have soap?" he asked.

"Yea, um. Yes." She glanced around, trying to not be completely befuddled that a naked warrior was in her chamber. As if he'd jumped out of one of her paintings—only the live one had a full male member and bullocks attached. "I'll get some."

As she walked across the floor planks to her dressing screen, she looked down the bodice of her gown to see the top of the dagger's hilt to gain courage. The knife was well hidden in the folds of her wedding dress. How odd to be fully dressed—and dressed so elaborately—whilst he was naked.

Once behind the screen, she unpinned the butterfly headdress, set it on a small table, and refastened the veil on her head to cover up her cropped hair. How did her sister wear such contraptions without having an awful headache?

Taking a rag and a cake of soap, she brought them to the edge of the tub. Her heart began to pound as she realized he expected her to scrub him.

Such an opportunity to explore the male body! The knowledge would add life to her paintings. She tamped down a niggling of guilt that she would be using him in this way. Her father oft railed at her that she should focus on important matters. She should be thinking of escape and saving her family, not artwork.

Trying not to seem too eager, she bent and wetted the rag in the side of the tub. The back of her hand grazed his leg, and even more interest sparked inside her.

No matter how beastlike the man within it, his body would be a joy to capture on parchment—nay, on canvas. Parchment would be too crude for such a subject. Brother Giffard assured her that canvas was aplenty in Italy.

Rounding to where she stood behind him, she rubbed the cake of soap on the rag and squeezed the cloth out across his shoulders. The water trickled down the curve of his spine. He leaned forward and she ran the washcloth up one side of his back and down the other in a slow circle.

"Mmmmmmm," he said.

She smiled. Getting him relaxed and off guard was good.

Leaning forward, she pressed her hand lower in the hot water. She allowed her greedy fingers access to his skin, trying to memorize every fiber and muscle so she could transfer it to the canvas later. Heat rose inside her. Who knows but this might be her last chance to ever see a naked man so close.

In her mind, she knew it was evil that she did not feel properly ashamed or beset with nerves. Surely God would forgive her this one sin. She tamped down her guilt: she would save her confession for when she reached the convent.

Water slopped on the bodice of her gown as she worked her hands over Montgomery. She soaped his neck and rinsed it, then moved to the side of the tub so she could reach his torso. The area betwixt her legs seemed wetter than usual, and she felt a little dizzy.

His skin was not as soft as hers, and his chest hair felt interesting against her palm. Crisp and slightly rough. His firm muscles, alive with vitality, flinched under her touch. She dipped her hand lower.

Montgomery drew in a sharp breath as her hand touched the inside of his thigh.

"Of a truth, wife, you please me greatly. I had thought we were ill suited."

Shocked at his words, she paused in her ministrations. The pulse in his thigh beat against her palm.

She swallowed, forcing herself to continue washing him in long strokes, running the cloth up his chest and over his neck. His member stiffened, and she felt a heady rush of power that she could have such an effect on him.

Soaping up the cloth again, she ran it over his shoulders, mentally counting the hand spans across his shoulders. The lye smell of soap mingled with the scent of warm male skin.

More water wet the front of her gown as she leaned across him.

How weird to be performing such a task dressed as she was. The houpelande was a far cry from her two tattered kirtles. She had not worn anything so fine in years and this seemed a bizarre task to do in such a garment. The musky scent of the wedding gown's ermine trim intensified as water dripped on it.

Montgomery had a bumpy crescent shaped scar on his right shoulder and four freckles on his left. Those would make nice touches on her next miniature.

Standing, she fanned her face. The chamber seemed over-warm. Wetness seeped from her woman's core. *Forgive me, Father, for I have sinned. I have lusted after a man and planned murder in my heart.*

Montgomery rose from the tub, skin glistening. Rivulets of water wiggled down his chest and arms.

Dear saints! His sex had become enormous. Her

prayer cleared like incense on a windy day. Her nipples tightened, and more heat pooled in her groin.

He chuckled.

A prickling sensation crept up her cheeks. Heavens, her eyes must be wide and round as feasting goblets. She blinked, trying to regain her composure.

"You're not afraid?"

"Afraid?" she said dumbfounded.

"Of having me inside you."

The gentleness in his tone disconcerted her. "I—uh—" At once she realized that she was not scared because she had not been thinking of the sex act itself, only on the beauty of his male member. Of how she would mix the colors to paint it. She would need lead white, cinnibar, and massicot.

She hid a grimace. She had no need to be afraid of copulation because she planned to slay him afore the night went that far. Bowing her head, she started her confession again. *Forgive me, Fath*—

"Come, wife, you have had enough of knowing my body. 'Tis time that I saw yours."

"Nay!" She caught herself and smiled tightly at him. If her clothing was removed, he would see the dagger. Their plans would be ruined. Her father would be hung. Her sisters raped.

She could not allow herself to go weak now.

"Forgive me, my lord," she coaxed. "I seem to be more nervous than I had first thought. If only you could lie on the bed that I might touch you a little longer. As you said, we have all the day and night to consummate this union."

The gleam in his eyes was predatory, but he walked to the bed. The tight round muscles of his buttocks flexed in a fascinating erotic dance. He lay across her mattress, propping his head up slightly on a pillow and lacing his fingers behind his neck.

Her mouth went dry. She took in his chest, trying to discern the exact location of his heart.

It seemed a shame to kill a man so perfect in form. Mayhap—

At that moment, a loud scream and frantic barking sounded outside the chamber.

She gasped. 'Twas Adele and Panthos!

Quitting the bed, she raced to the door and yanked it open. In the tower's stairwell, Adele was being pulled down by two burly soldiers. Her cane lay on the stones, and her dark hair flailed around her as if in a windstorm. Her skirt flapped about her knees.

"Adele!" Brenna screamed. "Cease! Cease!"

Ignoring her, the men laughed as one dove atop her sister and yanked her skirt up above her thighs. To one side, a man held back the snarling mastiff.

"Adele!" Brenna lurched into a run to rescue her sister. She slammed into something that felt like a wall. Montgomery! She blinked, stunned for a second, then sidestepped him.

He caught her and pulled her back. "Nay!"

"They are hurting my sister!"

Holding her by one wrist while she fought to get away, he peered down the hallway.

Adele scrambled for her cane, and one of the men struggled to get his breeks down. The mastiff spun and bit the man holding him who, in turn, kicked him, but neither let the other go.

Frantic, Brenna struggled against her new husband.

"Cease!" Montgomery bellowed out. His voice rang through the hallway bouncing off the castle's walls.

The men looked up. Montgomery gave them a deep

glare and made a short swipe across his neck with his finger. The message was clear: continue and be slain.

Brenna gasped, surprised at his action. He was a beast. What would he care about her sister being raped when all of them were there to conquer her family's castle? This union was naught more than legalized rape.

Adele wobbled to her feet. She was unsteady without her cane. She gazed around dazedly and caught Brenna's eye. "Do it!" she commanded. "Do it now!"

Brenna had no doubt what she meant.

"'Tis our only chance."

Panthos barked, lunging upward to her. The men wrestled the dog to the ground.

Stark reality slammed onto Brenna. There were only two things that would happen in the wedding chamber—either she would be swived or The Enforcer would be killed. If she didn't destroy this man, 'twould be both her and her sister lying beneath Montgomery men. And no doubt Panthos would be put down.

"Do it!" Adele cried. "Afore they rape and murder us all! We can get away if we act now! I know the way out and men are waiting!"

Now was her best chance, whilst Montgomery was naked, unarmed and unsuspecting.

Without another thought, Brenna yanked the dagger from her bodice, and lunged it at Montgomery's heart.

"What the—" Montgomery twisted aside, as lithe as a tiger caught off guard.

The knife struck skin, slicing in a clumsy arc across his chest and glancing off his shoulder blade to stick shallowly in his flesh.

He grunted. A thin red line oozed blood down his chest.

Her heart lurched into her throat and she backed away, realizing what she had done. She'd been too close. This was not how she had practiced; she should have thrown the dagger, not lunged at him. Her stomach felt sick and her knees liquefied as if they had turned into water.

He scowled at her, dumbfounded, his hand grasping the hilt of the dagger. "Christ Almighty, wench."

Her underarms prickled and her palms turned clammy. Terrified, she turned and fled down the hall.

Chapter Five

Justice demanded that she be charged with treason, the same as her father.

A red haze of fury clouded James's vision as he snatched his wife's upper arm, hauled her to the bed and threw her across it. His pride stung, demanding retribution. In his mind, he heard his father jeer. *Stupid fool! You are too soft to be a leader. An unworthy son.*

She landed with a thump, and James forced himself to unclench his fists to keep from beating her to death with his bare hands.

A sharp twinge throbbed in his chest, slashing across the knife wound. The blade was stuck shallowly into his shoulder and the dagger's quivering hilt caused wave after wave of stinging pain. He drew a breath, forcing himself not to look at her lest he be tempted to turn the knife straightaway on her.

With a mighty wrench, he yanked the dagger from his shoulder. He grunted. Blood trickled down the blade and wetness ran down his chest.

She scrambled to her knees on the bed. Her fingers trembled, but she glared at him all the same.

Taking a deep breath, he released his anger and refocused on his duty to the king.

Milksop, his father taunted, speaking to that dark part of himself that wanted to rashly slit her throat, to damn the consequences and slander of having a murdered bride in his past.

With strength of mind, he shushed his father's voice. His rage was not the best way to serve his country. But, all the same, insolence would form in his ranks if it were believed that he could not handle his own wife. He would be the laughingstock of the army. The King's Enforcer would become The Wife's Dunderhead.

The blade shook, but, through force of will, he made his hand open and dropped it to the floor. It clattered on the planks, and with deliberate, slow motions he commanded himself to don his hose as he decided her fate.

Earlier he'd thought the note to bring him to this castle was prompted by her father—now he realized that she, too, was a key player in the rebel scheme to unseat the king.

If he took her to London, the king would have her beaten and tortured. Likely, she'd be passed around the army. *Pass her around to your men*, his father taunted, *only a sap would give her the benevolence of a quick death.*

Nay. He would not allow that. Not even for her.

He would execute her here . . . but he wouldn't do it in the bedroom to have the castlefolk and all of England's rebels able to clamor around her as a martyr.

His mind made up, he reached for her leg.

Brenna scrambled backward on the bed, her

pearled veil and the enormous wedding dress twisting around her body. Ermine trim fluffed in the air.

At her insubordinate action, fury fogged his brain, giving a hazy quality to her wide-eyed face.

"Move off that damn bed and I'll kill you right now."

A strong pulse beat in her neck; she glared at him, but she didn't get off the mattress.

He stepped back, determined to make it to the courtyard before executing her for treason. To not give in to the rage that coursed through him.

Milksop, the dark voice sneered.

Brenna swallowed against the hard knot in her throat as she watched Montgomery buckle his leather belt around his waist and slide on his boots. Should she scream? Fight? Run? She straightened her skirt over her legs. His anger was a tangible force in the room and, feeling like a dog sent to its kennel, she dared not test his threat to leave the mattress.

"What are you going to do wi—"

Her mind froze, the words dying on her tongue, as he straightened and looked at her. His eyes were no longer cobalt, but steely blue with a red mote glowing in the left one.

Vengeful eyes. Determined eyes.

And she knew. Knew beyond a doubt, she was a condemned woman. He may not have turned the knife directly on her, but he planned to execute her all the same.

As was his right as The Enforcer.

Panic radiated through her limbs. For a fleeting instant, she recalled her sister's warning that he had murdered his first wife.

Glancing at the door, the window, the garderobe, she searched frantically for a means of escape. Her chest constricted so tightly she could barely breathe. Cornered. Trapped. Nowhere to run.

"The battle is lost," he said as if reading her mind. He stepped toward her, his jaw hard.

Not allowing herself to think, she lunged, attempting to race past him, to go somewhere, anywhere besides here. He grabbed her arm in an easy twist as if he had expected such a move and hauled her upright until her nose nearly touched his.

"You will have three lashes for every defiance you give me between here and the woodchopper's block." A tight tic pulsed in his jaw as if he was just holding himself back from striking her. As if he feared that once he started beating her, he would not stop. "I can have the skin stripped from your flesh and leave you to die from the wounds or have your execution done with one stroke to your neck."

Her knees began to shake. In her mind, the cold metal of the axe was already biting into her neck. With a bravado she did not feel, she squared her shoulders. "I'm not sorry for what I've done."

"Three lashes."

She lifted her chin, her ire rising. "Do what you will with me, I won't cow down to you."

His hand on her arm tightened into a biting grip. "If you care naught for your own flesh, I can have the skin stripped from your sisters' bones as well."

Hot, angry tears pricked the backs of her eyes. Before she could compose an answer, Brenna found herself pulled upward and slung over Montgomery's shoulder. The room spun, her paintings forming blurs of colors. His scent, which had enticed her only moments earlier, terrified her now.

"Put me down!"

"Nay."

She beat on his back with her fist.

"Six lashes."

She stilled, his shoulder pushing into her stomach. There was no sense in acting the fool. She would face death with dignity.

He paced to the door, opened it and began his march down the hallway. If the wound she had inflicted bothered him, his movement did not indicate it.

About halfway down the steps leading into the bailey, one of his men met them.

She cringed, embarrassed at being held in such an undignified position.

"My lord?" The man was a tall, thick-limbed brute with a crooked, ugly nose and deep frown line betwixt his brows. He took in the bloody red slice across Montgomery's chest, silently nodded and moved to follow them outside. As if he too understood what would happen.

Flashes of light flickered before her eyes; she bounced against Montgomery's shoulder as he strode down the steps into the courtyard. The bright sunlight stung her eyes, making them water. Hanging her head down, she allowed the pearled veil to cover her face and peeked through the folds.

Slowly, he set her down. Her legs trembled so much only his grip on her shoulders held her upright as her toes sank into the cool, wet earth. Her gaze darted to the castle's gate. Could she make it? Lose him in the woods?

"Run and I'll burn the keep to the ground," he said, following the direction of her gaze.

She shuddered.

A crowd gathered, soldiers and servants rounding on them. They stared at the two of them, and Brenna felt her underarms sting with terror.

Montgomery stood tall and firm, allowing the castle-folk to gawk at the open wound and the blood oozing down his bare chest. So this is what facing death felt like? A cold, icy feeling that won't let your knees stop shaking no matter how hot the sun gets.

Squeezing her eyes shut, she determined not to cry. Not to plead. Time seemed to slow so that the people moved like sluggish snails.

"Move. Walk forward."

Toward the side of the bailey, a tall woodstack leaned against the outer wall of the castle. Logs scattered haphazardly on the ground and a heavy block that the woodcutters used to split logs was nearby. Two axes leaned against the pile, their sharp crescent blades gleaming in the sun. Ogier, the head woodchopper, took pride in having a sharp shiny blade.

Brenna trembled, thinking of all the times she'd seen the men pop open a log. Breathe. Breathe. But she couldn't breathe. At least not deeply. Her breath came in short, panicked gulps as if her body was trying to inhale life itself.

What was left of it.

Montgomery's hand between her shoulder blades pushed her forward. Her feet tangled and she had to make several quick steps to keep from pitching forward.

Angry, she whirled around. "You needn't push me like a pig to slaughter!"

"Nine lashes."

She clamped her mouth shut, fury swirling inside her like a storm.

With a hard hand on her shoulder, he forced her to her knees before the woodchopper's block and motioned to one of his men. Her knees ground into the earth, further dirtying the wedding gown. Buttons popped and the points of the sleeves dragged in the mud.

She squeezed her eyes shut and when she opened them a man was nailing a spike into the block a dagger's length from her face. Every thunk of the hammer reverberated through her skull.

Bile rose in her throat. Clenching her jaw, she refused to give into panic.

The crowd grew larger, murmuring in hushed voices. To one side she saw Jennet, the laundress, holding her basket of linens. Brenna closed her eyes against the sight, and covered her ears with her hands.

She shivered as she felt strong male hands on her arms. One hand and then the other was brought in front of her to the spike and tied there. The ropes swirled around her wrists in symmetrical loops like some beautiful exotic snake. They cut deeply, biting into her tender flesh.

The crowd's voices strengthened into a roar. She wiggled to escape, to put her hands back over her ears, but her efforts were puny. The rough hemp scratched her skin as she pulled against the rope.

Breathe. Breathe. She couldn't seem to get enough air. The block pushed against her chest, the hewn wood smashing her lungs.

Behind her she felt Montgomery's presence. His anger. His largeness. Fury radiated off his body like heat from the hearth.

Anxiety rose higher and higher inside her, choking her like steel bands around her chest. *Our Father Who art in heaven*—

She bit her lip to keep from begging for mercy.

Hallowed be Thy name—

Beyond Montgomery, she felt the eyes from the crowd. Gooseflesh popped up on her arms and legs.

Thy will be done—

She stopped the prayer, suddenly angry with God that he'd made her a woman. If only she were a man, able to fight, able to choose her own destiny. She didn't want God's will if it included being female.

And then she heard a rip and air rushed across the skin of her back. She gasped.

Glancing backward, she saw Montgomery standing legs apart holding a whip. He wore only hose, boots, and a belt. Blood ran down his chest, dripping on the ground. Resolve gleamed in his eyes.

Terrified, she pulled against the rope binding her to the block. She tried to scramble off her knees and onto her feet. Why, why, why had they crossed him? They knew his reputation, his station as The Enforcer.

What a daft plan it had been to try to stab him.

The crowd drew in a collective breath as Montgomery unfurled the whip and silenced them with a wave of his hand.

"This woman has committed acts of treason. She has gone against the orders of the king and against the order of God by attacking her lord and master with the intention of murder. As The King's Enforcer, I now sentence her to a public whipping and beheading."

Oh, God.

Brenna squeezed her eyes shut, awaiting the feel of the whip. She wouldn't beg, she vowed. She wouldn't.

Around her she heard the sounds of the shifting crowd, of their approval of the punishment.

And then the whip cracked across her back and all thoughts left her brain. A line of white-hot agony laced across her skin.

Black spots formed in front of her eyes. Thrice more the whip sang through the air, landing with perfect accuracy across her shoulders. She screamed; feeling tears begin to leak from her eyes, and knew five more lashes would follow.

Sweat beaded on her upper lip. She pulled to one side, fighting the rope and dreading the next stroke. Gritting her teeth, she vowed to not scream again. She would not give him any more satisfaction.

With a soft pop, she heard the whip being flung to the ground.

Startled, she looked back, blinking the tears out of her eyes.

He paced to her, knelt and forced her neck down on the chopping block. She didn't fight, but looked at him with questioning eyes. Why had he stopped?

"I take no joy in another's pain. This was to keep order only and my point has been well-proven."

His face was blurry through the veil of her tears, but, even so, she could see that his anger was gone. His eyes still looked hard, but the red mote no longer shone. In a flash, she knew he still planned to kill her, but the public whipping and humiliation was over.

"Gramercy." Her voice sounded like a croak, her mouth dry as dirt.

He looked genuinely taken aback that she'd thanked him, and she felt her face heat. She wasn't thinking straight. If her hands had been free she would have covered her mouth with her palm.

Turning, he picked up an axe, running his fingers over the smooth wooden handle as if afraid that if he did not hurry he would lose his will to kill her altogether.

"My lord—" she started, trying frantically to think of something that would stave off the deathblow.

"Lady of Windrose, do you have any last words?" He raised the axe.

A gurgling sound came from her throat. She opened her mouth to speak but no words came forth.

Her heart beat like a drummer's frenzy. The seconds seemed to drag on, each one a year in length. The wood felt cool and hard against her cheek; four dark rings and endless others of lighter colors looped on the wood. Tans and blacks and browns all faded one into another as she stared at them, her eyes going blurry.

"Would you tell my sisters that I am sorry?" she finally managed to choke out, then squeezed her eyes closed and awaited the blow. Odd disjointed thoughts scattered through her brain. Would she die right away or would her head live for a few moments, severed from her body? Would her blood paint the earth in crimson? Would her miniatures be discovered? Perhaps this was her punishment for painting such things. For only wanting to enter the convent to follow her own selfish ambitions, not religious conviction.

"James!" A voice cried out from the crowd. "Halt! You cannot slay her."

The axe stayed high in the air, right over her neck. "Leave be, brother. This is not your concern."

Brenna opened her eyes to see a large man pacing toward them. He was similar in height and size to Montgomery, but his hair hung freely about his shoulders, wild rather than sharply contained like her husband's.

She could not see his face. He drew near Montgomery and stopped. "She is not to blame."

Montgomery glanced down at his chest. Red stains marred his hose and little splotches of blood fell from his torso to the ground. Damning evidence of her handiwork.

"You are here to bring peace to the region and to oversee the port. 'Twill cause discord among the castle-folk if you slay her."

"And if I do not then I'll not be able to sleep another night with my eyes closed."

"Then throw her in the dungeon, make her a slave or send her to a nunnery."

A convent! Hope soared in her heart.

"Stand back, brother. My duty is clear and this is the only way for peace."

Her hope crushed, she winced as the axe lifted even higher.

"Your position as The Enforcer has addled your brain. Use her as an asset, a pawn."

Brenna twisted her head as far as she could so she could to see Montgomery's face, to see if he was softening any. She wracked her brain to think of something to say that would tip the argument in her direction.

"Prithee, my lord," she said. "Give me my life and I will fight you no longer." Her pride kicked her for breaking her vow to beg. But she could be no help to her family dead. Mayhap she could poison him later. They said deceit and poison were women's weapons, but 'twas men who made it thus. What choice did a woman have in this world of men's power and men's wars?

Montgomery stood there, axe poised. "Offal is worth more than your word."

She swallowed, holding her breath. No words came to her to fight his claim. Pressing her forehead into the wooden block, she closed her eyes and began to pray again despite her fury towards God for making her a woman. She would not beg Montgomery again.

Slowly, he lowered the axe until its blade rested just on the nape of her neck. The sharp, cold metal chilled her to the marrow.

Moments ticked by.

Apprehension rose higher and higher, banding her stomach, squeezing off her breath. She opened one eye, angry he drew out the moment, that he stood there so calmly while she trembled on her knees. Pressure built inside her seeming to fill all her being until she felt she would burst. The fear, the terror overwhelmed her. If she must be a woman, why could she not be a fainting one?

"Zwounds! Just get it over with, man!" she cried out when she could take no more.

The axe twisted, raking to one side and nipping her skin. Her taught nerves registered it as strongly as a deathblow and her whole body convulsed. A stinging line burned her neck.

Another wave of terror went through her that it might please him to saw her head off slowly rather than lop it off all at once. The edges of her vision blackened and the voices of the castlefolk faded. Her head swam.

Mayhap she was the fainting sort of woman after all.

Chapter Six

"Awaken, Brenna. We must make plans. They are making talk of taking Father to London."

"Huh?" Midmorning sunlight streamed over the mattress in long yellow streaks as Brenna opened her eyes and blinked sleepily, trying to fathom what had just been said. "Am I dead?"

Adele hovered over her, shaking the bed. St. Paul paced back and forth across the pillows while Duncan licked her nose. "Get up, Brenna. We must rescue Gwyneth and Father."

At that, Brenna came full awake. Outraged, she threw back the covers and swung her legs over the edge of the bed. "Gwyneth and Father? It's their bloody fault that I nearly had my head chopped off!"

Adele and Panthos jumped backward as Brenna lurched off the bed.

Ignoring her stinging back, she scrambled to find the pack that Montgomery had emptied and refill it. "I'm leaving before the beast comes to finish his deed of beheading me."

"I do not believe Montgomery still intends to slay you."

Brenna remembered the hush of the crowd, the cool wood against her cheek and the terror in her heart. Her pulse sped, and she felt dizzy at the memory. "You are daft."

In sharp contrast to Brenna's panic, Adele calmly scratched the dog's head. "Panthos likes Montgomery."

"Panthos!" 'Twas the stupidest thing she'd ever heard. The world had gone mad. "Most likely my faint took the joy out of murdering me. Killing me isn't enough for a man like him—he could have done that here in the chamber." Her tirade rose in tone and pitch as she grew more and more determined to quit the castle. She accented her words by racing around her chamber, tossing random items for her journey into her pack. "He drew the whole process out to terrify me and probably sees my swooning as thwarting his plans. He may want to send me to the rack or worse for the mishap."

Panthos gazed curiously at her, ears upward as if he understood every word and thought she had lost her mind.

"Nay, Brenna, you must speak to Montgomery, see if you can lessen his sentence on Father. Both Gwyneth and I have been lock—"

"Father be damned! 'Tis his idiocy that caused this!" The thought of even seeing Montgomery made her queasy. In her mind she could see the red mote in his eye that bespoke vengeance. "And Gwyneth is as much to blame as him! Save yourself." Plucking her wedding garment from where it lay flopped over the trunk Montgomery had locked her painting supplies in, she flung it into the hearth. Flames burst around it. Duncan leapt onto the window seat as if to get away from the crazed humans.

Brenna hurried behind her dressing screen to find clothing for her journey. "Come with me. We will beg for shelter at a convent and pray Montgomery won't burn it down looking for us."

"But Gwyneth will be married off to one of the king's cohorts, and Father will be dragged through the streets and tortured if they take him to London. I know what Papa did to you was wrong—but he is still our sire. Montgomery is your husband; even with yesterday's events, he may still hear your plea."

Panthos barked once as if to agree with Adele.

A welling of dread clogged Brenna's throat at the word husband. "Not a husband in truth." She poked her head around the screen and scrutinized the sheets, searching for any sign of blood. "I am still a virgin. At least, I think I am. I need to get far, far away, have the marriage annulled and pray he never finds me."

With a pensive look in her eyes, Adele glided to the seat in the embrasure. Panthos followed and settled at his mistress's feet, flopping his large furry head on his paws.

Brenna scurried behind the dressing screen and peered at her wild red hair in the looking glass.

Someone had placed a sleeping cap on her head— Gwyneth? Adele?—but the curls had already begun to spring this way and that. Wearing the cap was a habit she'd let slide some when her hair had been freshly shorn, but she'd need it again soon to protect her locks. Her skin looked sallow and freckled.

"Ugh." Even if she wasn't dead, she looked like death. In this state, the convent nuns would think she was a harlot, hung over from a night of swiving randy men.

She hurriedly splashed water on her face, rubbed her teeth with a hazel wood stick trying to make the best of things. She needed to look respectable enough to not be mistaken for a whore or someone with the plague if she expected to find shelter along the way.

Picking her kirtle from her trunk, she inspected it. Three paint smears marred the faded blue bodice and the embroidery hung unraveled around the square-cut neckline. The sleeves had once been long, pointed, and graceful, but she'd cut them off and sewed them so they fit tightly around her arms and would not interfere with painting. The lack of embellishment made the dress look sad and out of fashion. But it would have to do.

Surely she could convince the nuns that she was simply a noblewoman down on her luck. She would explain her family's lands had been taken by cruel men and offer her talents as an artist to restore the convent's books and statues. A resident painter would be an asset.

Adele fingered her cane. "Montgomery intends to marry Gwyneth off. He says her beauty will cause discord."

"I cannot save Gwyneth." Nor anyone here. With one last glance at the looking glass, Brenna hurried from behind the dressing screen. "Gwyneth should count herself fortunate that Montgomery is only marrying her off and not having her whipped and beheaded. I'll have no part in provoking him further." She retrieved a wimple, secured it on her head and snatched her pack. "We must leave post haste. Come with me, Adele."

Challenging him with the knife had been daftness incarnate. She might rant to God about the unfairness of being born a woman, but ranting did not change the fact that it was so. Her safety lay in running.

Her father had shown an unholy disregard for their lives and the lives of the castlefolk by annoying Montgomery in the attack. She would no longer be a part of his schemes. Hurrying to the exit, she reached for the door.

The door flung open afore she could touch it. The terrier set off a shrill yapping, but Adele shushed him quickly.

Brenna yelped as Montgomery appeared in the doorframe. 'Twas as if speaking of escape had conjured their jailer from the pits of hell. He wore black hose and a black tunic and was larger even than she had remembered. In his hands, he carried a chain.

Yesterday's memory of being dragged to the courtyard, pushed to her knees, tied and whipped loomed in her mind. Her chest squeezed, choking off the air in her lungs. She looked for any signs of softness that he might have forgiven the ambush and stabbing and saw none. His jaw was set in a sharp line and tension pulled across his wide shoulders.

He had come to finish the beheading.

With a wave of his hand, he dismissed Adele who leaned on her cane and headed to the door. St. Paul scrambled into her arms.

Panthos wagged his tail and licked Montgomery on the hand as he followed her. Adele's familiar uneven gait faded. The terrier growled at him and Montgomery bent and held out his palm for the dog.

Duncan paused, reached his nose warily forward and sniffed the outstretched hand before following the pack out.

Montgomery straightened. "I have new jewelry for

you, wife." The last word was spat out like a bitter curse, his generous lips lifted into a snarl.

Warily, Brenna stepped back, her gaze darting to the open door and then the window. Obviously his softer side, if indeed he had one, was reserved for animals and not humans.

The metal clanked in Montgomery's hand and then unfurled. Five loops of iron connected by chains hung on his palms.

Brenna's eyes widened and sweat beaded on her upper lip.

Fetters of a slave.

Bloody hell. "Chains! You plan to chain me?" Despair rose in her chest as all her plans to shelter in a convent disappeared like smoke in the wind.

He began to stalk toward her, obviously planning more than to merely behead her. Humiliation and torture lay in her future.

"You cannot be serious," she gasped.

"You are a traitor. The chains should be the least of your worries."

Her legs turned watery thinking of prisoners sentenced to have their skin stripped from their bodies and their muscle and bones torn and broken by large hammers and hooks. Their screams of agony could last for days. 'Twas the price of treason.

She frantically scanned the chamber, looking for a way out. If she could make it to the window, she could fling herself into the courtyard—die a quick death. Taking her own life would land her a place in hell. But surely the devil had more mercy than The Enforcer.

Brenna edged toward the opening. If she moved too quickly, Montgomery would suspect and thwart her purpose.

The chains clanked as he paced closer, looming like a dark shadow. His eyes were steely and full of purpose, terrifying in their intensity.

Her heart hammered, beating so furiously she thought she could hear the sound thudding throughout the chamber. She stepped toward the window, her thighs tensing to make the final leap.

As if anticipating her move, Montgomery closed in on her.

She lunged; death beckoned her like a generous mistress of light. Her fingers touched the windowsill, her knee on the embrasure seat.

His hand closed around her calf just as she scrambled up on the window bench to make the final leap toward freedom and the safety of hell.

"Nay!" She kicked back at him, frantic for him to release her. "Let me go!"

He pulled her back. Her knees and thighs bumped on the edge of the seat and her chest scraped across the top of it. "Cease fighting, wench! There will be no such swift end for you."

She screamed, panic flooding her mind, and tried to wiggle away.

Undaunted by her efforts, he picked her up and carried her to the bed. "Shhh. Shhh. Be calm, wife." This time the word didn't sound like a curse. It was low and deep and soothing. He held her tightly, squelching her struggles.

She pushed against him, pressing her arms and legs outward to get away. 'Twas like trying to fight an iron cage, but she struggled until her strength was spent.

Tears rolled down her face. 'Twas pointless to combat him. Utterly, completely pointless.

He was a large man. She was a woman. A wedded

woman under the hand of her lord and master who could punish her at his whim. Furthermore, he was The Enforcer, a powerful man, legally empowered to torture and execute her as he saw fit.

More tears fell down her cheeks as her helplessness sank in. She furiously wiped them away, angry at her defeat.

Slowly he eased his grip. "Do not try to escape."

She tried to rally her strength, to give one last nod at getting free even though she knew it was futile. Weakness filled her limbs; her legs felt like lead weights. Her shoulders slumped and she nodded. "Yes, my lord."

Her own voice startled her. So this is how it would be—a world filled with "yes, my lord" and "of course, my lord" and "as you wish, my lord" until he finally tired of torturing her and finished the beheading.

"Stay here." He stood and the straw mattress jiggled.

Numbly, Brenna stared at him as he bent to retrieve the loops and chains from the floor. There may as well have been devil horns poking from his dark hair. She curled into a fetal position, hugging a pillow. Her stomach churned.

Straightening, Montgomery held the device up, his face as merciless and cold as a Roman warlord. Five iron manacles linked by a lightweight chain slid across his palms. Two for her wrists, two for her ankles, and one for her neck.

Her breath clogged in her throat. The cold, hard iron would wind around her neck and link to her limbs in a way that every step would be hobbled. She would not be free to run, or stretch or even climb stairs without trouble.

Worse, she would never be able to paint again. Even if she could break into the locked trunk, the chains would slop in the colors and drag across the canvas, inhibiting her from freely moving the brush.

She would be a slave in every sense of the word.

"There is truly no nee—"

"I won't have you jumping out of windows or trying to stab me at every turn." The links of chain slid across his long, blunt fingers. Clink. Clink. Clink.

She shivered.

The mattress ropes creaked as he sat on the edge of the bed. "Come, captive wife"—he patted his lap—"stretch your neck o'er my knees so I may fasten on your new necklace."

Every bit of pride she possessed crashed to the surface. Lay her head over his knees and allow him to snap a collar around her neck like one of Adele's pack?

Demeaning!

"Unless you would prefer to stretch it over the axeman's block again." The words were spoken as mild and politely as if he were offering her a choice between a slice of bread and a sweetmeat.

"I have no fear of death," she said shakily. Had she not just thought to kill herself moments before?

"Then perhaps we could stretch you o'er the spokes of the wheel."

She swallowed, a touch of ice shooting inside her veins. She'd once seen a man executed by that means. The victim had every joint broken in his arms and legs. Then his limbs were braided through the spokes of a large wheel, which was hoisted atop a tall pole. Around and around he spun as ravens plucked bits of bloody flesh from the man's body.

Her hand went instinctively to her throat as she scrutinized Montgomery's face for any sign that he was bluffing.

His jaw was hard as flint. No flicker of compassion shone in his eyes, and he gazed back at her as if he knew the battle was already won and merely waited for her to acknowledge it.

His long fingers skimmed over the links of the chain, one by one, as if counting them.

She shuddered. No doubt The Enforcer had sentenced many to death on the wheel and felt no measure of guilt over the pain they would suffer. "Is that how your last wife was murdered?"

His fingers stilled on the chain. "Nay."

"But you did murder her, didn't you?"

The mote in his eye reddened. "Some say that. Not the wise ones."

A deathly silence hung in the room. And she knew the battle was won.

Angrily wiping the tears from her cheeks, she moved to a kneeling position. Her face heated at what she was about to do. "'Tis vile to treat one's wife such," she said, unable to contain her tongue.

He glanced down at his chest and she knew that beneath his tunic he would have a long red gash and a small hole above his heart where *l'occhio del diavolo* had stuck him.

A tremble began in her knees and quivered up her legs to her stomach, so strong that she could scarcely hold herself upright. Of a truth, they were mortal enemies, bonded together by the church in marriage.

Unfit partners.

An unholy match.

If only she had been able to enter a nunnery as she had wanted! That life was sterile and dry, but at least she could have worked her way into a position of power and then used her spare time to paint and enjoy her artwork. Painting crosses and halos would be a form of torture, but even at its worst, it was painting. And, likely she'd have novices to mix the colors.

Taking a deep breath, she pushed her regrets behind her, placed her hands palm down on the bed, her fingertips nearly touching his thighs, and stretched her neck across his lap. The bed rustled with the movement. His thighs were warm and firm and she could feel the vitality pulsing within them. He wore soft spun hose of high quality. From this position, every fiber of his muscles seemed to bulge through them. He smelled of sandalwood and maleness and some other scent she could not discern.

Lifting the wimple slightly in the back, he looped the metal around her throat, his fingers sure and steady as if he'd done this a thousand times before. She grimaced at the cool hardness of the collar on her skin. Her pride stung, and she set her jaw so that no more tears would fall.

Her mind spun, trying to find ways to make the best of her circumstances and to change things to her favor. Surely the blacksmith could forge a key. Or she could write to her brother Nathan and he would know a way out.

There was a small snap and a click as the manacle was locked in place. She gritted her teeth and set her jaw, tamping down the urge to yowl with outrage. His hands loosed and she was allowed to raise her head. She swallowed against the iron. The ring was thin and strong. It wasn't tight, but the weight felt heavy against her neck.

"Sit up," he commanded, shifting his position slightly to take hold of one of the smaller metal loops.

She complied, smarting at his tone and her mind still whirring with ideas on how to set him off guard.

"Give me your arm."

Resisting her pride, she did so, allowing him to snap the manacle around her wrist without incident.

"No pleading?"

Bowing her head slightly, she regarded him through her lashes. "Nay, my lord," she said, trying to attain the proper conquered demeanor.

"Good."

Bastard. She burned at the arrogance of his tone.

He took her other wrist and she forced herself to not withdraw it. This was her right hand and once it was bound, she would be unable to hold the brush steady enough to paint. A knot formed in her stomach. What if she was never able to get free? What if the manacles crippled her hands?

She forced herself to stay compliant. Fighting The Enforcer would be a battle of wills, not a battle of strength. If she resisted, no doubt she would be whipped before being locked into the fetters. If she told him how much her painting meant, he might even break her fingers.

The lock clicked into place and she swallowed. She *would* find a way free. And a way to paint again. She had to. Painting was her escape. Her sanctuary. Her sanity.

"Stand up, and spread your arms."

Heat rose in her cheeks as she slid off the bed. The loop around her neck fell against her collarbones and the hard metal rubbed her skin with every move she made. The two ankle bands hung lifelessly downward, still unattached to her legs.

· Montgomery scrutinized his handiwork, running his fingers around the manacles. The sensation of the pads of his fingers running across her skin was a cross between a tickle and the rough feel of sand.

She shivered. "Surely three bands are aplenty. There is no need for five."

"Place your foot on the bed."

"It is unnecessary for—" she started.

"Nay," he said not allowing her to finish. "Lift your leg."

Her cheeks prickled even further as she obeyed, feeling like a mare going through her training.

"Prithee," she said softly, holding out her hands and letting the chain dangle between them. "I already have arm hobbles."

The red mote was gone, but his eyes were unreadable as his gaze flicked to her face. His smooth, well-shaved jaw neither tightened with annoyance nor slackened with compassion.

She held her breath for a moment, hoping that he debated her request.

He shook his head and patted the bed, indicating where she should place her foot.

She let out her breath. No mercy would be forthcoming.

"Hold my shoulder for balance if you need."

The smug coxcomb!

Glaring at him, she shifted her weight and bent her knees for balance so she would definitely not have to hang on to him while he bound her. She raised her leg and placed it beside him, focusing on staying upright without help.

His lips twitched, the first sign of emotion he'd given since this ritual had begun.

Was he laughing at her, or had she been mistaken?

The manacle snapped closed, and she wavered. She

bent her knee further. Do not fall. Do not fall, she willed her body.

"Other leg."

With an effort, she lowered her limb, proud that she had not needed to clutch him like a puppet. She shifted her weight onto the manacled leg, feeling the metal circle move about her ankle, and began to raise her unbound foot.

She hated him. Hated him! If she could think of a way to crugal him on the head she would have.

His gaze snapped to her face as if he had suddenly read her mind and she wobbled to one side.

Just do not fall. Do not fall.

"Do not make this harder on yourself than it is already. Use my shoulder for support," he commanded, taking hold of her calf. "Wobbling or falling because your pride does not wish to touch me will only hurt you."

Forcing her face into a bland mask, she gave him a tight smile that felt more like a grimace and placed her hand on his shoulder. If she stumbled now, she'd never recover even a shred of her pride—better to use his body for support.

She felt steadier on her feet using him as a brace. His shoulder was undoubtedly the thickest, most solid one she'd ever seen or touched—not that she'd had much experience touching men's shoulders, but she *had* painted plenty of them. The muscle formed a tight knot under his tunic, unenhanced by the pads that were so popular these days.

Once the manacle was locked, he allowed her to set her foot back on the floor. Her skin tingled, as if burned from his touch. A shudder went through her. He was the devil, and this was hell.

"Can you walk?"

Brenna looked down at the chains, which made a large spider web in front of her body. She stretched out her arms and the links made tiny metallic clinks. There were two sets of chains that radiated out from the wrist manacles. One set slipped through a loop at her collar, and she could stretch either her right or left arm out fully, but not both of them at the same time. The second set connected the wrist manacles to a metal loop near her bellybutton, which was connected by another chain to her collar as well. The leg chains slipped through this loop so that she would not be able to lift her hands unless her feet were fully in the air.

Her chest constricted as the extent of her bonds sank in.

Helpless. Unable to run.

"Walk to the hearth, captive wife," he said, taking her by the shoulders and turning her toward the fireplace on the opposite side of the chamber.

She smarted at his command and almost shook her head in refusal. She *would* find a way free.

"If you cannot walk, I will adjust the length of the chains."

She glowered at him. "You do not care if I walk or not; please do not condescend to me by pretending otherwise."

He took her chin in his hand and lifted it. "Do not presume to tell me what I care about and what I do not."

Jerking her chin from his hold, she turned and stalked to the hearth. The chains made small sounds and it felt awkward to be unable to stretch her legs out fully, but she had no trouble moving about so long as she did not try to run or hurry. At the hearth, she whirled around and placed her fists on her hips. "Satisfied?"

"Very well. Now walk back."

When she returned to him, he nodded in approval. She wished she could wrap the chains around his throat and throttle him.

"Am I to remain thus for all of my life?"

His lips lifted into a wicked half smile, and he ran his finger along her collarbone in a claiming gesture. "If it pleases me."

She bit her tongue to keep herself from retorting. A hot glaze of anger clouded her vision and her hand itched to slap him as she had in the chapel. She moved her arm slightly and realized that even if she had enough daring to do so, she no longer had the physical ability. She could not fully lift her arm to his cheek without leaving the rest of her limbs at awkward, unbalanced angles.

"I wish you would have beheaded me yesterday," she said.

"Me too." He fastened the locks' key onto a leather cord that hung around his neck. "Instead we are bound together 'til death do us part."

She swallowed, wondering what would happen next. Would he toss her on her back and demand his marital rights? All he would have to do was tether the chains to the bedposts, and she would be exposed and lifted for him to do his worst. She would have no hope of fighting him off. A long shudder ran through her at the thought of that indignity. Lifting her chin, she vowed to face whatever evil he had planned for her with self-respect.

"If you mean to swive me, I won't fight you—"

"Good."

"—but do not mistake that for consent."

He tucked the key within his tunic and scrutinized her for a long moment as if wondering what to do with her. "We will save that discussion for tonight."

Her stomach twisted into a knot.

His gaze flicked to the bodice of her dress as if he could see beneath it. His lips turned down slightly as he took in the three paint spots and loose embroidery.

Well. She lifted her chin. How dare he look down on her clothing when he was naught but a barbarian.

Slowly, Montgomery curled his hand around the nape of her neck. He leaned close so that his breath tickled her ear and she could smell the male musk of his skin.

She shivered, a confusing heat spiraling through her. The same as she'd had in the chapel. Mentally she shook herself. Had she been locked away so long, so starved for attention that even a brute such as this moved her?

"Did you really mean you would not fight me?" he whispered.

"Nay—Yea—nay—" she stammered, then stopped, realizing she sounded like a fool.

His lips grazed her ear sending a line of heat streaking through her belly. She started to pull away then remembered she was going to retain her dignity and not put up a pointless fight. For a long moment she just stood there while his lips ran softly across her earlobe. The hair on her nape prickled.

A betraying desire welled inside her. Ne'er in her life had a man touched her thus.

She'd expected rutting violence, for him to toss up her skirts and plow into her. Something she could block out of her mind through sheer willpower. But this . . . this seemed so much more intimate. Soft, warm kisses.

Her teeth chattered.

Abruptly, he pulled away. A half-smile graced his face and once again she was struck by how perfectly handsome he was. She lifted her hand to her ear touching the slightly damp spot where his lips had been. Inside, anger and confusion swirled in a dangerous whirlpool.

"You should not have done that," she said.

"Why?"

Flustered, she grasped for her fury. "Because I am chained like an animal!"

"Only so I can sleep, eat, and walk without concern where the next dagger thrust will come from. Save for your bonds, we may as well try to get along as well as any other married couple."

"I cannot even move about!"

He shrugged. "The bonds are light and smooth. In time you will become accustomed and not even notice them."

She held her arm out angrily. "Not notice them!"

He shrugged. "On my travels I have seen many women in such."

Shocked, she willed herself not to allow her mouth to gape. "Ladies wearing chains?"

"Nay, slave girls."

She glowered at him. "I'm no slave, sirrah."

"The women learn to move so that it does not interfere with their duties," he continued as if she had not spoken.

Duties? Did he mean *wifely* duties?

"I won't be your whore."

He laughed aloud and the sound infuriated her. "You will if I so desire it."

"You dam—"

Before she could get the curse out, his lips topped hers, claiming. Possessing. Dominating all her senses with his presence. His tongue slid into her mouth, licking the front of her teeth.

Heat shot through her. Her brain went fuzzy. His tongue danced with hers, and she waffled between the urge to bite down on it or to surrender to its caress.

When he released her, she grasped her bodice, trying vainly to still her thrumming heart. Her brain felt befuddled, and she realized she was panting. Whether from fury or some base need she did not know.

She glanced at the door, desperate to put some space between them. To give herself a chance to think.

He must have sensed her confusion and had mercy on her reeling emotions, because he latched her wrist and pulled her toward the exit. "Come, captive wife, so I can introduce you."

"Introduce me?"

"Aye. To my men and their ladies."

Her pride forced her spine to stiffen. "I am no festival monkey to be paraded around."

"Nay, you are my wife. As such, you will obey me."

"I am in chains!"

"Which, I have explained," he said as if speaking to a child, "will not interfere with your duties."

He emphasized the word "duties" in a way that left her again wondering exactly what duties he was talking about. He paused. "Then again, mayhap you would prefer to finish what we began here. There are other duties asides attending my men that I will require of my wife."

She swallowed, feeling ill as he headed toward the door. She didn't want to ask about these other duties.

Being introduced in chains was still better than staying here in her chamber and being swived.

She moved her fettered feet to keep from tripping. He did not give her time for shoes, likely did not even notice she wore none. Cursed barbarian.

Dread welled inside her as they entered the hallway. The scents of rosemary, fresh hay, and tallow wafted in the air. Ne'er had she enjoyed social affairs as Gwyneth did and it had been a year since she had roamed the keep.

How could she possibly face all the castlefolk disgraced as she was? She could scarcely walk in her bonds. Her heart skipped and she knew her face was flushed. Their curious, pitying gazes would overwhelm her.

She tarried, dragging her feet on the planks to hold off as long as possible. She was well aware that 'twas common practice for knights to display their captives bound and subdued, but somehow it seemed an obscene practice.

"Come, my lady."

She ground her teeth. "Yes, my lord," she gritted out, vowing to not let him know the depth of her humiliation.

Somehow, someway, she would get free from him.

Chapter Seven

A short while later, Brenna suppressed the shivers that threatened to engulf her as she climbed down the tower's narrow stairwell with her wrist encircled by her captor's fingers. The chains clanked so that each step drove a stake into her pride.

She pulled her wimple further around her face, looking for tools she might use to pick the locks. Could the decorative metal on the sconces be broken and used?

They reached the bottom and started down the hall. Montgomery did not look at her, but marched her as one would a military prisoner. His boots gleamed; nary a speck of dirt dismayed their surface. Light from the arrow slits flickered across the black linen of his tunic winking the fabric from dark gray to black in a precise pattern as he paced past them. With scorn she noted that the linen had been ironed to crispness—likely he had a staff of servants whose sole duty was to care for the meticulous and demanding way he kept his garments. She imagined an army of sweating women, stooped from hours of using smoothing stones.

Seething, she vowed that when she escaped, she

would steal one of his tunics and pound it into pig shite for the sheer pleasure of the act.

He walked slowly so that she could keep up, but part of her wished he would drag her and show the world what a horrid brute he was. They turned a corner and the sounds of revelry could be heard from the great hall.

Ysanne the baker's daughter and Genna the alewife stood in an alcove speaking in hushed tones behind their hands. Brenna slowed even further, wanting to catch their eye and somehow indicate for one of them to tell her sisters to find her.

"She always was a bad girl, apainting those pictures when she should have been helping her father," she heard Genna whisper.

Anger shot up Brenna's spine. How dare they look down on her when it was her sacrifice that kept Montgomery from burning the castle to the ground!

"I do *not* deserve this," she hissed at the two women as she walked by. "Go get Adele and bring her to me."

Ysanne sneered at her and lifted her chin.

Brenna smarted. Obviously no help would come from that quarter.

The manacles bit into her wrists as Montgomery yanked her forward. "No gossiping with the servants."

She set her jaw and stared hard at *l'occhio del diavolo* tucked into Montgomery's belt as if gazing at it could make it fly from his hip and land in her hand. The blade moved in time with his precisely ordered steps, gliding against his hips back and forth with each swing of his legs. Even knowing that brute force was not the way to fight her husband, her palm itched for the dagger.

As they passed more and more armed guards, the

futility of such an action bit into her soul. Huge men wearing swords and gleaming armor lounged in doorways and leaned against the walls. They snapped to attention as Montgomery passed. Her husband must be a rich and powerful nobleman to afford such a personal guard to accompany him to a wedding.

The noose tightened around her throat, threatening to strangle her. Of a truth, she belonged to The Enforcer. To whip. To punish. To swive. To lead around in chains.

She was a prostitute of peace.

A man's plaything.

A prize of war.

What an evil, awful role.

And so very far removed from the life of independence and strength she envisioned for herself when she imaged herself as a high-nun in a convent.

"Harlot," a soldier sneered as she passed, but Montgomery gave him a stern look, and the man cleared his throat and looked down.

A welling of despair threatened to eclipse her anger.

What if she could ne'er get loose? She forced her mind away from that desperate thought. She *would* find a way to pick the locks or steal the key. She had to.

She would be observant and ready when opportunity came. She had already arranged passage to Italy if she could make her way to the docks before the ship left. Even if she were slain on the road before she made it to her brother's home surely it would be better than being Montgomery's toy for pleasure.

They neared the great hall. The rattling of the chains grated on her nerves as she shuffled along behind her husband. She shivered at the precision of his steps, at the determined set of his shoulders. He was a man of order and form; all of her life from her messy paintings to the hanging embroidery trim on her kirtle seemed rash and chaotic.

Mint and rosemary had been strewn into the rushes and the sweet, spicy scent floated around them as his boots crushed the leaves. By comparison, her bare feet seemed vulnerable.

He squeezed her wrist in a grip that was commanding but not hurtful. Her hand felt fragile in his larger one. Puny.

Her weapons were her wits and her courage. They would have to be enough.

She willed her face not to blush as they passed Jennet the laundress on the steps to the Great Hall. Jennet had been her friend before and she wondered if she would join Genna and Ysanne in their scorn.

"Milady?" Jennet offered, propping her basket on one of her hips.

Brenna unfocused her eyes, willing herself not to see her, to not see any of them.

"I'll get yer sister, milady." Jennet lifted the hem of her skirt as if to run. "She's the cause of this, she is."

Gratitude welled in Brenna's heart that all of them had not turned against her. "Gramercy, Jennet," she whispered, the words coming out rough.

The sound of clattering tankards and laughing men grew louder, gusting around the walls from the depths of the Great Hall. The scent of roasting meat and baking bread wafted into the air.

They passed more and more castlefolk lingering in the passageways and alcoves. Brenna caught little snippets of conversation as they passed.

"Serves 'er right," said one as he gawked at her

bonds. "She ought not astabbed him like that, she shouldn't of."

"Disobeyed her father, disobeyed her husband."

"'Tis a shame the way women act these days."

"Now if you get right down to it, women'll be the downfall of England, they will."

Taking a deep breath, she determined to not allow any of them to know of her turmoil. But her upper lip beaded with perspiration as they passed more and more curious onlookers and the full humiliation of being trussed up and paraded in chains sank in.

One woman caught sight of the bonds and gasped; the goblet she held clattered to the floor, splattering ale across three people who yelped and jumped back.

Brenna winced, wishing she could stare all of them down or could somehow cover that she was bound like a cur, following in her master's wake. Even the very bones of her cheeks seemed they would melt from the fierce hot blush on her skin.

Straightening her shoulders, she stared at unlit sconces on the wall and allowed her vision to unfocus so all the weight of their gazes would not seem so sharp and frightening.

Somehow she would find her way to freedom and independence. She would head to Italy, lose herself in her artwork and forget Montgomery ever existed.

If that were possible.

But she doubted she would ever forget this humiliation. Or the kiss he'd given her. Or the way his lips had felt on her earlobe.

The heady thought terrified her.

If only her aim into his heart had been true. If only she had not hesitated. She cursed herself for that hesitation—for being a woman. If only she were a man mayhap she would not have had such moments of weakness.

Mayhap she could steal an eating knife and try again.

They stepped over the threshold of the great hall. For a moment, Brenna halted, stunned at the changes in the room. She had not seen the chamber in a year.

Servants bustled to and fro; soldiers lounged on benches at the trestle tables. Adele sat by the window, petting Duncan; Panthos lay at her feet. Gwyneth was conspicuous by her absence and Brenna wondered about that. With luck, she would be able to speak to Adele afore the feast's end.

Her favorite tapestry depicting a foxhunt was missing. It had been in her family for three generations, and the wall looked lonely without it.

Bread trenchers lined the large table on the dais instead of silver ones. Beside the hearth, the comfortable padded seats where she had spent many pleasant evenings playing chess were also gone. In their place: hard, straight-backed chairs.

She closed her mouth. Montgomery knew naught of her imprisonment this past year; he did not need to know of her family's personal strife. 'Twas best she not appear like a gaping fish pulled from the lake.

Still, she glanced around uneasily.

Had Montgomery's men already started to rob her family's wealth? It did not seem possible for them to have changed so much in such a short time.

"Come, my lady," Montgomery said, his voice a low command. He shifted his tunic and *l'occhio del diavolo* glinted in the sunbeams streaming in through the windows. It bore both testimony of her failure and a silent warning. Her palm itched again, and she wished she could take the knife.

By force of will, she turned her gaze away from it and stepped into the hall. Naught would be gained by foolish gestures. She would wait and she would observe.

Montgomery tugged her forward and she stepped into the pandemonium.

All the castle's inhabitants had been invited to the wedding feast and the hall was loud and riotous. The cacophony caused the clanking of her chains to be lost.

Across the chamber, she saw Egmont the blacksmith sucking ale from a tankard. Her heart sped. The two of them had always been friendly in the past; mayhap she could secure his help with the manacles. She craned her neck, hoping he would look in her direction, but he did not even look up. She bit down a wave of disappointment.

"Wife!" she heard one of Montgomery's animals yell from across the hall.

Brenna cringed. If she did not escape, such would be her lot now: for a man to forever be ordering her about.

"Have I not told you to leave your hair unveiled?" the warrior continued in a bellow.

Glancing up, Brenna saw a huge scarred brute pluck a silken veil from a small beautiful pregnant woman's head. An abundance of red hair, darker than her own, spilled down her back and hips reaching nearly to the rushes.

"My lord!" the lady admonished, reaching for the shiny green fabric. Her wide emerald eyes flashed him a look of irritation. "I just had that made. 'Twas expensive! And we are guests!"

The monstrous brute gave Brenna and Montgomery a quick glance. With a flick of his wrist, he tossed the veil into the hearth. Orange and green flame brightened around the material, burning the delicate fabric in a flash.

"Aaagh!" the lady exclaimed.

Irritation curled through Brenna at the frustrating lot of a married woman. At the mercy of some oafish man's whims. 'Twas exactly why she planned a life of independence at a nunnery! She glanced down at the masculine hand that held her wrist and pressed her manacle into her skin. Loathing waved through her. Fighting the urge to pull away, she looked back at the new beast.

The unveiled lady raised herself onto her toes to glare into the giant's eyes. She grasped a handful of his blue tunic in each of her small hands. Her smooth alabaster complexion contrasted with his tanned scarred skin. Her delicate limbs with his brawny ones.

"You are the most vexing husband a woman could have. Arrogant, impossible, beef-witted blackheart!"

Brenna squirmed, wanting to close her eyes to what would surely happen next and yet was unable to turn away. She awaited the warrior to cock his arm back and club her for her impudence.

Instead, a slow smile lifted his lips into a lopsided grin that crinkled the white crescent scar on his cheek. His eyes lit with blue flame. He slapped his wife on the bottom, but the stroke was without heat. His hand lingered, folding over her buttock in a gentle, overly familiar caress as he pressed her into himself. Even with all his brutishness, 'twas obvious he was being cautious with her pregnant belly.

"I like your hair," he said simply.

The woman gave an exasperated long-suffering sigh, then yanked him close and kissed him.

"Barbarian," she said when the kiss was broken, but

she tilted her chin down and glanced up at him in a way that made Brenna wonder if the lady had worn the veil apurpose.

He ran his hands over her long locks, digging out a wayward hairpin and tossing it into the rushes.

Brenna blinked, running a finger across the locks on her manacles. Could she unlatch them with a hairpin?

Beside her, Montgomery cleared his throat.

The couple turned.

Keeping her gaze on the spot where the hairpin had landed, Brenna tried to memorize the exact position.

"Come, wife. You will meet my brother Godric and his lovely wife Meiriona, the lord and lady of Whitestone." He jostled her forward and the location of the hairpin was lost, eaten up by the multitude of rushes.

Devil take it.

Irritated with the loss of the ill-formed plan, Brenna scowled at the new intruders.

So this was the legendary lord and lady of Whitestone. She had heard of the great love and passion between them, but 'twas unseemly for them to act thus in the great hall.

Brenna looked from her new husband to his fearsome sibling. Of a truth, it must have been this man who her sister had seen at the tournament. He and Montgomery had a similar look, but scars laced this man's face and his hair was shaggy instead of set in close-cropped precision. In contrast to her husband's unadorned black tunic, he wore a blue paltock with delicate embroidery that looked to have been stitched with painstaking care.

Clothing of a man well-loved by a woman.

Montgomery caught Brenna's hand and drew her forward. "I will introduce you."

The giant tucked his wife's hand into his own as they approached. The lady had the grace to look slightly abashed. She pushed a strand of wayward hair behind her ear then held her hands out to Brenna.

Awkwardly, Brenna took them. The woman's long auburn hair swayed gently against her calves. Her green gown was of high quality with an empire waist, and she wore sparkling emeralds around her neck.

The clothing of a woman well-indulged by her lord.

Naught like her own marriage at all. As discreetly as possible, Brenna shuffled her toes around in the rushes, hoping to come across the hairpin.

"Congratulations on your marriage and the union of our families," the woman said, as if no hostilities had occurred. Mayhap she was daft.

"Th–thank you," Brenna stammered.

"I am Meiriona of Whitestone and this barbarian is my husband Godric."

Leaning forward, Brenna tried to determine if the woman's mass of long hair contained any more pins. Surely such an object could pick the locks.

"Ho, brother!" The scarred warrior drew Montgomery into a bearlike hug with cuffs and claps that would have left a smaller man bruised. The giant eyed Brenna and nodded. "I like her. She suits you." When he moved his head, she suddenly recalled where she'd seen him: he'd been the one to stand up to The Enforcer during yesterday's hurly burly. "And lovely wedding jewelry," he continued, eyeing the chains.

Brenna flushed, indignant anger rising inside her. She wished she could crawl beneath a trestle table to hide from the prying eyes of others.

Apparently heedless of her discomfiture, the

warrior winked at his wife. "Might need to get a set for you, love."

Brenna felt her face grow hotter. She was some big joke for them all. She wiggled her toes more furiously in the rushes, determined to find the hidden hairpin and set herself free.

The lady shook her head at her husband and pulled Brenna across the hall, her pregnant stomach wobbling this way and that as she went. "All bark, no bite," she murmured to Brenna. "Treat him well and you can have everything you've ever wanted."

"Freedom?" Brenna asked bitterly.

"Of course. 'Tis only his pride you must soothe to gain such."

His pride. Bah. And what of her own?

At that moment a loud screech sounded across the hall.

Gwyneth barreled toward her wearing a blue woolen dress with long embroidered sleeves. "He put you in chains! Oh, blessed Lady of Mercy." She stopped before Brenna and threw her arms around her. "Brenna, forgive me."

A hush fell on the hall as men, women, and servants turned to look their direction. Brenna felt Montgomery's eyes watching them. "Get up, Gwyneth."

"Dear heavens, sister. Are you all right?"

"Yea," Brenna answered, unsure if it was entirely true.

"But the chains. Oh, Mother of Mercy, the chains. I am so sorry. I never meant for it to end like this. There has to be a way out. This is not what I intended at all."

Unease prickled Brenna's neck. Her sister was talking much too loud, attracting too much attention. "Shh . . . shh."

The hall grew quiet. Montgomery's boots scrunched on the rushes and Gwyneth turned as he approached.

"I will set things aright."

Zwounds. Not another of her sister's bedlamite ideas. "Nay, he doesn't need to kn—" Brenna whispered, but halted as Montgomery closed in on them.

Both women turned to gaze up at him. He scowled, imposing as ever.

"Doesn't need to know what?" he asked.

"Naught, my lord. A small matter betwixt my sister and I," Brenna said, latching on to Meiriona's plan to soothe her husband's pride. She licked her lips.

Gwyneth held her hand out to him. "My lord, I beg you to release Brenna from this union."

"And you are?"

"Gwyneth, her sister."

When Montgomery made no indication that her name meant anything to him, Gwyneth dropped into a deep curtsy.

A feeling of impending doom welled inside Brenna like that moment when a brushstroke has gone astray but the paint smear had not yet appeared on the canvas.

"My lord, this is my fault," Gwyneth began.

"Shush, sister," Brenna implored, trying to reach for her sister's mouth to cover it with her palm. The bonds made moving quickly awkward.

"I beg you to release my sister and take me." Gwyneth held her hand out to Montgomery.

Frantic, Brenna lunged for her sister, clapping a hand tightly over her mouth. "Shush, you ninny! He doesn't know."

God only knew what Montgomery would do when he found out they had switched places at the altar.

"Know what?" A tight tic started in his jaw and

Brenna's heart dropped into her stomach. Would he lead her out to finish the beheading when he discovered their trickery was not yet over?

Gwyneth pushed Brenna away and dropped into a position of fealty.

"Gwyneth, cease, you milksop!" Brenna tried to hoist her pea-brained sister to her feet, but, fighting, Gwyneth remained on her knees with her palms toward Montgomery.

"I tricked you, my lord." Gwyneth lifted her hands even higher in an obvious beg that he take hold of them. "I am your bride, not she. I will willingly become your wife, your concubine, your slave, whatever you require, just, please, please, I prithee, do not harm my sister. 'Twas my fault and mine alone that she attacked you in the bridal chamber."

Brenna felt her fingers itch, wanting to smack her sister across the cheek and beat some sense into her. "Get up," she hissed. "Get up before I smack you."

Silence permeated the hall.

Dead silence.

Lifting her chin, Brenna glanced at her new husband to see what his reaction to Gwyneth's nitwitted declaration was.

His eyes were alight with an unholy gleam as he gazed from her to her kneeling sister and back again.

Queasiness poured into her stomach. Whatever he made of this new development, it would not be good.

Chapter Eight

James stared back and forth from the beauty kneeling before him to his new wife. Tricked *again*! These two had made him out to be the stupidest sort of fool.

The blood of generations of warriors ran through his veins and a battle cry rose in his soul. Fury coursed through him in thick waves, and for an instant, he wanted to behead both of them. He wanted to see them vanquished and conquered, their pride crushed beneath his heel. From their remains he wanted to pull his tattered honor and then force them to sew it back together.

He clenched his fists, determined to formulate a plan before embarking on his quest. For years his life had been controlled and ordered, his inner demons kept at bay by duty and honor and rigid demands. He would not let women's trickery tear his self-control apart. Honor was not gained by beating women physically.

Beyond a doubt, Gwyneth was the most stunning woman he had ever seen. She had a sweet, heart-shaped face, pale translucent skin, and glorious yellow hair. She looked like sunlight with bright turquoise sky for eyes.

As dazzling as Helen of Troy, she gazed up at him with a look that no doubt could conquer nations. A woman who fully understood her own beauty and wielded it with keen precision.

"You are offering yourself to me to save your sister?" The words came out with more control than he felt.

"Yea, my lord." The blonde looked ready to cast herself prone on the floor.

"I see." He would marry her off to someone who was blind to her beauty and unaffected by it. Someone who was wise to women's ways. He turned from her to the redheaded wench who was trying to haul her to her feet.

As if sensing the moment of reckoning was upon her, his wife let go of her sister and straightened, standing stiff and proud as any queen.

He stroked the hilt of the dagger in his belt, wanting to draw out the moment, to build worry inside her mind. Yesterday, she had cracked for an instant and begged him to strike her with the axe. Mayhap her impatience was a weapon he could wield against her better than the whip had.

This mission should have been simple: bring a measure of order to this area by marrying Lecrow's daughter, taking control of the busy port and flushing out the rebels who had made a laughingstock of the king by selling illegal erotic artwork to build up weapon supplies.

Instead he'd been ambushed. Stabbed. Tricked.

Reaching out, he thumbed the scar across his wife's cheek and felt a satisfying shiver run through her despite her warrior-like stance. She was comely, but his bride had been rumored to be a beauty, an English rose of such loveliness that men wept. He should have known that this woman's scar would have kept her from earning that title. Society rarely saw past a few scars or supposed imperfections.

Frustration coursed through him like a raging river that threatened to spill over the top of its dam that he had not suspected he had married the wrong woman. They had played him for a fool because he had acted like one. He'd been struck by her courage in the chamber, her willingness to push her sister behind her own body and face him squarely, just as she was doing now. As he had looked into her flashing eyes, the discrepancy between her scar and the rumors of beauty had not registered.

He curled his hand around her shoulder, resisting the craving to haul her from the Great Hall, toss her across his bed and show her who would be master here.

Mentally, he kicked himself for not paying more attention to the missive from the king that had demanded this marriage. He had not even bothered to check his new wife's name. One noblewoman was pretty much like the next. Or so he'd thought until his new wife had stabbed him and he'd been forced to put her in chains.

But not even the sight of seeing her trussed with manacles soothed the howling beast in his chest. Not while she was standing so unyielding and pompous.

Quivering and mewling at his feet might have a different effect.

Seeing his obvious interest in the hoyden he was married to, Gwyneth licked her lips in what seemed like a very calculated gesture. "I want to make things right. Take me as wife. I can please you. I want—"

"Gwyneth"—James cut in, deliberately sneering her name—"I have a wife already. Mayhap she will give me the same bargain to spare your life that you have offered to save hers."

His wife gasped, her little pink mouth forming a perfect "o," and he allowed himself a dark, satisfied smile. The beast of his own pride still circled in his mind, but it no longer howled with outrage.

Establishing dominance in private would definitely soothe its wounds. The thought of having the hellion who'd stabbed him as a biddable partner in his bed shot a streak of wicked desire through his groin. She'd looked erotic as hell bent in two with her neck stretched over his lap.

But, he didn't want to take her by force—he wanted to take her of her own compulsion, to make her body fully and completely his so that she craved and longed for his touch. He'd leave her shivering and trembling, her pride vanquished.

"But, my lord," Gwyneth protested, shuffling forward on her knees. Her lovely skirt dragged behind her, sweeping the rushes aside and exposing the planks beneath.

"Get up. Serve ale to my men and make yourself useful until I decide a husband for you."

She sank her teeth into her lower lip as if biting back words, then gave a jerky nod. Her blue skirt bounced around her as she flittered to the kitchens.

James took a deep breath before looking at his wayward wife and contemplating her fate.

She stood, hands on hips, glaring at him, and he

doubted she would have been as compliant if he had given her the order to fetch ale.

Hoyden.

All her pride and defiance affronted him. He wanted her crushed, mewling at his feet, panting and lustful in his bed, a slave to passion, as her sister had promised.

Her hands fisted at her sides as if she longed to punch him. The chain formed an X in front of her, but she looked more warrior than captive.

Theirs would be a battle of wills, but in the end, there *would* be only one master here.

"Your name, again, wife," he demanded. The act of having to ask something so trivial pinched his pride. Damn the woman.

Around them, he could feel the gaze of his men watching him.

To one side, Meiriona rustled. "Cease, James, you are frightening her."

Good. With a wave, he dismissed his sister-in-law. "This is not your concern."

Meiriona slid between them, her deep green gown swaying as she moved. "She has done no more wrong today than yesterday."

Noting the quietness of the hall and the many eyes watching them, he gave his sister-in-law a glower. "Stand aside. This is betwixt me and my *wife*." And my honor.

"Brenna," his wife said through clenched teeth. "My name is Brenna."

"Brenna." He tasted her name on his tongue. It was a strong name. Not flighty or girly. It suited her.

Brenna swallowed, and he could see the pulse fluttering in her throat. Her obvious fear did little to soothe the beast within him that demanded he conquer her.

Milksop, his father's voice said in his mind. *Beat her as is your right.*

He latched on to Brenna's wrist and pulled her toward the exit.

Meiriona gnawed her lip, but she didn't try to stop them. Her long hair quivered as she shook her head at him. He did not fault Meiriona, 'twas in her nature to step in when she saw one being intimidated: she'd done the same for him against his brother.

As soon as they were out of sight of the many people in the Great Hall, he whirled his wife around and pressed her back into the wall. Her unique scent— warm skin and gesso—teased his nostrils.

Placing one hand on each side of her head, he loomed over her. In spite of her bravado, her lower lip trembled.

Good.

"Why you, Brenna? Why did your sister not try to slay me herself? For all her emotional ways, 'tis obvious she cares for you."

Her gaze flicked to the dagger in his belt. "Gwyneth has not the heart and I did not think I would actually *be* married to you."

"Were you so confident of your knife skills then?"

"I felt I had naught to lose. I thought you would kill me if I failed."

Glowering, he grasped one of her arms and held it up so the light from the arrow slit sparkled off the chain. How vexing she was. "You were wrong. You aren't dead."

She lifted her chin. "Do you plan to execute me now?"

He smirked, glad he'd spared her life. Glad for the challenge of conquering her. "Executing you would be too easy." He ran his finger down her arm, enjoying the shiver it elicited from her. She was not as totally unaffected by him as she pretended. The chain made a soft chink.

Pressing her lips together, she stiffened her spine like a soldier caught by the enemy.

He stared down at her noting the fluttering pulse in her neck that beat against the tattered neckline of her kirtle. Her clothing was practically rags compared to the finely stitched and trimmed gown her sister wore.

"Your sister offered herself as my concubine," he whispered. "What is your offer?"

She stiffened so fully, he thought her back might fly apart from the effort. "Rape me if you will, but I'll not cede the same promise my sister gave." Her voice shook, but she did not flinch away from him. "My family has brought me much trouble and I had planned to flee afore you arrived. I'll not become your compliant puppet to save them from themselves."

He scrutinized her face, noting the stubborn set of her jaw, the fierce frown furrowing her brow. She had wide green eyes with two spots of brown in the left one. They burned with resolve as she gazed back at him. The scar crossing her cheek was thin and somewhat faded. In any event, the red line did not distract from the comeliness of his new bride.

"Tsk. Tsk. Such sisterly love."

Her eyes flashed. "Do not chide me for lack of sisterly love when you are scarce more than a brute and know nothing about my family."

Her words pinched his conscience, but he shoved the feelings aside. "Explain to me these issues. 'Tis clear that you are not so esteemed as your sister. Your clothing is plain to the point of near raggedness while your sister wears fine embroidery."

Brenna lifted her chin as if to show off the scar on her cheek. Did he see hurt in her eyes before haughtiness had covered it up?

"Methinks you are not so immune to your sister's plight as you pretend or you would not have switched places with her in the first place."

"As I said, I thought we would not stay married."

"But we are."

Her brow furrowed even more. "You cannot keep me bound forever."

Her insolence goaded him. "But I can," he said darkly. "I can keep you bound and force you to my will for the rest of your life—serving me night and day in any way that pleases me."

She swallowed. "I—I'll find a way free."

"Your easiest way to freedom is to please me."

She caught his fingers beneath hers. A calculating gaze formed in her eyes. "And how may I please you, my lord?"

Heat, hot and fast, filled his groin. He knew— knew!—she had not meant the question the way his body took it, but something about her fired an interest he'd thought long dead. She was being smart and cunning, not truly wanting to please him, but his cock did not care.

At once, he determined to have her agree to the same terms Gwyneth had offered. No matter her protestations that she would not agree to such to save her sister, he did not believe she would be so cold.

"It would please me to have you on your knees, naked and begging at my feet with the same question," he said, allowing the dark goal to turn over in his mind. His member tightened. 'Twould be true and complete abolishment of her pride. He'd seen her anger. Her fervor. To have all that passion as his to command was a very, very heady idea.

"And if I do so, will you release me from these chains and leave my sisters alone?"

"I thought you cared naught for your sisters," he taunted.

She turned her face aside, but not before he saw the pain on her features. She cared deeply for her family, and it angered her that she did. But, no matter, if there was to be peace between them, it would have to start in private. And her concern for her family would be a sharp weapon indeed.

"Methinks you care deeply for your sisters, both the beautiful one and the uncanny one. And there is your father and the castlefolk to concern yourself with as well. Your dishonesty does not please me. Why was I not told of the switch in brides sooner?"

She huffed. "While you were busy imprisoning my father, attacking my home, nearly beheading me and locking me in chains, there was no time."

Her wit caught him off guard, and he lifted a brow. For certes, the wench had nerve. She intrigued him in ways her beauteous sister did not and he felt stirring in his loins.

"Come, captive wife," he said, "we go to the bed-chamber to make a bargain."

Chapter Nine

A streak of cold terror shivered through Brenna at the direness of the situation and the sort of bargain that a demon like Montgomery would propose. For certes, it would involve the taking of her virginity. She had expected that act for hours—but she feared he had more in mind than merely pushing his rod inside her and consummating the marriage. The unholy interest in his eyes when he'd said he wanted her naked and begging at his feet terrified her.

Light flowed through the arrowloops, and dust motes danced in the sunbeams as they walked down the hallway. She gazed back and forth, trying to find a place to run and hide. But, chained as she was, she was well and fully defeated and they both knew it.

She squared her shoulders, determined to submit to her wifely duties with resolute bravery: she would become as still as one of her miniatures—not fight him no matter how he humiliated her. She would think about paint and colors and the smell of gesso, and try to memorize what she could to add to her next set of miniatures. Surely, the act, no matter how heinous, would not take long, and she could treat it as a way to enrich her art.

If she was ever allowed to paint again.

Images of how large his manhood had been in the bathing tub interrupted her vow to stay calm. She'd drawn her own private parts enough to know he would not fit inside her without a great deal of force. Her opening slit was small, tender . . . and his manroot had been thick. And hard.

Her trepidation intensified as they neared her chamber. What sort of bargain did he want? She could not imagine anything he had not already taken from her. Her home. Her freedom. Her pride. They were all toys crushed in his monstrous hands. He had even locked away her paints and brushes.

At last they reached her chamber. He flung open the door, hauled her inside and turned to stare at her.

She ran her hand across the edge of her wrist bond, feeling as conspicuous as a lone spot of paint against a white cloth. Would he pound into her while she was still chained? That would be the ultimate humiliation.

For an instant, she wished she would faint again.

Anger at her sisters and her father swam through her in a red haze. If they had not defied the king with the wedding, she would not have to mop up their mess with her very life and body. It would serve them right for her to deny Montgomery's every wish and leave them to their folly.

The door slammed shut, a horrid echoing sound like that of a future of independence being closed.

"You will give your enthusiastic willing consent to fulfill my every whim in bed in exchange for your father and sister's life," he said without preamble.

Enthusiastic! His every whim! Did the man expect

her to pretend some sort of feeling for him or thrill for what he was forcing on her? She fisted her hands on her hips.

"Just rape me and be done with it!" 'Twas a wonder the bloody beast had not jumped on her already. "I'm already bound. Do your worst."

He stalked to the bed, leaned a hip against one of the posts and crossed his arms over his chest. "That is not the bargain I wish to make."

"I do not want to bargain with you at all!"

"But you want out of the bonds. And you want your family and home to be safe."

She glared at him, furious that he spoke truth and enraged by his smooth control. If he had tossed her straightaway to the bed, she would have had defenses against that. But, this, this disgusting, calculated assault incensed her.

"I want your active support to bring peace to the region."

"Bah. What do men know of peace? All they think of is war."

"I'm not thinking of war right now."

She stared at his overly perfect face, at the thick biceps that bulged against his tunic and the trim hip propped against the mattress. His calm goaded her. If he was waiting for her to come offer herself, he could damn well wait all night.

"We are married—the church would claim that I belong to you and it would be neither force or rape," she spat out, angry she bespoke the truth.

"Point taken." He lifted a brow, and for an instant she feared he would do just that. Mayhap a softer approach would be more prudent.

"Why don't you take a willing woman to fulfill your needs instead of me?" she said reasonably.

"Because you are my wife, and that is adultery."

"But I would not mind, I swear it."

His lips lifted into a small smile, as if he was enjoying their discussion. The blackheart. "Swiving one of them would not consummate our marriage."

"We could put chicken blood on the bed if you need proof of the consummation."

He held up a hand. "Peace, Brenna. There will be no chicken blood here. 'Tis the two of us that need to work out our own union. Asides, I want children."

Children!

"Of all the horrid things." A lump settled in her throat. The vision of her quiet career as a convent artist crashed to the ground as she imagined herself being pulled this way and that by a passel of brats, her stomach as rounded as Meiriona's had been.

She looked around her chamber, wanting to focus on the desk, the window, the floor—anything but what might occur on the bed. The consummation alone would have been bad enough. But children?

"I am *not* a broodmare."

"Women love children."

She snarled her lip. "Not this one." Children were the epitome of duty and concern. The noose of responsibility that would suck her artwork dry. Already Bishop Humphrey had refused to show her paintings at the town's cathedral hall because of her gender. He had railed at her for doing artwork instead of doing her God-given duty to marry, stay home, and raise a family. She wanted naught to do with having children.

He gave her one long blink. "I need an heir."

She stared at him, again angry with her family

and with herself for not completing the act of slaying him. Of course, she *could* breed from the first act of consummation—from the taking of her virginity—but she knew that was unlikely. God only knew how many times they would have to copulate in order for her to become pregnant with his brats. "Nay."

He cocked his head to one side. "What do you understand about the relations between a man and a woman?"

She shrugged, uncertain where this conversation was going now or why he had changed the focus. "The usual things."

"And what would those usual things be?"

If he thought to intimidate her with frank talk, he was mistaken. Brother Giffard, who she sold her miniatures to, and she had had many such discussions. 'Twas not talking about the act or painting the act that frightened her . . . but the thought of actually doing the act and then the inevitable results of it that left her shaken to the core.

"A woman opens her legs and the man pushes his manroot inside her," she said, wanting to meet his crude talk with bluntness of her own.

"I see. So you understand what is expected?"

His enigmatic mannerism crawled under her skin. Why did he have to seem so smug, so sure of his knowledge? She knew as well as he how the act was performed. She had been painting that sort of picture for years. "Of course. I'm not a ninny, you know."

He thumbed his jaw, as if debating the next question to ask, and she realized her uppityness was not helping the situation. She needed rationality if she was going to take any control of this situation.

"I understand what is expected of me, my lord," she said with as much calm as she could muster.

His eyes smoldered, like twin blue coals from the pits of hell. "Nay, my lady. I do not think you understand at all. I want a willing and submissive wife."

"I will not fight you, if that's what you mean!" She held up her fist and shook the chain. "I could not do so, no matter how much I want to." If she thought it would do her any good, she'd beat on the door and yell for help, but she knew it would not.

Without moving from his position by the bed, he smiled outright then. A perfect, feral grin.

Only . . . his smile wasn't perfect.

Stunned, she blinked: his teeth were dazzling to behold, white, large . . . but the front two overlapped slightly.

Overlapped!

Not much, just a tiny amount, enough to add warmth to his presence and make him adorable and boyish rather than such a cold beauty.

His smile made him human. It was the first imperfection she'd seen on his otherwise magnificent form. There was no way to iron out his teeth the way he had his servants iron the wrinkles from his tunics. Had she seen his grin on their wedding night, she would have been unable to use the knife altogether. His smile was boyish. Charming. Almost sweet.

Shaking her mind clear, she willed herself back to the present situation. There was nothing sweet about the man. Especially not with his demanding goals of raping her until she was breeding with his brat. She needed to formulate a plan, to turn the tide in her direction.

"My lady," he continued. "I want so much more

than merely the absence of having to force you. I seek a bargain."

"A bargain?" That sounded horrible. Especially if it involved having his heirs. No matter what other bargains were foisted on her, she would not have babies. Silently, she made a vow to speak to Adele or one of the maids about ways to prevent children until she was able to escape.

"I want to be able to walk around without worrying where the next knife stroke or trickery will come from. The lives of your father and sisters in exchange for your vow that you will ne'er fight me in any way. I seek a quiet, calm marriage"—he lowered his voice— "and all that that entails in the bedchamber."

She gasped. "Never could I agree to a quiet marriage. Oft my tongue gets the best of me."

Straightening, he fisted his hands on his hips. "Then you should learn to curb it—for the sake of your family."

Another threat. She gritted her teeth. "'Tis a devil's bargain. My family does not deserve my concern."

He shrugged, and even that seemed precise and calculated. Both terrifying and thrilling in its masculine display. "Concern for our families rarely has anything to do with whether or not they deserve it. 'Twas what your sister offered in exchange for your life— complete submission in my bed."

A horrifying image of herself in twenty years bit into her imagination . . . she would still be wearing chains, but now stooped and humpback from the daily bowing to his every whim. Her fingers would be rubbed raw from the grinding daily tasks he set her about—and all to save a sister and father who cared so little for her that they locked her in her room for a year and embroiled her in a desperate plot to kill The King's Enforcer.

"I–I cannot do it," she stammered.

He must have caught the look on her face, because his demeanor softened slightly. "I will offer you this, Brenna: I want a wife, not a puppet. You may speak freely so long as you are respectful about any concerns you have about politics, the people, my policies or the running of the castle."

"How bloody magnanimous," she muttered sarcastically. She wanted to be free in her own right, able to paint and fight as she willed. Why had God cursed her such to be born a woman?

"But concerning the intimate acts between us, you must allow me free roam of your body and give yourself to me without question."

For a moment she fought the urge to scream, to rail at God for the unfairness of it all. She was glad Montgomery did not mention children again, because she *would* have screamed then. But, there were herbs to take so that babies could be prevented without his knowledge. Ne'er would she bear his heir!

"And in exchange for these things you will free me from these cursed chains?"

"Nay."

She narrowed her eyes at him. "But you will allow my family to be free?"

"Nay."

Breaking away from his nearness, she paced to her bare art desk. The need to sit and hold a paintbrush just so that something would seem normal nearly overwhelmed her. But her paints were locked away and her fingers felt empty and restless.

Silence engulfed the chamber like a heavy cloud.

Exasperated that he did not lead the conversation further or seem to be in any hurry with this damned bargain, she huffed out a breath. "What *is* my consent buying, sirrah?"

"My good graces. And do not call me that."

"Your *good* graces?" She rattled the band around her wrist and glanced out the window into the bailey, noting the various guards stationed around the walls. At the new targets that had been set up for the men to practice with their swords and bows. "You have taken my father captive, forced a marriage upon us, locked away my paint supplies, whipped and enchained me. What good graces do you have?"

"Your father would not be captive, nor your castle be under guard had your family followed the king's orders. As I have already stated, 'tis within my power to have everyone in your castle not only displaced from their land, but to have them beaten and imprisoned as well."

Brenna sucked in a breath as she was reminded again of the power The Enforcer controlled. They were all at his complete mercy. Her footing here was as dangerous as taking her illegal paintings to market. The lot she had been dealt was not fair.

But it was not only Gwyneth and her father at risk. But Adele. And Brother Giffard. And the servants at the castle. Like Jennet and those two bitches Genna and Ysanne. And the peasants in the village.

"And if I give my willing consent in your bed, you will not harm the people?"

"Not so long as they give an oath of fealty to me."

"And my family?"

"The same."

"You mean to imprison them?" She squirmed on the stool, and tapped the table with her fingertips.

"Nay, only detain. Unless there are further disturbances."

"Detained?"

"Better the dungeon than the gallows."

"My sisters?"

"I will choose husbands for them."

Her stomach cramped painfully. Adele despised the thought of marriage, and Gwyneth needed a man who could see past her beauty to the caring woman that lay beneath.

"What of the land?" she asked.

"I am claiming the land as payment for wrongs occurred. The king has already granted me the port in the contract for this marriage."

Her father would never agree to that. He had powerful contacts everywhere and hated the king with a loathing passion. Even from a dungeon, he would rally men, and then all of them would die in the aftermath. "But the land is my brother's inheritance."

"Then he should pay more attention to the happenings on it."

"He is . . . occupied." She could not tell him of Nathan's semi-exile into Italy. Of the issues he had with her father or how much she resented that he was able to leave—because he was a man—while she had to stay here, locked in her chamber. Still, she would not abandon him. "Mayhap if he were to make recompense? He is a good man and would no doubt swear fealty to you as overlord."

Montgomery straightened, walked to her and laid his hand on her shoulder. His eyes were merciless, as blue and stormy as the sea. "I tire of your delays. Deal or no?"

She ran her finger along the edge of the desk. "And if I say 'nay'?"

"You won't."

Anger flashed inside her. "I might."

He smirked. "Then I can call the priest and insist he witness the consummation. The union won't be as agreeable as a truce just between the two of us. But it will be as effective."

The blackheart. He knew she would not leave her family or the castlefolk to their folly, fools that they were.

"You said that was not the bargain you wished to make."

He smiled, but it did not reach his eyes. "I could easily change my mind. I do not think you would find my touch as gruesome as you pretend, even without a bargain for your sisters' lives. Asides, as you have stated, we are already properly wed so it would not be considered force."

She hated him. Loathed him. "Just because I do not fight you physically, does not mean my consent is not forced."

He shrugged, an appalling arrogant gesture.

Her mind raced for a way to even the battlefield, to bargain for better terms of surrender.

For one, she needed Montgomery slightly off balance. All during this negotiation, his gaze had roved over her plain kirtle in the same way she herself scrutinized a blank canvas to see what lay within it.

She had no particular qualms about losing her virginity—she'd long thought that being a maiden was a hindrance to her artwork.

She stared at him for a moment, at his tall, warrior form, trying to take it all in. Shadows and light shifted across his body.

"Why do you want me and not my sister?" The question jumped awkwardly from her lips as if it were a one-legged frog. Still . . . she wanted to know. Every man wanted Gwyneth. None wanted her.

He cocked his head to one side, his perfect jawline forming a sharp line against the backdrop of the swinging bed curtains. "Who is to say that I do not want you both?"

The bastard!

"Did you not just say that I could take whom I wanted as a willing bed partner instead of you?" he asked.

Humiliation clogged her throat. "So, I am to sacrifice myself—fulfill your every whim, but you are still free to make a sham of our marriage?"

"If you are holding your bargain of fulfilling my every desire, then there will be no sham of marriage."

She huffed. "That's disgusting."

At once, he stepped toward her and ran his thumb along her collarbone.

Shivering, she turned away, but he caught her chin within his fingers and turned her face up to his.

"Do not pretend there is no heat between us. Brenna, you need not fear that I will humiliate you by taking both you and your sister to my bed. *You* are interesting, *she* is not."

Brenna blinked, stunned. A shot of desire streaked through her betraying body. Interesting? Her, the scarred one? She pressed her lips together, unsure what to make of this development or how to play it to her advantage. She had no experience in seducing men to her will.

Without giving herself a chance to think it through, she pulled the string on her blouse and let it gape down so that the deep curves of her breasts and the soft pink skin of her areola showed.

Montgomery took in a sharp breath.

She smiled, glad his arrogance was not as much a

stronghold as she had first thought. The flow of power turned slightly her direction.

"You surprise me, my lady."

Gazing fully into his eyes, she pulled the string down lower until the fabric hung just under her nipple. "Afore I agree to your devil's bargain, I insist you treat my sisters with fairness and allow them to remain unmarried."

Montgomery's eyes darkened. "'Tis enough that they are allowed to live."

"They do not want husbands."

"'Tis a noblewoman's place to marry."

"I'll not have you send my sisters to be wives to ogres."

"I will give them a choice of several men, but they will marry. Deal or no?"

Brenna rushed the rest of her words, not wanting to lose courage. "I want my father kept out of London and you must give my brother audience and a chance to make recompense for the harm done to you. That you will take the land only as overlord, not dismiss us altogether."

Her indignation seethed; her family did not deserve the bargain she had made for them. But she could not leave them to suffer.

She held her breath as Montgomery's brows slammed together and his gaze moved from her breast to her face. She had already asked for a lot in granting favor with her sisters. Asking for her father to stay out of London and her family to remain in possession of the land was an impossible boon.

"And," she continued recklessly onward, "I would like my paints unlocked."

Montgomery's fingers tightened on her shoulder.

Her heart slammed into her ribcage as he deliberated for what seemed like hours.

Embarrassed that she was playing the part of a tawdry whore, she lifted her blouse back over her breast and gave him a glower. She knew the effect was ruined by the chains, but didn't care.

Gripping both of her shoulders, he lifted her to her feet and turned her around slowly. Warmth radiated from his skin.

Her heart dropped. Victory had been so close. "What are you doing?"

"Inspecting my prize."

"You did that already!" she huffed.

"Nay. Afore I was checking for weapons. You have sweetened your pot, and I would like to sweeten mine as well."

She clenched her jaw, unsure what to do or say.

"So your negotiation," he said, continuing to turn her around in a tight circle, "is that I remain as overlord only rather than owner, treat your sisters with kindness, not send your father to London, and agree to parley with your brother."

"Y–yea." Her cheeks heated and she felt hot. Very hot. His scent teased her nostrils—something about it reminded her of ocean adventures and salt spray, but that made no sense at all. "And to paint," she added. She waited for him to agree to the new terms.

A moment stretched. Then another.

"If I allow you to paint, my pot needs to be sweetened indeed. Painting will take time from your wifely duties."

If she could kick him, she would. Frustration burned inside her, and she longed to move, to fidget, to ask him what the bloody hell he was doing. But such action would reverse the subtle power that had flowed in her direction.

"And in return," he continued, "you will vow to ne'er lift a hand to injure me or any of my men. In addition, you will cater to my every whim, allow me complete reign over your body and serve me with a kind and properly submissive spirit. And you will bear heirs for me."

She wanted to scream. Her lot sounded like death. But surely she could escape and take her sisters with her. And she would just have to hide the fact that she would be taking herbs to prevent babies.

"Yea, my lord," she said.

"You do not ask that the chains be taken off?"

Was he tempting her to push him? This game he played confused her. She licked her lips, weighing her words. "I would very much like the chains to be taken off, but I will not ask for small favors when large ones hang in the balance. I'll wear them gracefully so long as it pleases you for me to do so. But I hope you will consider removing them in the future."

Her answer seemed to gratify him, but he made no comment on it. "Will you ask that I be gentle?"

She looked him over, from his short raven hair to his tall black boots. Standing there in front of her bed, he looked like some ancient king, ready to conquer. Her earlier fear that he would not fit inside her returned in full force.

"I have seen the size of your manhood, and I do not believe that it will fit with gentleness."

At that, he actually blinked. And then he grinned. A twinkle formed in his eyes.

He ran his finger around the area of skin where her

veil connected with her forehead. His touch was whispery soft.

"If you give yourself to me, I can assure pleasure for both of us."

She scoffed, the sound coming out like a strangled laugh. Pleasure? For both of them? What pleasure could her enemy offer her?

"You are a handsome man, and I assume you have some skill as a lover. If you intended to brutalize me, we would not be having this discussion at all. But pleasure?"

He quirked a brow and ran his fingertip slowly up and down her arm. The calluses on his fingers hinted at how enticing his touch would be on other areas.

Heat pooled into her woman's core. Bloody betraying body!

"Trust me," he whispered.

Trust him? Ludicrous! His condescending mannerism made her want to hurl a rotten egg at him.

The moment lengthened between them, and she realized he was deathly serious. The arrogant dunderhead.

It was the same as it had been when her neck was stretched over the chopper's block, and she just wanted to hurry the seconds along.

She gritted her teeth. Painting had always been her pleasure. It had always been enough, and he had taken that from her. "While you can command my compliance, you cannot command me to have pleasure." She felt stronger just saying that. She wanted to keep something for herself. "Do not speak of pleasure when we both know my willing compliance is all you desire. I tire of your delays. Deal or no?" she asked, turning his own words back on him.

Instead of answering, he turned her until she stood

with her back against his chest. Snaking an arm around her waist, he pulled her upward onto her tiptoes.

She gasped as she became slightly off balance, held in place only by the strength of his massive arms. "Wh–what are you doing?" she asked, then wanted to slap herself for stuttering. Mentally, she reached inside herself for her earlier bravado. But she felt off-kilter.

He leaned forward until his lips touched the crest of her ear. "If we do come to an acceptable bargain, I won't harm you. In this you can trust me."

She shivered as his breath caressed her cheek. Regardless of the evil between them, there was something heady about being so close to such an attractive warrior.

"Will you allow us to keep the land?" she asked, trying to steer the conversation to less treacherous topics. To pretend he did not entice her, that his voice wasn't as enchanting as a warm summer day. She hated herself for the lapse in judgment.

Slowly, he slid his free hand up her spine until it rested betwixt her shoulder blades. She quivered, fragile as a broken limb after a storm.

"And if I do, will you agree to comply with whatever I ask of you without question?"

"I–I agree," she said slowly, shuddering at the finality of the words and for the horrid betraying shiver of lust that spread through her.

"Bend forward," he commanded, pressing firmly on her upper back.

"What are you doing?"

"Testing your sincerity. Let me take your weight on my arm."

She did so, feeling herself pitch forward toward the floor and be suspended on his arm like a rag doll.

What an awkward, disconcerting position! In all her paintings, nowhere in her imagination had she ever conjured a scene such as this.

Breathless and slightly dizzy, she stared at the floor planks. The patterns in the wood swirled before her eyes.

He scrunched her skirt up over her hips. Ne'er in her life had she felt so vulnerable and helpless. Or so disconcerted. Or hot. The whirl of emotions made it hard to think.

Should she fight? Remain still? Just as he promised, he wasn't hurting her, just holding her.

The hand between her shoulders trailed once again down her spine, made tight circles on both sides of her upper back then caressed over her bottom and down one of her legs. Tightness tingled in the area betwixt her thighs as if her body had no qualms whatsoever about the graceless and un-artful pose it was in.

Her cheeks prickled with embarrassment as she realized he was staring at her buttocks. She could only imagine what she must look like from this position.

Squeezing her eyes shut, she waited, knowing this was merely a test of wills.

She *would* win. Like a strong warrior queen, she would clench her jaw and bear whatever he planned, she vowed silently.

Separating her buttocks slightly, he ran his finger down the sensitive crease where her thighs joined her bottom. The movement was slow and gentle, teasing.

More dizziness. More heat. Wetness formed within her woman's core. The world seemed to lose focus save for the feel of his fingers drawing close but not quite touching the sensitive area just to one side of his hand.

What a horrid, terrible sensation. If he knew in any

way that she felt even the slightest desire, he would crush her in a way that would leave her devastated. She vowed to not react.

He made another slow burning line with his finger, and she gasped, devastated to realize there was no way to merely tolerate his caress. She was floating, tethered to the earth by his touch. For a daft moment, she just wanted to hang suspended in his arms forever.

The thought sent a terrifying knot through her body, jolting her back to the present. She had assumed he was interested in simple compliance from her, no matter how grudgingly it was given. But now she understood better: he intended to break her spirit and master her as one would a pet.

Humiliating! Disgusting!

She opened her mouth to tell him their bargain was off.

"I agree to your terms," he said. "The land will remain in your family's name until the Martinmas Tournament where your brother will be given opportunity to make recompense. Your father will remain with my brother rather than be taken to London, and your sisters will have some say in choosing a husband."

Choking back her words, she clenched her teeth. If she could reach her brother, they could put the issue aright. Then somehow, she would find a way to escape from this marriage. She could not stay here and allow herself to be vanquished by this man.

She would have to be very careful to only grant him leave of her body but keep her soul intact.

Chapter Ten

Her smooth rounded bottom tempted James to untie his brais and plunge into her even knowing she wasn't ready. Her position of being draped over his arm, open and available for his every desire stretched the limits of his control. He wanted to take her, to bury himself inside her. To not even take the time to remove her chains or soothe her humiliation of wearing them while he swived her.

He held her for a second longer, enjoying the feel of her stomach pressed against his forearm. Her little whimpers of vulnerability ignited a dark urge.

The woman addled his brain. How could he be so bloody stupid as to allow her family to remain in possession of the land!

The desire to swive her, to possess her, coursed through his mind. *She's yours. Take her. She's a wife to tup, not a mistress to seduce. She's already given her consent.*

She was trembling, partly in fear, he knew. But there were other levels of complexity to this woman. And not all her quivers came from fear. He would deal with her pleasure later, for now he would take what was his. All the trickery that she'd done left little room for mercy where she was concerned.

It was on the edge of his tongue to tell her to hike her skirt and get on her knees with her arse facing him. He yanked her upright, the dark thought sending a quiver of terror through him. Passions of that sort would tear down the tightly controlled life he'd spent years carefully building.

The chains clanked. The short cap she was wearing fell aside. It tumbled to the floor planks. Red-blond curls sprang loose and frizzed around the top of her scalp.

Gasping, she hurriedly covered her hair with her hands and lunged for the covering. Her bonds toppled her off balance, and she stumbled to the floor, falling onto her buttocks as she scrambled for the covering.

"What the hell?" He stomped the linen cap with his boot, preventing her from snatching it so he could get a good look at her uncovered head.

Not attempting to rise, she trembled and covered her head with her hands.

Dear Christ. Her hair was horrid. Unruly. Uneven. It looked as though someone had taken a battle-axe to it.

"What the devil happened to your hair?" he bellowed. Had he been given a plague victim to wed? Was that why the sisters had switched places?

Cowering on the floor with her arms and hands covering as much of her hair as she could manage, she turned wide-eyed to him. She looked terrified, as though afraid he would beat her or take back the compromise she'd fought for.

"Are you ill?"

"Nay."

"Have you been ill?"

"Nay."

"The plague?"

"Nay."

"Smallpox?"

"Nay!"

He loomed over her, wanting to intimidate the truth out of her. "I swear, Brenna, if I catch you lying again and I've been given a plague-infested wife—"

"I do not have the plague! I just cut it!" Her vehemence took him off guard and fear lurked in her gaze as she tried vainly to cover her head with her hands.

He almost laughed. She'd been defiant when he'd tied her to the woodchopper's stump, angry when he'd locked her in chains—and now . . . she was afraid of her hair showing?

When would he ever understand women?

He reached for one of the curls.

She jerked her head aside, her knees shuffling against the floor. "D–do not."

He tsked. "Your promise was to allow me to touch you in any way I wished. Have you forgotten already? Let go of your head."

She swallowed. Her cheeks flamed, her arms slid from her hair, and she turned her face back to his in a show of defiant surrender. "As you wish, my lord."

He wondered at what that act must have cost her. More than taking her virginity would have he imagined.

"Kneel up to me."

She obeyed, a look of distress lighting across her face. The chains make a soft metallic sound as she changed positions from cowering on the floor to kneeling before him.

Taking a frizzy strand of her hair, he rubbed it

between his thumb and forefinger. She trembled in some sort of odd terror he did not understand.

Her hair was soft and smelled like her—of paint and turpentine. Odd scents for a woman, and yet, it suited her.

"You cut it like this apurpose?"

She nodded jerkily. She seemed so vulnerable that he wondered where her warrior princess attitude had gone. Mayhap he should have snatched her cap from her head in the Great Hall as Godric had done Meiriona's.

"What happened?" he asked again, this time in a gentler tone.

Her lips quivered. "I cut it to prevent a marriage betwixt my sister and a man not suited for her." She shook her shoulders as if warding off a chill. Or warding off her vulnerability.

He raised a brow. "Is it a habit for you to prevent your sister's marriages?"

Despite her tears, her eyes flashed. "Mayhap."

"Do not play coy with me, Brenna."

"'Twas a year ago," she said bitterly. "He was a very bad man."

"Like me?"

"Nay. Much worse than you." She drew a sharp breath, and for a second he feared she would start bawling again. Instead she covered her lips with her hand as if she had not meant to admit that she thought anyone could be worse than him.

Taking her wrist, he pulled her hand from her mouth. "Tell me about this marriage you prevented. Is that how you got your scar?"

Her eyes widened at the word "scar." "Nay, the scar

is old, from when I was a child. The marriage was to Gwyneth—"

At once she seemed more naked to him than when she was bent over his arm with her skirts upturned. Obviously the strain of the bitter battle and the strange passion between them affected her much stronger than she had let on. He had wanted her humiliation to be complete, but seeing her cowering, terrified that her ugly hair was showing, did not give him victory as he had expected.

Without allowing himself to over-think his actions, he pulled her to her feet and enclosed her in his arms.

She didn't fight him.

"You *are* beautiful." Zwounds. What a dunderhead he was. He should be reveling in the vanquishment of her pride, not speaking love-words to her. There could be no tenderness for a betrayer such as her. She'd already used his fascination with her body against him, had him agree to terms he never should accept. What would she do with this new weapon?

She sniffed.

Sniffed?

He looked down to see if he had heard correctly. Was this more trickery? More of women's games?

She blinked furiously. Tears? Of all the blasted things.

Tilting her chin up, he scrutinized her face. She did not resist although she seemed to be fighting the urge to do so. She was so utterly unique and complex, both so strong and so vulnerable, that he could not imagine why she was still unmarried, that men had not been fighting to possess her.

"No one has ever noticed your beauty, have they?" It wasn't a question.

Her lips parted, and she touched the scar on her cheek in a telltale motion.

"'Tis no wonder," he continued, "dressed as you are." His first order of business would be to buy his wife a new wardrobe. In all the ways he wanted to prick at her pride, wearing rags was not one of them.

"I–I–" she started, shifting in his arms. "I had lovely hair once."

"Hmmm . . ." Reaching up, he fondled her ill-cropped locks. Her hair was soft and thick. It curled around his fingers with a life of its own. Her hair was still lovely, 'twas just cut badly.

"It was long," she added. "I could sit on it."

"'Twill grow again."

Her body grew rigid against his and he felt a trembling sob push through her before she uttered a loud snort. "'Tis been a whole year and I have naught but frizz." Her breath caught several times in a snivel of distress. "I have no need for beautiful hair," she sniffed. "Truly I don't. Nor for beauty of any kind. I want to be an artist. I can paint all the beautiful women I want, I don't need to be one myself." Then, oddly, she began to weep.

James tightened his grip on her body, completely at a loss of what to say. His little hellion was crying over beauty? She was already beautiful.

The innate urge to protect those under his care swelled inside him.

"Gwyneth is beautiful. Adele is beautiful." She sobbed. "My father calls me scarred goods, the one too ugly to get rid of."

"Is that why you were foisted off on me?"

She buried her face in his chest and twisted his tunic into her fists. Her tears wet the linen causing a large spot in the pristine garment. A flicker of guilt ran through him that she was chained. He could bond the defiant warrior princess—but this woman left him at a loss.

"Nay. I chose to marry you. At first I refused, but I didn't want to see my sister crushed. I thought I could kill you and then go to Italy." She sobbed louder.

"Italy?" he pressed.

"I was meant to be a nun," she wailed. "My father didn't want me to join a convent, and he locked me in my chamber. My family hates me and now this marriage is a disaster."

"You *wanted* to be a nun?" There was so much about this woman that baffled and intrigued him.

"Yea," she sniffed.

"That profession would not suit you at all."

"So everyone says." Her hands wrenched his tunic. The fabric would forever be ruined, its perfect tailored lines irreparably damaged.

At a loss for how to extract her fingers from his garment, he hugged her closer and was inexplicably pleased when she did not resist the embrace.

"Marriage is much more suited for someone of your fiery nature than some dull life in a convent."

Stiffening, she moved away from his arms and wiped the tears from her cheeks.

He let her go, but the chain clinked softly, reminding both of them of their positions as master and captive.

"Bah," she said with a wave of her hand. "What do you know about what marriage does to a woman? To ne'er be able to go where she will or make her own choices or even have a cow to call her own."

His lips twitched. "You do not wish to be married because you want to own a cow?"

"Nay! I want to make my own choices."

Stifling a prick of guilt, he slid his hand down her arm. "You are a noblewoman, Brenna. Our marriage was ordered by the king. 'Tis your duty. And I swear I can make the marriage bed a pleasure, not a chore."

She trembled against him, but he determined to not allow any sympathy toward her keep him from what must be done. The marriage must be consummated. He would do well to remember she had tried to kill him. That this play of emotion might only be a bid to gain his sympathy so he would let her go.

He could make their marriage bed pleasant for her; it would have to be enough.

At that moment the door burst open and Godric followed by two guards entered the chamber.

"Lecrow!" Godric exclaimed, his wild hair whipping around his shoulders. "He's missing!"

"Damn!" James sprang into action, glad he'd not gotten around to unchaining his wife. "Be here when I return, wife."

Chapter Eleven

"Wait!" Brenna called, but was only answered by the stomping of boots down the tower steps. She glared at the door, damn tempted to help Montgomery look for her father and turn him over to the king. She had just humiliated herself grandly to save his sorry hide, and now he had betrayed all of them and left them to fend for themselves.

Here she was, locked in her chamber once again, only this time in manacles.

She raised her fist and shook it in the air. The chain clattered against itself. "Curse you, Father! Curse you, Montgomery! Curse you, King Edward! And curse the rebels too!"

Perhaps she could find a way to pick the locks on her manacles and escape as well.

She prowled the chamber, searching for some small instrument she could fit into the latches. All her small paintbrushes were locked away—Montgomery had even found the pack and taken the tiny hog's hair one out of it. She had no hairpins—she'd had no need of any since her hair had been cut.

She plucked at the springy curls as she made her

way around the room. Her cheeks heated with the memory of Montgomery's bellow asking her what the devil had happened to the mass. Her hair was longer than it had been, and she ought to feel some spark of happiness that it was growing, but the strands sprang back into tight, frizzy loops when she let it go. When it was longer, the curls had stretched out.

Irritated that no instruments to pick the lock could be found, Brenna stopped her pacing, raised one arm as far as it would go, then switched and raised the other. She watched the chain slide through the circular link. The sound grated on her already tight nerves, and she wanted to howl with outrage. Why must women be pawns in men's war? It was unjust. Unfair.

Sighing, she plopped down on her stool beside the painting desk, disgusted with her father and disgusted with herself for getting caught up in his personal drama against the king. All she had wanted was a chance to sit and paint and make her own way through life. She should have left when she had the chance, when Gwyneth had first come into the room with her wedding garment on.

A wave of despair passed through her as she realized how fully caught she was. Even if she could get free of her bonds, she could not simply leave as she wanted.

If her husband returned and found her missing, God only knew what he would do. She was the only thing standing between Montgomery and the destruction of her sisters.

She tried to tell herself that she didn't care about what happened to Gwyneth and Adele, but she could not make her conscience believe the lie.

She could leave her blasted father to his own devices, but she must find her sisters and formulate a plan of escape that included all three of them. If they could scrape together enough gold to make it to Italy, Mother Isabella had already promised to accept her into the convent and Nathan could surely buy her an annulment.

Opening one of the rough drawers in her table, she ached at the empty space, then glared at the trunk pushed against the wall. Painting had always been her sanctuary in a world gone mad. Her fingers itched. She wanted to paint something violent and passionate, to lose herself in the glory of color and brushstrokes, to forget her troubles for a time. Part of her bargain had been that he would unlock her art supplies, but with him out searching for her vagabond father, they were still locked away.

Frustrated with her lot in life, she slammed the drawer shut and ran her finger around the metal encircling her wrist before standing and marching toward the door to bang on it, to insist they let her out.

She would start moving plans into place to get ready for her escape. She would go down to the Great Hall and supervise the removal of the rushes so she could find Meiriona's hairpin. Perhaps she could even steal a knife. She would find her sisters. Brother Giffard had been here for the wedding; she would speak to him about making secret travel arrangements. And she would speak to Egmont the blacksmith about forging a key to the chains.

The marginal plan gave her a small hope. She banged on the door with her fist.

It swung freely open.

Not locked! She stifled a small thrill of victory and another wave of disgust that she had been so beat down by the past year of confinement that she had not even checked to see if the door had been locked.

Anticipation sprang in her chest as she looked into the hallway. A year of imprisonment and now she was free to move about the castle.

A gangly youth wearing a purple cape and an overly large mustache for a boy of his age leaned on the stone wall. The hair above his lip was twisted with beeswax so that it poked outward from his face like a bushy walrus.

Ridiculous.

He was barely more than a boy. 'Twas as if the only reason he'd grown it was, because, by some fluke of nature, he could do so. It certainly did not fit his youthful looks or suit him in any fashion.

"My lady," he said deferentially, stroking his facial hair. "Is there somewhere you would like to go?"

She stared at the mustache for a moment wondering if she should compliment it or ignore it. "Who are you?"

"Your guard, my lady."

Harrumph. So she had a guard. As if the chains weren't enough to keep her bound to the keep. Irritating, but not surprising. At least she was not locked in her room. She looked him over. He was just the sort who fell in groves at Gwyneth's feet spouting courtly love.

"I am to accompany you wherever you need to travel," he said.

"I would like to visit my sister."

He made a flamboyant bow with his purple cape. "My deepest regrets, my lady. I was told you were not to speak with any of your family."

She wanted to scream. Instead, she composed her face. "To the Great Hall then?" She would go and search for the hairpin.

"Of course." His long gawky fingers twirled the mustache round and round.

Bloody hell, the thing was awful. As if a hairy worm crawled across his face.

He shifted back and forth, his face reddening as she continued to size him up. He would be a handsome youth when he grew into his shoulders and shaved that hairy thing off his face. He turned awkwardly and began walking down the hall toward the tower's steps.

She gave him a cheerful smile, deciding that if he was to be following her around, 'twas best she win him over as soon as possible. "What a lovely mustache you have."

The boy beamed, nearly missing a step.

Ha! She was right. He was damned proud of the thing.

"Your name?"

"Damien."

"Damien, do you know if my father is well?"

"I haven't heard."

He motioned for her to go ahead of him in the stairwell. The steps were steep and narrow, concave and slick from years of use. The iron rail had given way years ago and her father had not seen fit to replace it. What need was there when 'twas only his wayward daughter, the one too ugly to get rid of, that was here in the tower. The chains made climbing up and down hazardous and she clung to the chilly damp stones of the wall moving very slowly downward. There were no lit candles in the sconces to illuminate the way, and the tight passage felt as gloomy as she did.

"Has my new husband returned?" she asked.

Behind her, she heard the rustle of clothing indicating Damien had shrugged.

Harrumph. If she was to be given a guard, why could she not be given one who was more useful?

* * *

More than a fortnight later, Brenna still had no word from her new husband. More and more an anxious despair clouded her thinking and she felt desperate to escape, even if only so that she could change clothes. After several days of coy searching, she had found the hairpin and now sat at her stool furiously trying to jam it into the locks to unlatch the mechanism on the manacles.

The skin around the bonds itched and her tattered kirtle was wrinkled horribly. She had washed herself as best she could, but wearing and sleeping in the same clothing day after day made her feel bedraggled and unkempt. Her plain clothing had never been fine, but she had always made a point of keeping her garments neat and washed.

"Bloody hell!" she cursed at the locks as they refused to give.

"Be you alright, my lady?" Damien called from outside the door.

"Yea, Damien, fine. Just cursing my husband, 'tis all."

"He's a good man, mistress."

Good man! "He's a damn bastard," she muttered, tugging furiously at the manacle out of sheer impotent frustration. She resisted the urge to rail at Damien for his lord's sins. "It's unfair that I cannot converse with my sisters!"

Rising, she marched to the trunk that had her paints locked inside it, poked the pin into the lock and fiddled around with the device. It would click, but not open.

Damn.

Damn.

Damn.

She kicked it, as she'd gotten into the habit of doing every time she entered and exited her room, then yelped as her toe smarted in protest. When her husband returned—please, God, let him return, she could not bear to spend the rest of her life in this itchy, dirty garment—she would give him a piece of her mind. Especially about his promise concerning allowing her to paint.

She wrenched up the floor plank that was her secret hiding place and took out the nude of herself. On the morning of the wedding, after Montgomery had left so that she could get dressed, she had pleaded with her sisters to give her a moment of privacy and go to the chapel ahead of her. In that moment, she'd hidden the miniature here. She lifted the painting into the air. Was this the last thing she would ever create?

"Pox-ridden dunderhead," she cursed her husband again.

"My lady?" Damien asked.

Hiding the miniature in her pouch, Brenna marched to the door and hurled it open. "I would like to go pray," she gritted out. Brother Giffard should have returned this morning—perhaps he had some solution to her quandary. And perhaps she could sell this painting for gold.

Damien must have sensed her outraged frustration because he gazed at her with sympathetic eyes. "I can ask Master Gabriel for some leniency that you could visit with your sisters under strict guard. I do not know what he will say, but I can ask."

Pressing her lips together, she nodded. "Gramercy, Damien." He was a good youth, he truly was. And his mustache was growing on her. No doubt guarding her was as dull and tedious for him as it was for her.

"To the chapel then?" he said.

"Yea."

A few moments later, she knelt at a prayer bench in one of the alcoves with her head bowed. Damien stood outside the sanctuary doors, stationed as he always was.

As always, she wished she could fix the position of the lands and the proportions of the torsos on the screen. It irked her that she had not been chosen to do the art-work to begin with. A man *had* gotten the position simply because he was a man, not because he was a better painter. If she would have been able to get her art supplies, she might have brazenly whitewashed them and repainted over the inferior work today. With both her father and husband gone, no one would be able to stop her. A statue of the Virgin Mary stared down at her and several painted screens—not her own work—gave some privacy.

Brother Giffard slid up to her, his robe rustling as he walked. He was barefooted in the manner of the Benedict monks and great tufts of hair curled on the tops of his feet like fur.

She gazed upward, not wanting to look at his large, misshapen feet and uneven toenails.

He was a tall man with kind eyes, an easy demeanor and a loose-limbed gate. He threw his cowl back off his tonsured hair in a carefree gesture.

His easy manner made him well loved and welcomed at many tables across England. But his mannerism seemed more suited to that of a court entertainer than a monk, and the bishops in several dioceses openly de-spised him. The town's local Bishop Humphrey had taken him into custody on several occasions, but some-how Brother Giffard had always managed to get free.

"Brenna, my child, I heard what happened and came as soon as possible." He looked down pointedly at the chains and gave her a pitying look as he rested his hand on the tall back of the prayer bench. Candle glow flickered around them. "Why did you not follow through with the travel plans we had arranged?"

She nearly groaned. Mother Isabella, the abbess of La Signora del Lago had been expecting her, indeed she had encouraged her to come by telling her how desperate the abbey needed artwork and promising all the canvas and paints an artist could ever desire. Brenna had met the aged nun years ago and they had exchanged friendly letters ever since.

"I cannot get free of the chains. All the gold is lost?"

"With regret—" Brother Giffard started.

She waved a hand at him dismissively, nearly knocking over the nearby candlestick. "The past cannot be returned. But I need help."

A glint formed in his eyes. For one vowed to poverty, Giffard seemed to have a large propensity for smelling gold. "What can I do?"

She shuffled on her knees and fingered her manacle. "I am turning lunatic being chained all the daylong while my new husband is scouring the countryside to chase down my father. I cannot speak with my sisters or send a message to Nathan. I have tried to speak with Egmont the smithy, but am guarded oppressively night and day."

Giffard's robes rustled as he patted her shoulder. "Have you been painting? Oft the colors have soothed your troubled soul."

Despair touched her. "My husband locked my paints in a trunk!"

"My child."

She leaned back, casting a wary glance at the massive church door. "Where is Father Peter?" she whispered.

"Gone to the town to converse with Bishop Hum-

phrey, for certes. Have you any paintings to show me?"
He nearly licked his lips, the lecherous old toad.

She gazed around. The two of them were alone in
the sanctuary and if anyone burst into the church the
alcove should provide some protection and give her
time to re-hide the erotic miniature. But one could
never be too careful. If they were ever caught selling
the illegal artwork, both of them would be burned at
the stake as devil worshipers.

Satisfied they were alone and that Damien would
stay outside the church, she undid the stays on her
pouch and withdrew the small parchment.

The monk's robes swirled around his furry feet as
he reached for the miniature. The paint was slightly
smeared in one corner because she'd had to hide it
quickly, but otherwise the self-portrait was in good
shape.

Lifting a brow, Brother Giffard gazed at it critically.
"'Tis quite good," he said, his gaze lingering on the
open crook of leg the young noblewoman in the painting sported.

"Do you think it will fetch a high price?" she snapped,
impatient with his lingering. She was used to his pe-
rusal of her work and it annoyed, but no longer embarrassed her.

He shrugged. "'Tis hard to say. Times are perilous
with The Enforcer watching our every move. People
are afraid to bid."

Her heart sank. One more reason to hate her hu
band.

"Perhaps if you would release the other two paintings of *The King's Mistresses* . . ." he pressed.

She shook her head. For the most part, church and
crown would turn a blind eye to a few scattered erotic

works, but she was not so foolish as to outright provoke the king.

"Well." Brother Giffard tucked the miniature into his robe and patted it. "Be of good cheer, child. Your artwork is exquisite. I will find a buyer for this but perhaps will have to go farther north out of harm's way."

"Do you think that it will sell for enough gold to buy passage on a ship?"

Giffard blinked a few times and shook his head. "Not this one alone, child."

"But you *can* arrange passage?"

His lips thinned. "That will be nigh impossible. A ship's captain will not want to risk hauling The Enforcer's wife."

Wife. 'Twas a word akin to death. Tight bands seemed to press all the air from her chest.

"Then mayhap a message to my brother Nathan?" She withdrew a sealed scroll that she had prepared days ago and held it out to him.

He sucked in a breath and did not reach for the missive as he had the parchment. "'Tis dangerous."

"Prithee, Brother Giffard. I have no one."

"If they catch me I'll be branded a traitor."

"If they do not and Nathan comes, I'll see that you are well-rewarded and welcome all across Italy." It was an empty promise and they both knew it. She shuffled on her knees, rocking the prayer bench. "Brother Giffard, you must help me."

He frowned down at her, his hairy misshapen toes tapping on the tiled floor of the church. At last, he took the scroll. "I will do my best but make no promises."

"Gramercy." Some relief flowed through her. At least she had a chance now.

Chapter Twelve

Rain. Rain. And more blasted rain. Wet and exhausted James entered Windrose Castle over a month later, a foul mood wrapped around him even closer than his damp cloak. He had not caught the baron, damn the man, but he had too many responsibilities to keep traipsing the countryside looking for him.

In the morn, he'd send Gabriel after the old man. Gabriel had an uncanny talent for tracking the untrackable, and it had been plain bad luck that he'd been unreachable when they had left.

James heaved a long, weary breath as he and the few men with him made their miserable way across the bailey. As soon as he finished his mission of finding the painter of *The King's Mistresses* and securing the keep with its nearby port, he would allow himself a long waterbound journey.

He longed for sunlight and freedom, for the open swells of the sea. For the scent of the salt, and the sting of the spray across his cheeks. Here, he was so bemired in duty and responsibility it suffocated his very bones.

Silence hung like a pall. No servants with torches

came to greet them. No child splashed in the fresh puddles. No laughter wafted out the windows. No smoke curled from the chimneys. The scents in the air were of rain and mildew, not fresh bread or hot stew.

The lack of greeting seemed indicative of the state of his marriage. Bleak. Forlorn. Like that of a battlefield on the morning following a skirmish.

His hellion wife's face floated in his imagination and he cursed himself for being every kind of fool for marrying into this family. He should have outright denied the king's wishes rather than be saddled with these betraying devils.

His marriage had not even been consummated.

Planting an heir should have been a duty he was anticipating, but he felt too drained at the moment to take heart for the battle.

Right now he longed for a welcoming fire and a hot meal—as Godric no doubt had gotten when he returned to Meiriona and Whitestone. He could well imagine his sister-in-law rushing from the keep to greet his brother in the rain.

He gazed about the bailey, telling himself he was not looking for his own wife. Mayhap, even if there was no warm greeting, at least the month away had given Brenna time to reconcile herself to the marriage. He did not have a patience or inclination to seduce her with pretty words tonight. The union must be formalized, a babe planted in her womb and his duty here completed so he could get back to the sea.

Urging his mount forward, he looked up at the looming turrets of the keep, wanting to find his wife and get one more duty accomplished afore morning.

The tips of the castle spiraled dark and ominous

into the night, their tops hidden by the inky sky. Only a sliver of moon, mostly covered by black clouds, hung in the heavens. No stars shone in the bleak darkness, as if the relentless drizzle had washed them away.

A blood-curdling scream echoed from inside the keep.

Hurriedly dismounting and tossing the reins to a groomsman, James drew his sword and sprinted toward the sound. His blood pumped through his veins, chasing away his exhaustion. He wound into the bowels of the castle, once again shackled with the responsibility of setting the situation aright.

Ahead, at the foot of a stairwell that led upward onto the wall walk, a clump of people gathered.

Several men, including Gabriel who had been in charge, were there already. Servants hung about. Loud, excited gibberish echoed against the walls.

James pushed his way forward, sliding between members of the crowd.

A woman with short curly red hair lay on the stairs, her body at an awkward angle. Brenna!

Gabriel bent over her, checking for signs of life.

"Damnation," James muttered. Had his wife thrown herself down the stairs when she saw his arrival? Had the month apart done naught to reconcile the wench to their union? He knelt, his blood pounding in his ears.

A kick of guilt pricked him that he had left her chained but he quickly stifled it. The woman and her whole bloody family were a damn menace.

"Brenna?"

She lay unmoving, with one arm twisted back. She wore a wretched brown kirtle and had a large gash on her forehead. Dirt stained her face so he could not tell the extent of the damage. He swiped at the grime, but his hands were damp from the rain and it only smeared into mud.

He placed his hand on her chest. She did not stir, but her chest rose and fell in a deep regular movement. He checked her arms and legs and determined they were not broken. With luck, she was only knocked out and not injured.

Brushing one curly lock away from her face and further staining her face with filth, he tried to stir her. "Brenna? Wake up, girl."

No response.

Her features were relaxed as if asleep and, despite the grime, she reminded him of something innocent and guileless, a far cry from the woman who had yanked a dagger from her bodice and stabbed him. He would do well to not be fooled by the sweetness of her face.

"Where's Damien? Why was my wife alone?" James snapped at Gabriel as he scooped her into his arms. His shoulder where she had stabbed him gave a little protest of pain, reminding him that this woman did not deserve any mercy.

"She was here when I arrived," Gabriel answered. "I know no more than you."

Her head lolled back, and she let out a small moan. Candlelight flickered over her face highlighting the scar on her cheek.

James pushed through the crowd, carrying her to the bedchamber. "What happened?" he asked the servants.

More loud confusing gibberish issued forth as several stepped forward, talking all at once, offering their own take on the situation.

"Fell, she did," someone answered.

"I saw a man with her."

"Shouldn't leave a woman chained like that."

"She was pushed, me lord," a tall thin woman wearing a wrinkled peasant dress said.

All thoughts of a restful evening disappeared. No matter the issues between them, she was his responsibility now. He had to take care of her and investigate the situation. He needed to get her cleaned up, access the damage and then determine if she was pushed, trying to escape or had simply fallen.

Gabriel and the other men followed as he rushed down the labyrinth of hallways and up the tower steps to her chamber.

Damien lay asleep before Brenna's door. Not stopping on his way in, James kicked the boy in the side and hurried into the chamber to lay his wife across the bed.

The boy groaned and blinked dazedly.

James hurled orders at the men and servants to bring a tub and water. Reaching beneath his tunic he withdrew the key to the locks of her chains. He ignored the little prick of guilt that she had been bound for so long.

He hurriedly unfastened the manacles while servants rushed to do his bidding.

Lifting her arm, he inspected the skin around her wrists. It was red but not broken or bruised. He squeezed her fingertips watching the nails turn from pink to white and back to pink again.

Not damaged.

At least not by her bonds.

He let the chains slide to the floor. They clanked against the planks and landed in a heap beside the bed. Frustration coursed through him. His well-ordered life had been turned upside down with one crisis after the next since the wedding.

He gazed around the chamber, trying to determine what to do first to get the situation under control.

The servants were rapidly filling a tub with steaming water. Damien was by the door, wobbling to a sitting position and holding his side where James's boot had caught him.

"Damien! Boy! Where were you? Why was my wife unattended?"

Damien blinked sleepily.

James stomped over to him, grabbed the youth by his overgrown mustache and hauled him onto his feet. "I said, where the hell have you been?"

"I've been right here." The boy began to shake as he glanced at the woman lying across the bed. "Oh, sweet mercy!"

"You were supposed to be guarding her!"

Damien's eyes widened. "B–b–but I've been right here!"

The urge to pluck the boy's mustache out whisker by whisker coursed through James. He gave it a good yank before letting the youth go. "If you weren't Meiriona's brother—" he growled.

"But I am!" Damien nodded his head vigorously.

"You still deserve a good walloping."

True to his nature, the boy sank into a flamboyant bow.

"My lord, I most humbly apologize for any wrong I have done. Mistress Brenna has been most kind to me and I would cut off my right arm to save her."

James glowered at him. "I don't want you to cut off your arm—I want you to obey orders."

"But, my lord, I was here—the whole evening—lying in front of the door. And before that I went with your lady everywhere, just as you commanded. I did not abandon my post—would not abandon my post." He thumped his fist passionately on his chest.

A moan issued from the bed before James could give the boy the railing he deserved.

They both turned and rushed to the bedside. Brenna was wide-awake, sitting up in bed, looking hearty and hale instead of weak, as he had expected. Her hair fluffed around her head, a misty red cloud like the horizon at dawn. The mud on her cheek made her look like some underworld princess, and she quivered with indignation. The bed curtains fluttered.

Damien sank to his knees beside the mattress. "My lady, forgive me."

She pointed at James and shook her head forcefully. "This is not Damien's fault!" Her voice was strong and loud, as if she had not just been lying helpless at the bottom of the stairs. "You were the fool who left me chained for weeks."

A streak of anger bit through James that he had even been concerned about her. That he had thought for one moment that she was innocent. That he'd felt guilty that she might have been injured.

Likely she'd planned the whole ordeal.

"I've been a fool alright," he snarled, "but not for leaving a hellion such as you in bonds. Why were you not with your guard?"

She jumped off the bed, nearly landing amidst the chains piled on the floor, and shook her fist at him. The mattress ropes creaked. Her brown kirtle fluttered around her ankles. "Mayhap I was tired of being followed around all the daylong as if being in bonds alone is not enough!"

The room grew quiet as the servants stopped their duties and stared at their mistress. Her hair was a fright; the curly strands poked outward from her scalp like a disheveled, frizzy mop. Dirt smudged her cheek. Mud mingled with the paint splotches on her worn kirtle.

But, oh, she looked magnificent in her outrage. Her eyes flashed as if she could burn them all with her spell. She stood beside the bed—her posture sharp and full of pride. He had seen men go to battle with less passion.

She marched toward him and poked him squarely in the chest. "'Tis shameful for you to treat me such, unable even to bathe. I'm dirty. Disgusting!"

A smile tugged at his lips. Leave it to a woman to be concerned about bathing when there were rebels running all over the countryside.

"There you go," he said, jerking a thumb toward the steaming bathing tub.

She pointed at the door like a queen, as if completely heedless that only a moment earlier she'd been fettered like a slave.

"Leave," she commanded. She glared around the room at the servants, which were staring gape-mouthed at her. "All. Of. You. Leave. Now."

Her audacity rankled him. He crossed his arms over his chest.

The servants shuffled toward the door. Damien gave several low, low bows and scooted out backward as one would do in the presence of royalty.

James stifled the urge to cuff the lad; 'twas clear that her being loose in the keep was not the boy's doing. No doubt Damien had been as fooled by his hellion bride as he had been, but it irked him that he would show her any deference at all.

The door swung shut with a bang, leaving them alone in the room.

Glaring at him, she stomped her foot. "I said *go*!"

"Nay. If you want to bathe, you will do so with me in the room."

Her eyes flashed. "I will do no such thing. You are a hideous horrid monster. Leave now or I will stab you again, you son of a whore."

He stepped forward and scooped her into his arms. His pride had taken enough dents from her and her family. Tonight, there would be only one master.

She flailed, but was so much smaller than him, her efforts were ineffective. "Put me down!"

"As you wish." He dumped her into the bathing tub. Water sloshed across the floor planks and splattered on his tunic.

Sputtering, she came up for air. Her skin was red and blotchy, especially the scar crossing her cheek. "You dolt! You dog!" Drops ran off her hair and the water darkened with mud.

All at once a brick of guilt hit him as he remembered a time from his past when his father had locked him into a closet for seven long days because he had been digging in books instead of practicing with a sword. Terrified and thinking he would die, he'd flown into a blind rage when the door was unlatched and attacked the first person he'd seen. Which turned out to be Molly, the old woman who oft snuck him sweetmeats while he was studying. He'd stopped himself from truly harming her, but not before she'd been pushed down and scraped her knees and hands. One of her fingers had been broken. Guilt bit into him at the memory.

Now he saw himself in Brenna.

While he'd been chasing after her father, she had been chained, facing the stares and scorn of the castle-folk, unsure when, or even if, he'd return. He had not even unlocked her paints or allowed her to converse with her sisters.

"Brenna." Taking a deep breath, he gazed down on her in the tub.

She did not try to rise, although he could tell it irritated her to remain in the water.

"I had not intended to be gone so long," he said.

At that, she slammed her hands down on the tub's edge and looked as though she would scream.

"Peace, girl."

"Peace? That's a fancy word."

He rubbed the back of his neck. As much as he'd like to feel sorry for her, he could not afford to let her get the upper hand. His men needed a leader, not someone who was led around by an out-of-control wife.

"Bathe, wife, or I'll do it for you myself."

She glared at him but began undoing the fastenings on her dress. With a heave, she flung the sopping kirtle into his face. The stench assaulted his nostrils. He drew it aside and tossed it beside the chains on the floor, more amused than annoyed.

Glowering at him, she raced through the motions of soaping herself.

Her hands flew fast and furious on her skin as if trying to peel off the filth of the past month's dirt.

'Twas clear that although she did not wish to be where she was, being unclad in front of him didn't embarrass or humiliate her. That fact fascinated him. His experience with noblewomen were that they were a silly lot, overly concerned about fashion and elaborate clothing, yet Brenna had never shown modesty, even when she'd bathed him the night of their wedding or when they had made their ill-fated bargain.

"Are you a virgin?" he demanded.

She stopped, the bathing cloth a thumb's breadth above her skin. "I've had dozens of lovers," she sneered. "You can tell that to the priest and have the marriage easily annulled."

Cocking his head to one side, he scrutinized her. Her audacious declaration called to the conqueror within him, to rise and prove her wrong. She was lying. She had to be.

She went back to scrubbing her body, this time even harder. The skin around her wrists and ankles was red and tender—attacking them with lye soap was not going to help her.

Bending down, he pulled the cloth from her fingers. "Cease, Brenna, afore you rub yourself raw."

She snatched at the cloth, coming partway out of the tub. "Give me that!"

"Not if you are going to harm yourself with it."

"I won't. Give it back."

"Cease fighting me, Brenna. You cannot win. This can be easy for you or difficult—either way, there is only one ending to this evening and it does not involve annulment."

They glared at each other for a moment.

With a glower, she sank back into the water and drummed her fingers on the edge of the tub.

Kneeling behind her, he cupped her upper arm. He would do well to be wary of her unpredictability, but he intended to conquer her one way or another.

Her back was rigid, but she did not fight him as he ran the cake of soap across her shoulders. Good. At least she'd given up on trying to fight him physically.

He sniffed at the soap. It was harsh lye, not well made at all. Certainly not suitable for a noblewoman. Setting the soap on the floor, he decided to use only his hands to wash her.

He drifted his fingertips up her neck and then down her spine. "Relax, girl. Trust me, just for right now."

Chapter Thirteen

Trust him! Of all the daft notions. Brenna seethed silently as Montgomery ran his fingers over and down her back. If fighting him would do any good at all, she would fly out of the tub and hurl herself at him.

But, even without the chains and manacles, he was too large. Too powerful. Too masculine.

He loomed over her, his big body with its wide chest and long muscular legs eclipsing everything else in the room.

Wearily, she slumped forward and leaned her head on one side of the tub, fuming that she had to submit to his ministrations. She had planned to state her case with some form of dignity, but instead had attacked him like an animal. Her brain felt foggy and bewildered. This past month she'd become more and more frightened, terrified she'd be living in chains, dirty, exhausted, and helpless, for the rest of her life.

Despair welled inside her as he ran his large hands over her shoulders. She hated that they felt good; the calluses on his fingertips rasped her skin, cleansing away the feel of grime. Had she sank so low that even her enemy's touch was welcomed?

He had said that there was only one ending to this evening. Likely as soon as he had her clean, he'd be slamming into her, consummating their marriage, finishing what he had started weeks ago.

She hated him. Hated him!

Vowing to face her fate with dignity, she tried to conjure up images of Italy, of how her life in the convent would be when she was able to escape.

"I am sorry, girl, truly I am."

Blackheart. Liar.

He did not rush to clean her as she assumed he would. His fingers lingered over her back and shoulders, rubbing up and down in slow, sensual strokes. Over and over again his hands roamed, smoothing away knots and washing every trace of filth from her skin.

"I know you do not believe me, but 'twas not my intention to be gone so long and leave you chained. Two bridges were washed out by rain so that we had to take a much longer route home. We were waylaid twice, attacked by thieves and two horses fell lame from slipping in the mud so we were reduced to walking until we could secure more mounts. I sent word back with a key, but we found that man dead days later."

She didn't believe him, but the words sounded like balm anyway.

"Forgive me, Brenna." He kissed her shoulder and the rough feel of his beard rasped her skin.

He hadn't shaved.

There was something telling about that. Everything about the man had been so precise: from the creases in his tunic to the spotless shine on his boots. But, here, he returned as bedraggled as she felt.

"I'm sorry, Brenna," he murmured, his generous lips brushing the top of her shoulder. "Truly, truly sorry." He massaged down her arms, then her legs. He caressed the crevices between her fingers in unhurried motions. Despite her nudity, not once did he reach for her private parts or attempt to jump on her—his fingers remained on her back and arms sliding slowly up and down.

Little by little she felt herself being sucked into his spell. He kept murmuring gentle words against her neck and his breath caused her skin to heat and tingle. Slowly, she lost track of everything but the present. He massaged her lower back then took her arm and placed little kisses all around where the manacle had braceleted her wrist. The skin was no longer red or itchy.

The knots beneath her shoulder blades eased, and, against her will, she felt her betraying body begin to relax.

She sat up in the tub, not wanting to feel that languid sensual sentiment, not wanting to enjoy the touch of a man who had brought her so much grief. For an instant, she wished her back was whelped and scarred, that her wrists and ankles were bruised, that somehow she was injured to prove how horrid and evil he was.

But she knew she was not. She had been dirty, not harmed.

Montgomery slid to the side of the tub. His hand dipped lower into the water, cupping beneath her knees and back, and he lifted her effortlessly into the air. Water dripped onto his tunic and she felt vulnerable being naked while he was clothed.

She stiffened, then forced herself to relax. A man who took his time massaging her and gave her the courtesy of both explanation and apology for his absence, did not plan to harm her, no matter his size and strength.

He carried her to the bed, pushed the curtains back and laid her across the mattress. Her stomach churned nervously as she waited for what lay ahead. Anticipation warred with dread. Would it hurt? His member had been enormous.

She swallowed. "About our bargain—"

"Our bargain still stands and you are still mine. The image of you off-balance, bent over my arm with your skirt upraised and a trickle of woman's fluid wetting your thighs has kept me warm these past weeks."

Her face flooded with heat at his words and the memory of how his fingers had felt as they traced their way down her spine and between her buttocks.

"You wanted me then," he continued.

She shuddered. "I don't want you now," she said, but the lick of heat in her woman's core belied the words.

"Hmmm." He rolled her onto her stomach, his sleeves brushing her bare skin. "Stay here."

With unhurried movements, he backed away and shrugged out of his tunic. Brenna watched with lowered lids. Despite her anger at him, the artistry of his body fascinated her. His shoulders were so wide and tanned. Muscles moved beneath his skin, rippling and undulating.

He stretched casually in an obvious display to show off his body to its full glory. It was vulgar. Shameful. Magnificent.

He was beautiful and he knew it, how horridly arrogant. She tried to turn aside but couldn't seem to make herself do so. She nearly moaned as he moved his hands to the waist of his breeches and teased at the laces. He watched her, observing her with all the casualness of a coiled snake ready to strike. If only she had done a better job at hiding her fascination with his large, male body all those weeks ago when she had bathed him. This purposeful onslaught to her senses was not fair.

With infinite slowness, he unlaced the ties and peeled off the rest of his clothing.

Her mouth went dry.

His member stood partially erect, but still relaxed.

The lines of his body were as well drawn as any painting. All sinew and strength. Round buttocks. Long, long legs. Thickly corded muscles. The curve of his hip was sculpted with such beauty that it would have made a master artist weep.

Devastating.

How could such evil be held in such a perfect body?

He stepped into the tub, his thighs flexing in a compelling masculine display.

She cursed herself for watching, but her eyes seemed to follow his every move of their own accord.

Water trickled down the sensuous line of his back as he ran the cloth over his shoulders. The gesture was slow, practiced, as if he were a merchant displaying his wares. *Like what you see? Isn't this muscle interesting? How about this arm?*

As if he was testing the truth of her statement that she did not want him. How utterly, utterly horrid.

His thickly corded biceps danced beneath his tanned skin as he moved the cloth slowly over his wide chest and down the bumpy dips and valleys that made up his stomach.

Her breath caught in her throat. How could she resist such beauty?

For a wicked instant she remembered how it had been when she had bathed him. Heat seeped into her core in a hot wave of desire and she wanted to slide off the bed and follow the paths of the water rivulets with her finger.

She slammed her eyes closed, squelching that daft thought. He was her captor, not her lover.

"Look at me," he commanded in a low voice.

Swallowing, she reopened her eyes—and nearly lurched off the mattress. The bed ropes protested her sudden movement.

He stood right beside her, water dripping off his torso in interesting rivulets. Intensity swirled in his eyes like a sea storm. In his hand, he held the blade she'd tried to kill him with.

She yelped and shrank back with a shudder, holding her hands up in a feeble attempt to protect herself. "Y–y–you don't need the knife; I wasn't going to fight you," she stammered, horrified to realize she spoke the truth, and equally horrified to realize that if he planned to slit her throat, she was completely at his mercy.

"Peace, girl," he said, proffering the blade. "I want you to shave me. We need new memories between us with this knife."

Taking the dagger, she scrambled off the mattress, wrapping the sheet around herself as a makeshift garment. He loomed over her. The bed curtains flittered and she stared at the blade. The glow from the low fire in the hearth flickered across it, showing that he'd sharpened it to a razor edge. The handle was warm, heated by his skin. Should she try again to stab him? To slit his throat?

Her fingers tightened.

He caught her wrist in his hand, latching around it like the manacle had been. "Think carefully before you act," he said, as if reading her thoughts.

Blinking, she leaned her head way back so she could scrutinize his face.

He was watching her intently, the blue of his eyes gleaming like dark sapphires. Releasing her wrist, he indicated the cake of soap and the three-legged stool beside her table. "Shave me."

She smarted at the command. Shaving him instead of stabbing him would just prove how fully captive she was. She had to at least attempt to rid herself of him. She *had* to. Didn't she?

He turned, giving her an open view of his back, and walked to the stool. Arrogant bastard! As if he thought her so puny he did not even have to look at her and that she would heel like a dog.

Her fingers slid down the length of the blade, resting lightly on the tip between her thumb and forefinger. Afore, she had stabbed him instead of flinging the knife. Stabbing was not her skill. But now he was across the room like one of her targets. And this time the knife was very sharp.

She *could* kill him.

He had apologized. Relentlessly. The thought struck her as sharply as if a paintbrush had jabbed her in the eye. *He washed me, bathed me, massaged me, carried me from where I had been laying on the stairs.*

Those were not the actions of a monster.

But he kept me dirty and terrified, chained for over a month, her mind argued.

But he bathed me.

"Brenna?"

She blinked, coming back to the present, glad of the distraction from her warring thoughts.

Montgomery sat at her table desk, his legs splayed as he sat on the stool in a pose worthy of one of her paintings.

A commander, a husband, a man, yes. But not a monster. Not worthy of death.

She could not slay him. She stifled a sigh at that revelation. If only she had the nerve to slay herself instead. But, alas, she wanted to live. Even if it meant consummating the marriage.

She looked him up and down. His member hung to one side, relaxed and much smaller than it had been before. Even in its flaccid state, it did not look like a scrawny sausage. She allowed herself a small smile at her folly of sketching a man's member incorrectly. She would do better in the future.

"I would like to paint," she blurted, the words coming out of her mouth before she could stop them. "The bargain was that I would be able to paint."

He ran a hand against the stubble on his cheek. "We were talking about you shaving me."

"Nay, we were *talking* about whether or not I would try to stab you again and if you were going to be able to swive me without putting me back in chains." She held up the blade to punctuate her words. Her fingers were no longer on the tip, but wrapped loosely around the hilt. Harmless.

He slapped his thigh and laughed. "How perceptive of you, my lady. And your decision?"

"I want to paint. I want you to open that damn

trunk and let me paint. I cannot bear this marriage or my lot in life without my artwork."

"Another bargain, my lady?"

"We have made bargains aplenty," she said sharply. "I've been chained like an animal this past month, and if you intend to keep me thus, I want you to open my blasted trunk." She wondered if holding the dagger to her own throat would tighten her argument, but she imagined he would know she was bluffing.

Pursing his lips, he stood, retrieved the key from his pouch and unlocked the trunk. He flipped the lid open.

A wash of relief sped through her and she wanted to race to the chest and dig through her supplies.

That he could command her pleasure and pain so easily irritated her—painting had been what she had longed for, obsessed over these past weeks. Even more than the chains or the lack of bathing.

He straightened, standing wide-legged, hands on hips in front of the chest. His member twitched, lengthening some. If he was unsettled in any way by being fully naked, he did not indicate it.

"A kiss in return for your paints, my lady?"

"A kiss?" she scoffed. "The paints are what you owe me already."

"True. But your father's escape changes our bargain some, so I insist on a kiss in return." The dark sapphire of his eyes twinkled like sparkling sand in the clear blue depths of the ocean.

A lazy butterfly swooped into her stomach. A kiss was so—simple. Especially in light of what would surely occur later. Squaring her shoulders, she walked to him, holding the knife with one hand and the sheet with the other.

Heat flowed off his skin as she neared him. He did not move to grab her, but she could see the tension in his shoulders. His mannerism might appear relaxed, but he was ready to pounce if she attacked.

Standing on tiptoes, she slid her hand around his neck and leaned her face forward. Hesitating only a moment, she brought her lips to his.

His arms closed around her, not frightening or imprisoning as she had imagined, but simply holding her. It felt . . . nice.

When she broke the kiss and stepped back, he did not try to stop her, but instead smiled his boyish grin. His overlapping teeth showed, as did the dimple on his chin, and for a moment, he could have been an Atlantian god instead of a conqueror.

She took a deep breath, not wanting to acknowledge the thrill that slid through her betraying body. His manhood pressed against her stomach, proving he was not so impassive to the kiss as he pretended either. A curl of heat unfurled inside her.

Feeling awkward at the sudden change in tension in the chamber, she held up *l'occhio del diavolo.*

He caught her arm in a motion so swift that she gasped. Clearly, the mistrust between them ran high.

"I–I was going to ask you about that shave," she stuttered, ashamed that she had not even considered the dagger.

His intense eyes burned into her and she felt he could see right through the flimsy fabric covering her body.

She held her breath until he nodded stoically and ran his finger down her jawline.

"Take off your sheet first."

A punishment for lifting the blade too suddenly?

Shivering, she untucked the sheet and let it fall. "I meant you no harm," she murmured. "This is what I would have done if I had." Whirling, she slid her fingers in the tip of her *l'occhio del diavolo*, cocked her arm back and threw the blade in a flash. It landed with a solid thud into the bedpost.

His eyes widened.

Satisfaction flowed through her at this small victory. "If I had intended to harm you, I would have done so when I was across the room from you."

He lifted a brow. "You are full of surprises, my captive wife."

Chapter Fourteen

Brenna took in a deep steadying breath as she turned to gather the supplies needed to shave her husband. Emotions churned inside her. She was accustomed to moving about her chamber nude, but his gaze on her body as she moved around made her skin tingle and burn.

Brenna retrieved *l'occhio del diavolo*, gathered rags and heated water in a pot that hung over the fire for such use. He watched her the whole while, barely shifting on the stool.

When the supplies were ready, she moved in front of him. Candle glow flickered over his beautiful muscled form, dancing along the sculpted planes of his torso. Dipping the rag into the water, she wet his face then lathered his beard with soap. His whiskers pricked her palms. So different from her own skin. So masculine. So very interesting.

With careful precision, she ran the blade across his cheek, then dunked it into the water. "How did you know I would not strike you with the knife?"

The area around his eyes crinkled. "I did not. But you

seem intelligent enough to reason out that attempting murder again is not the wisest course."

He tilted his head as she ran the blade down his neck. "Mayhap I just wanted to get closer to you," she reasoned.

"Brenna, love, you are no murderess, and I could strike you dead with one blow even with the dagger sticking from my throat."

She shuddered at his words, all the more frightening because of the ring of truth in them. Glancing down at his large hands, she rinsed the blade in the bowl. The power radiating from him both fascinated and repelled her. Like a moth whose wings were singed by a candle.

She finished her ministrations carefully, then ran her fingers along his cheek to inspect her work. The whiskers were as close cut as they had been that day in the wedding chapel, and she felt oddly proud when he nodded approval.

Slowly, he reached for her, and when she did not resist, he pulled her into his lap. The shock of skin on skin snaked through her. He traced his fingers down her neck and between her breasts then rubbed gentle circles around her bellybutton.

Heat flooded her woman's core. She wished she could pretend he did not affect her so, but she could not.

Instinctively, she closed her eyes and allowed his hands to roam freely over her skin.

He *was* her husband. Surely that lessened her guilt that enjoying his touch was betrayal. She should be angry with him—too angry to receive pleasure.

Warmth spread across her as his hands moved. Enthralling. Spellbinding. As if they were floating, alone in the world. Her body felt relaxed from his massage, and stimulated from this new touch.

"My pretty lady," he murmered into her ear, his breath sending spirals of heat across her skin.

Pretty?

She sucked in a breath, wondering if he called all his lovers by such name.

"Come, let me see you." Leaning her back across his arm, he slowly ran his finger from her neck to her navel and then lower.

She wished she had the strength of character to resist.

But the v betwixt her thighs tingled.

Almost of their own accord, her hips raised, meeting his touch. She wanted . . . wanted him to touch her there, between the curls of her nether lips.

All at once, he stood and set her down on the desktop so that she was facing him. He knelt, pushing her knees outward so that his face was at the level of her privates.

Heat crept up her face, and she knew her face flamed as red as her hair. Many times, she'd gazed at herself in the looking glass, painted her sex, and sold off the miniatures. She knew what he saw: she had red curls between her legs that crept out a little further on one side than the other. The inner lips were pink and swirled a little like the crinkly edge of a rose. Nestled betwixt the folds was a nub of sensitive skin—her woman's pearl.

But the paintings were so much less personal than another person—a magnificent conqueror, looking at her down there. And she was never this wet or slick when she painted.

"Spread your legs, love." He threaded his fingers through the red-gold curls and she shivered, barely resisting the urge to lean back on the desk. Moisture beaded on the pink flesh.

And she felt hot. Hot all over. As if a furnace burned inside her.

Spreading apart her nether lips, he licked one side of her slit and then the other. She moaned. Zwounds! No wonder the maids spoke of copulation as such pleasure. Surrendering to the sensations, she closed her eyes, leaned back and spread her thighs apart.

His hand touched her elbow and she opened her eyes slightly. She gasped as she realized he was holding *l'occhio del diavolo*.

"Shh, Brenna. I will not harm you. I want you to see how beautiful you are." His voice was low and bewitching. He smiled wickedly, his eyes glowing. With one hand he lathered soap into her nether curls.

She frowned, trying to fathom what he was about. Or if she should resist or submit.

Then, stretching the skin slightly, he took the knife and shaved off a swath of her pubic hair.

She gave a little shriek and slammed her legs together, capturing his hand between her thighs. The desk creaked beneath her. "What the bloody hell are you doing?"

He grinned. A pirate's grin, full of mayhem and mischief. "I told you I wanted new memories with this knife."

Her eyebrows knit together, and for an instant she wondered if she should up and run from the room. "But you can't shave me!"

"Why not? You shaved me."

"That's different!"

His fingers twitched, touching that pearl of skin above her womanly opening.

She gasped. Then shivered.

His smile widened, showing off his two overlapping teeth to devastating effect. "Open for me, my lady. I swear by all that is holy, no harm will come to you. You have naught to fear."

Naught save her own response to him.

"What does a blackheart like you know about swearing by all that is holy?" she countered.

Leaning down, he kissed her thighs, right where they came together, and eased his tongue betwixt them. "I know a bit about worshiping at this altar."

A mewl of desire escaped her throat before she could catch it. It felt so . . . heady, like when painting and the brushstrokes were sure.

She opened her legs, allowing him access.

The knife rasped against her skin. He scraped off another swatch of hair, this one a thumb's width longer than the first one, then ran his finger over his handiwork. Her skin tingled. The bare area felt so alive and sensitive, she feared his touch might send her bursting into pieces.

'Twas intoxicating.

Slowly, carefully, he shaved more of her nether hair off, stretching the skin this way and that as he worked with delicate precision. She didn't dare move and somewhere inside her, the flickering of fear lit into an inferno of desire. The blade was cool and sharp as it scratched against her sensitive sex, but his strokes were masterful and steady. No nicks marred her skin.

He gazed at her, with the passion of an artist, at work, transfixed on making the canvas to his liking. His hair was still wet from his bath and his wide shoulders held her thighs apart as he knelt between her legs.

Droplets ran from her woman's slit, joining the wayward splotches of paint on the desk's surface. Her pearl tingled. He didn't touch her on that sensitive nub, so she lifted her hips in invitation. But he paid no attention, only continued his work of making her sex free of anything that would stand between it and his gaze.

Swallowing, she gazed down at the smooth, pinkened skin. Ne'er in her life had she felt so exposed.

And yet, so safe. 'Twas obvious he knew what he was doing and an arrow of jealousy sliced into her that any other woman would have enjoyed such close attention.

He ran his fingers across her shaven sex when he was finished; she flinched, her skin overly sensitive.

He gazed at her as though she was Venus, the goddess of love, not Brenna, the scarred daughter of a rebel.

Setting the blade aside, he washed off the soap and patted her dry.

She felt she would crumple to the floor with sensation.

Standing, he carried her to the bed. No longer fearing what would come between them, she wrapped her arms around his neck and surrendered to his touch. Any man that could hold a blade with such steady, slow precision could surely control his own manroot and not harm her.

"There may be some pain the first time, my lady," he whispered as he laid her across the mattress. "But not much, and I will not move until you are ready."

She already felt ready, but she did not say so.

His hand trailed from her neck to her stomach. Her heart fluttered, and she wanted . . . more. She wanted him to touch her sex on that newly exposed skin as he had done afore. She wanted to feel his large, callused hands slide between her woman's fold and find that pearl of desire that tingled and burned and ached.

She shifted her hips, trying to press his hand further down her body. He did not move his fingers, so she shifted.

He moved a dagger's width down her body. But not nearly far enough.

She wiggled again, feeling more womanly moisture drip from inside her.

His fingers walked another inch down her stomach. Oh, bloody hell. Why would he not touch her as he had before!

"My lord, prithee," she moaned.

Leaning down, he trailed kisses from her ear to her lips. His tongue swept inside her mouth, taking control of her senses. She arched her body upward and he slid his hand down between the folds of her slit. With a sigh, she sank into the mattress, savoring the feel of his fingers on her skin.

"You are so slick," he whispered, shifting slightly so that he was atop her.

She felt his manhood at her entrance, parting the folds of her sex. Spreading her legs, she rocked her bottom toward him, reaching for him. He entered slowly, as careful as he had been with the knife.

When he was crested inside, he paused and kissed her forehead. "Are you well?"

She wanted to melt, to take all of him into herself. She had braced herself for pain, but there was none— just tightness, and the sensation of being full and open to him.

"'Tis wondrous," she breathed. Her paintings lacked the element of passion found in the room between them. She would change the ones she did in the future.

Languidly, she gazed up at him. He rocked his hips

and pushed his cock all the way inside piercing through the barrier of her virginity.

She yelped, but he caught the sound in his mouth with a kiss that dulled the pleasure/pain.

"Only pleasure now," he promised, curling her hands into his and holding her arms above her head. He lingered, unmoving, letting her adjust to his body and she surrendered to the marvelous impression of simply being his.

She lifted her hips up to his, craving more. With the gentlest of strokes, he moved, sliding in and out in a slow, steady rhythm. She sighed. Her body tingled. The wondrous sensations built and built. She raised her legs, then lowered them, wanting to get the highest level of movement on that small nub betwixt her thighs.

A small part of her hated herself for enjoying this act between them, but she was too lost in her own feelings to care.

Tomorrow there would be time to fathom it all out.

She inhaled the warm scent of his skin and wiggled her hands against his palms. When he released them, she ran her hands along his back, enjoying the tight, thick muscles of his body.

Mine.

All mine.

Throwing her head back, she yielded to the friction between their bodies. She moved faster, bucking underneath him, moving towards the spiraling sensation.

Her body shuddered, as if an avalanche had occurred within it. "Bloody hell!" she gasped.

He laughed. Laughed! "Well, that's a new one."

Embarrassed at her outburst, she squeezed her eyes shut and tried to push him off. His chest was like a wall. Strong and unbending as it squeezed the air from her lungs.

"Get off me!" she cried, flailing her head to one side. How could he laugh at her when she'd just given him so much of herself? The bastard. The blackheart. The barbarian.

It would have been better if he had raped her than to have been so humiliated.

"Shh, shh," he soothed, "peace, Brenna."

She calmed, but the backs of her eyes stung with mortification. "I do not know how women are supposed to behave during copulation," she said sulkily.

"You are wonderful, girl. I am very, very pleased with you. You can scream 'bloody hell' all you want and I'll love every minute of it, alright?"

His words felt like cool water on her hot shame. She nodded sullenly.

"You were a virgin," he said as if inexplicably pleased with himself. "And now you are mine."

His lips captured hers, telling her without words that her outburst had been welcomed and his laugh been one of delight, not mocking. She sighed, feeling even more out of sorts than before. Her father had beaten her for using the word "bloody."

James pushed himself more firmly into her. Stronger now. Pumping. And then, he too cried out his own pleasure and slumped against her.

She wrapped her arms around his body, enjoying the soft slide of perspiration against her skin. Out of sheer curiosity, she stuck her tongue out and licked his shoulder, just to see if he tasted as good as he felt. He shuddered at her gesture and a surge of feminine power snaked through her.

She closed her eyes, intoxicated by the scent of

heated sex and the sweet, salty taste of male skin. In her most outrageous imaginations, she had never dreamed copulation would feel so astounding.

Or so wicked.

She relaxed against the pillows and stared up at the bed's canopy, her fingers itching to hold a paintbrush. She could scarcely wait to capture it all on canvas.

Chapter Fifteen

Brenna awoke to a throbbing headache and a whirling mind as unnaturally bright light glittered across her face. She ached. Her head, her shoulders, her back.

Miserable. Absolutely miserable.

Squinting her eyes in the brightness, she saw her husband sitting by the window at her desk, one leg crossed over the other at the ankle. He wore leather breeks and naught else. His relaxed vulnerability touched a heartstring and his wide chest and thick biceps fascinated her, making her wish she had a paintbrush in her hand.

His hair, normally so orderly, was mussed on his head. It was longer than it had been at the wedding, but his face was perfectly shaved. She groaned at the memory, her cheeks flaming. It wasn't just his face that was shaved. She resisted the urge to peek under the bedcovers at her bare sex to verify she had not imagined the entire evening.

A scrick, scrick, scrick bit through the air; he appeared to be sharpening *l'occhio del diavolo* against a leather strap.

Her face flooded with heat at the memory of that knife against her queynt. He had . . . shaved her. Touched her. Pleasured her.

She watched him for a moment, captivated by how smooth his strokes were, at how sure his hands were on the hilt. Warmth flowed into her at the memory of how he'd caressed her with the same precision, with the same surety. As if he knew of some inner secret passion that she herself did not know.

Her heart warmed as she remembered that he had apologized for keeping her chained so long. That he had taken his time in bathing her to make up for the time lost. That, despite her father's escape, he had given her back her paints for the price of a kiss.

There were still things to work out between them, but mayhap their marriage would not be so heinous after all.

He paused holding the blade just above the leather. "Good morning." His rich blue eyes were spellbinding against his tanned skin. Beautiful.

She felt her nipples tighten, and she wondered what he would do if she threw back the sheet and offered herself to him again.

Would he be shocked? Appalled?

Or would he caress her again as he had last night— seeking out her secret places and making her gasp with delight. Would his staff rise to wondrous heights?

Contemplating this pleasant thought, she swung her leg to move off the mattress, wanting to go to him, to touch him.

Her foot caught and a loud clank rang through the chamber.

Gasping, she looked down—a manacle was wrapped around her left ankle, chaining her to the bed.

Bloody hell. Her kind feelings toward him shattered like stained glass under the assault of a rock.

"You chained me?" she burst out.

"Of course, my captive wife," he said impassively, going back to sharpening the knife. "We are no more in love today than we were yesterday when you were attacking me and trying to escape."

"You—you—" Words failed her, and she nearly screamed. How could he do this! After what they had shared. She had dared think that somehow their tryst had meant something.

What a stupid, naive ninny she was. He was the one who had experienced dozens of lovers, not her.

Resisting the urge to duck her head beneath the covers in humiliation, she drew the sheet up to her neck and stared at the curtains swinging around her bed.

To him, she was simply another conquest in his bed. He had used his skills as a lover to bend her to his will.

And, damn the man, it had worked. She wished it did not hurt, but it did.

She wished he would leave so she could get dressed and put some sort of covering on her naked body. And pretend last night had never occurred. Pretend she hadn't just planned to offer herself to him like some lovesick slave before her master.

Pretend the sheet didn't rasp against the bare skin of her shaven sex.

She glared at him, but he bent over the knife, stroking it back and forth across the leather. Unruffled. Unaffected by yesterday's activities.

She should have stabbed him. Why didn't she stab him!

Irritated at her own weakness, she stiffened her spine, determined to carry on as if naught had occurred. As if the sound of the blade sliding across leather didn't scrape her nerve endings raw.

Shame curled through her gut and she wanted to hang her head that she had thought things might change between them.

But she was as captive today as she had been before.

"How do you feel?" he asked, glancing up for a moment.

Vulnerable. Embarrassed. Confused.

"Fine."

The light from the window streamed across his face, kissing his generous lips.

She smoothed a springy curl of hair behind her ear and lifted her chin. He would never know of how she'd lusted for him just moments earlier. She *would* find a way free from this entanglement.

"There is no reason to chain me," she said curtly.

He tilted his head to one side. "Naught has changed between us."

Despite her vow to carry on as if naught had happened, his plainspoken declaration felt like a blow in the stomach. Mayhap nothing had changed for him, but she felt vulnerable and fragile in ways she had not known possible.

"Who were you meeting on the wall walk?" The question was asked coolly, but she recognized the tension across his shoulders. He was as on guard as he had been yester eve when she held *l'occhio del diavolo*.

"No one," she answered, matching his tone in composure.

"I found this in the stairwell." He lifted a parchment

off the desk. The parchment she'd given to Brother Giffard to send to Nathan.

Devil take it!

She rubbed her temples, irritated with herself, irritated with Montgomery. And irritated that Brother Giffard had not sent the missive weeks ago when he had the chance.

Evidently he'd dropped it when they had met last night. Brother Giffard had sent her a message to meet on the wall walk—Father Peter was on a rampage and the chapel had been unavailable. He had secured a little gold for the painting she'd given him earlier. The amount wasn't enough for passage on a ship and Brenna had been ranting at the unfairness of her husband leaving her paints locked away when Montgomery had come into the bailey. She had flown down the stairs to make it back to her room before he caught her without her guard, and before he discovered whom she was conversing with.

She had tripped in the narrow stairwell, her steps encumbered by the chains, and had bumped her head.

"Who were you giving this to, Brenna?"

Her heart skipped. If she implicated Brother Giffard and he was questioned, all hope of arranging passage to Italy would be lost.

"I wasn't giving it to anyone—I wrote it weeks ago, hoping to pass it off to one of my sisters or someone going into the town."

"I see," Montgomery said, but it was unclear if he believed her or not. "Why was Damien not with you? Why did you say it was not his fault when I was angry with him for sleeping?"

Her heart sank lower and lower until she wanted to kick herself for her outburst yesterday. She had grown fond of her young guard and his outrageous mustache and had sought to protect him when she'd seen Montgomery loom over the lad. She'd slipped his watch, given him some herbs to help him sleep, because Brother Giffard and she were not meeting in the church where they could have some privacy.

Montgomery's eyes seemed to probe into her soul, ferreting out her secrets.

"Brenna." He moved right beside her and ran his finger up the side of her neck. "If you have a lover, I will kill him."

A harsh laugh welled in her throat. "I do *not* have a lover, as you well-proved yester eve!"

An odd look gleamed in his eyes and she wished she could tell what he was thinking.

"Why were you in the tower?"

Running her fingers lightly over the bed covers, she debated for a moment what to hide and what to reveal. Mayhap her best course was to be as forthright as possible.

"I found it wearisome to be followed around twenty-four hours a day, so I fed Damien a potion to help him sleep."

"Where did you get this potion?" Montgomery cut in.

"Sometimes I have trouble sleeping, my lord." She kept her voice deliberately non-inflammatory. "My sister makes it for me—"

"Which one?"

"Adele—"

"Have you spoken with her?"

"Nay—"

"Was she the one in the tower?"

His battery of rapid-fire questions left her reeling.

"Nay! I was carrying the note myself and dropped it when I fell rushing back to my chamber."

"Why were you rushing?"

"My intention was only to escape Damien for a bit, and when I saw you had returned, I panicked." It was close enough to the truth, and she held her breath, praying he would believe her.

He nodded in his precise, calculating manner.

Relief flowed through her. She wiggled her leg, rattling the chain. "May I get up?"

Before he could answer a knock sounded.

"Enter," Montgomery commanded. He stood, laying the strop of leather across her desk and tucking *l'occhio del diavolo* into his belt. Clearly, he had been expecting someone.

A caravan of trunk-carrying servants entered followed by a pudgy middle-aged merchant and a round-faced woman.

Montgomery indicated a place for the trunks.

What the bloody hell? Was this more of Montgomery punishment? She glowered at them.

The man bowed low, making a sweeping gesture with his hat. He was richly dressed in an elaborately embroidered paltock and finely made hose. "We came as soon as the rains would allow."

"We've brought the finest of our silks and velvet," the woman added. She pointed at a trunk, and a tall, bald servant wearing a well-stitched tunic opened it. Taking out a piece of blue velvet, she held it to the light.

"'Tis as good a weave as one can find anywhere, even in Paris or Italy," the man said, puffing out his chest.

Montgomery glanced at Brenna. "Well, wife?"

Brenna squinted at the lush material, confused.

He waved his hand toward the two strangers as they opened a second trunk. "They are clothing merchants."

She gave his back a sour look. "I'm not daft."

"Our garments were in disrepair from the soggy journey," he said, digging through the linens in one of the trunks. He pulled out a fine piece of green silk and draped it over his bare forearm.

She'd had to wear the same blasted unwashed dress for weeks and now he wanted to parade in front of her that he was having new garments made because a little rain got on them! What a peacock! She'd realized that he was meticulous with his clothing—every stitch perfect, every seam precise. No doubt fawning maids ironed those perfect creases with hot flatplates and smoothing stones every morning. But this was beyond anything she'd ever seen.

"What do you think of this?" he asked, holding up a scrap of silk trim embroidered with small roses.

"It is lovely," she said sourly.

"Excellent." He pulled cloth of gold from the pile of fabrics nestled in the trunk. "What else do you have?" he asked the merchant, who was busy folding and unfolding other pieces of fabric.

Soon the room was aflutter with color as they showed all sorts of fine silk and velvet in every length and size. Reds, blues, greens. 'Twas as if they were painting cloth rainbows in the room. They showed embroidered trim and linings of ermine and fox and mink.

Brenna rubbed her temples. Why Montgomery needed new clothing was beyond her. Even in its travel-worn state, his tunics were better than anything she'd worn for the past seven years.

She wiggled the toes on her manacled foot, irritated she could not get up and leave the room. No doubt it was testimony to his arrogance to have merchants come to their chamber while she was chained to the bed.

He lifted several more swaths of fabric, keeping some and discarding others. As always, his motions were keen and direct. Intense.

And finicky. Ne'er had she seen a man so versed in the weaves and makes of different material. He picked out flaws that she didn't even notice. What silliness. He was worse than Gwyneth.

Exasperating. That's what he was. And furthermore, she needed to pee.

Wanting them all to go away, she closed her eyes to pluck them out of her sight.

"Fifteen dresses then," she heard Montgomery say. "With undertunics and chemises too. Something for both everyday wear and things suited to go before the queen."

She opened one eye. "Dresses?"

He whirled to her, the movement as sharp as men training for battle.

Ignoring the tug of the manacle around her ankle, she sat up in the bed. "You are ordering these for me?"

"Of course."

Her world spun. Her last new dress had been years ago, shrouded by painful memories. And-fifteen? 'Twas an unheard of number of garments for one woman. Even when her father had taken all of hers, she had only had five. Realizing her jaw hung slack, she closed her mouth and relaxed back onto the pillow. "Why are you being nice to me?"

He looked taken aback by the question.

"Well?" Heedless of the discomfiture of others in the room, she rattled the chain around her ankle. "There is no reason for it. We are no more in love today than we were before," she said, parroting his earlier words.

The merchant and his wife exchanged a look, then rapidly began rooting around in the smaller trunks.

Montgomery opened his mouth to answer, but the woman quickly pulled out several yards of a silky green fabric that was so fine it was nearly transparent. "How about this, me lady? 'Twould look lovely with your eyes, yes?"

The fabric swirled into the air catching the light from the window and reflecting out a thousand colors. It was the most amazing cloth she'd ever seen. Nearly magical.

"My wife speaks truth," the merchant rushed before anyone could speak. "If you will just stand, me lady, for the measurements."

Brenna looked helplessly at Montgomery. She was naked beneath the covers: she had neither long hair on her head to cover her breasts nor curls of nether hair to cover her sex.

"Stand up," he said curtly. "I will not have my countess dressed in rags."

She crossed her arms over her chest. "But you don't mind if I'm naked and chained," she snarled.

Heat lit in his eyes and he lifted a brow. "Not in the least."

A curl of desire flitted through her belly at his words. She turned her face aside. Was this one more way Montgomery intended to humiliate her?

"Here." Montgomery chuckled and tossed her a chemise. "Put this on and get up so they can measure you."

Obnoxious toad! She frowned, recalling how impassive he'd been when servants had filled the bathing tub

for him. While he may be used to people invading his
privacy, she found the swirls of activity disconcerting.
She had been mostly alone this past year.

The merchants bustled around them, consummate
professionals as they rustled fabric and pins and scissors
pretending they were completely deaf and oblivious
to the conversation.

Gritting her teeth, she put the garment on beneath
the sheet and swung her legs over the side of the bed.
The floor was cold on her bare feet. The chain clanked
against the bedpost.

The merchant woman's eyes bugged, but she only
smiled. One does not anger well-paying customers.

Brenna scowled.

Montgomery stepped forward to stabilize her as the
tailor stretched her this way and that to make measurements.

If she had not been so irritated, she would have enjoyed such treatment. But she needed to use the garderobe. And being poked and prodded wasn't helping.

Setting her jaw, she stared at the wall. She couldn't
make water until Montgomery released her.

At last all the measurements were taken and the
fabrics packed back into the trunks. The merchants
left with their orders and the room felt quiet again.

"I need to use the privy," she hissed at Montgomery
when he still seemed disinclined to unlock her from
the bed.

He grinned. "Say, 'please.'" With his boyish overlapping teeth and the tiny dimple beneath his lower lip,
he looked like a pirate about to claim a hidden stash
of booty.

She glowered at him. She'd rather wet herself.

"Close enough," he said with another wicked smile,

pulling the key from his tunic and releasing her. "I would have done so sooner if only you would have asked."

Seething, she scampered to the garderobe. So, that was the way of things now, eh? To have to ask even to use the privy.

A wave of distress crashed over her that she had enjoyed his attentions last night. How could she have? He was the most awful ogre alive!

When she returned from the privy, he held up a dress that the merchants had left. It was a creation made of blue silk with tiny embroidered dragons on the sleeves and neckline. It was not quite as voluptuous as the houpelandes that Gwyneth wore, but for certes, the fabric was fine, soft and comfortable—a far cry from her homespun kirtle. Well suited for a lady of the keep—both practical and pretty.

She blew out a breath and wished she had the strength of will to defy him, to toss the garment down the garderobe shaft. All new clothing had been denied her for years and she had told herself she did not care. But, alas, she was a woman still.

She put on the dress. It was as luxurious against her skin as she had imagined. Like donning a sigh. The skirt rustled against her legs and she could not help but rub the fabric back and forth between her fingers. At least her cage was gilded.

"Go on," he said. "Go look at yourself in the glass. I know you want to."

She wished she could stifle the age-old feminine urge toward vanity, but instead she propped up the looking glass and backed away so she could see her form. The color of the dress brought out the green of her eyes. Feeling like a princess, she held her unevenly cropped hair off her neck and turned this way and that.

"Fabulous." He flashed another of his devastating smiles.

"You are still not forgiven," she said, running her palms over and over against the silk.

He laughed and picked up the manacles from where they were piled beside the bed. "And that is why you must put your jewelry back on."

Chapter Sixteen

Loud clanking, the clucking of a rooster and the squeals of a woman shouting reached Brenna's ears a few days later as Damien and she entered the east tower while searching for Montgomery to ask his permission to walk into the village.

A note from Brother Giffard requesting they meet at the town's cathedral was slipped to her during the noon meal. She had concocted an excuse that she needed to buy painting supplies and wanted to stop by the town's church to take them a painting she had done of the birth of Christ. It was a flimsy excuse since that ol' dried up prune Bishop Humphrey and her shared a mutual hatred for one another—but Montgomery didn't know that.

That she needed a husband's permission to walk into the town smarted. But judging from the sounds, she had found him.

She lifted the hem of her dress—one of the fancy new ones made of blue silk with slitted sleeves and a yellow undertunic, which looked hopelessly ridiculous with the chains—and went down a flight of steps. Every night he released her from the bonds and inflamed her body to a fevered pitch, but she was forced to wear the manacles as she went about her daily chores.

Irritating, for certes, but she had her revenge with her: she carried a wooden tube that contained two miniatures depicting the passion she and Montgomery had shared. They were hidden between the religious paintings she was taking to the cathedral. She planned to give them to Brother Giffard to sell. They were by far her best work yet and she knew in her heart they would fetch a high price.

Enough gold to take herself and her sisters to Italy.

Following the cacophony of sound down a narrow hall, they quickened their pace and hurried down another flight of worn steps that led to a large lower room.

And entered into chaos.

Montgomery and two of his men poked through drawers and upturned trestle tables. A rooster fluttered around the room, dropping feathers here and yon. Tunics, smocks, and undergarments looked to have been exploded about the chamber.

"You cannot go through that, my lord!" Jennet shouted at the men. "Catch Roger! 'Es terrified!"

Roger, Jennet's pet rooster, made short paths around the laundry washing chamber, landing briefly on Brenna's head before being caught by one of the men and released out the window.

"Roger!" Jennet yelled after the spooked bird. "Roger! Come back here!"

The rooster flew across the field, beating his wings like the devil followed him. Red and brown feathers swirled to the ground.

"Oh!" She stamped her feet. "Look what ye did, me

lord. Now I'll ne'er be able to get him back, I won'. An' 'e was such a good bird too."

Montgomery stood, sword drawn, in the midst of the confusion of dirty and clean garments. He wore an unadorned blue tunic, hose and high boots. As always, his tunic was crisp and his boots gleamed. A set of woman's underthings hung limply off one of his shoulders, no doubt a casualty of his battle against the laundry.

Brenna stifled a laugh.

"Bear, go get the good woman's bird back," Montgomery bellowed at a large one-armed man who had a head full of bushy red hair.

"Aye! You do that!" Jennet fumed, snatching fistfuls of laundry from where it was strewn out around the room. "All my work! Ruined by a pack of boorish men!"

Casting a wild look over his shoulder at Jennet, Bear hurried from the chamber. "A pet rooster, of all the daft things," he muttered under his breath.

"A word with you, my lord," Brenna interjected before Jennet could catch her breath and start railing at him. Pet rooster or no, the laundress liked her work done orderly and systematically. She'd be uncontainable unless Brenna could soothe her.

In fact, if this was the way Montgomery handled matters, it would only be a matter of time afore the entire household exploded in utter chaos. His return has certainly sent her own emotions into a muddle. All the more reason to reach her brother in Italy, and gain his help in gathering her sisters and escaping. She planned to ask Giffard why he hadn't sent the note today when she saw him. Everday she stayed here bound her more and more to the marriage; she had started looking forward to their eveinings together and she'd had no herbs to prevent a child either.

Montgomery turned and stared at Brenna. The blue of his tunic caused his indigo eyes to flash and spark. Sweat dripped down his temple and he looked for all the world like a demon come to life. But the effect was ruined by the lady's undergarments flopping across his shoulder.

She bit back a welling of laughter. "If you are looking for rebels, my lord, they have gone and left only their underpants."

Behind her, Damien giggled.

Removing the offending garment, Montgomery growled and gave the boy a curt look.

Brenna covered her mouth with the back of her hand. Laughing at her husband was not going to win her the trip into the town.

"Forgive me, my lord. What exactly are you hoping to find in the keep's laundry chamber?" she asked, changing her tactic. With forced casualness, she plucked a tunic from the floor and folded it. Her bonds rattled softly, but were unobtrusive.

He flung the women's undergarments onto the mountain of clothing. "I am searching for paintings."

Her interest peaked. "Paintings?"

"Aye." He moved closer so that only she could hear him. "A certain set of miniatures from this area has reached London and the king is most displeased. The paintings depict the king in various poses copulating with a number of courtiers. I have been sent to find them and take the artist to London."

A lead weight fell into Brenna's stomach. She remembered the questioning he'd given her after the wedding. He had been very concerned about the subject of paintings, but she'd never guessed why—or that it would involve the king.

Quickly, she bent to gather more of the scattered garments lest guilt show on her face.

When she was a girl visiting London, she'd painted a series of naughty portraits using what she remembered of the king's likeness. They had been a joke to heal herself from the bruising memory of the trip. A reckless moment of petty revenge for being embarrassed by the queen.

Five had been sold when she'd first began the plan of escaping her father's imprisonment—'twas what had started her erotic art sales. The other two were hidden in her room—she'd been afraid to sell them after Brother Giffard told her of the stir they had caused among the ladies of the court. She had not given any of the paintings a thought for months.

Montgomery watched her so intently that butterflies turned slow drunken circles in her stomach. He knew! He knew something.

The tube in her hand felt heavy. Inside, two miniatures crouched between the religious canvases. They were much better, much more erotic than the ones she had done of the king. But, if her husband took one look at them, he would have no doubt she was artist of *The King's Mistresses*.

This past week, he had moved into her chamber and gone through all her drawers and trunks. She had hidden her sensual artwork beneath the floor's planks, but had some thought that if he accidentally found one of the paintings, he would be amused. That she could claim she'd never done such before and that being with him had inspired her. She had no doubt that he was arrogant enough to believe such fodder. But if his duty was to find *The King's Mistresses*, she was doomed if he found the paintings.

She coughed to cover her reaction and set the tunic onto a rough-hewn table stacked with toppling piles of clothing. A castle of this size generated a large deal of laundry.

He patted her on the back. "Surely after what we shared, I have not shocked you too much," he whispered in her ear, the words only for her. "Are you well?"

"'Tis only the dust and feathers stirred in the hurly-burly." She coughed again for good measure and arranged a pair of hose neatly atop the tunic she had just folded.

"I see." He thumbed *l'occhio del diavolo* which was tucked into his belt.

She winced, hoping she wasn't blushing. His fingers against the blade ignited memories she did not wish to explore. And . . . the painting contained depictions of her newly shaven sex.

"Have you heard of these miniatures?" he pressed.

"Nay," she said, then realized she'd spoken too quickly. She smiled tightly.

"The miniatures are entitled *The King's Mistresses*," he continued. "They are quite good save for the subject matter. Surely you have heard of them."

"As I told you before, I was meant to be a nun; my paintings are of a religious nature," she denied, ignoring the selfish thrill that he had just said the paintings were good. Likely he knew naught about art and his opinion should be discounted. Still, in a world where criticism came more oft than praise, 'twas nice to hear.

Holding her breath, she held up the tube, deciding to brazen out his suspicions. If he checked what she carried too closely, she'd be taken to London so quickly her head would spin. "I would like permission to take these to the town's cathedral. One of the monks wanted to see them."

He stood too close to her; her nape prickled at his nearness.

She glanced at Jennet who was still muttering and picking the scattered clothing into piles and at Damien who stood by the door, his mustache twitching. There was no one here to help her if the worst was discovered. Chained as she was, she couldn't even run.

Sheathing his sword, Montgomery nodded at Damien to leave them. "I will accompany you."

"Oh." She pursed her lips, relieved that he was disinclined to inspect her goods but dismayed that he would be dogging her steps. Damien would never suspect a monk; Montgomery might suspect his own mother.

"You look pale, my lady."

"I–I had not expected that you would go with me on such a woman's errand."

He straightened his tunic, dismissed his men with a wave and offered her his arm. "It will be good for us to be together . . ." *Somewhere besides the bed*, was the unspoken ending for his statement, but neither of them acknowledged it.

Swallowing, she took her husband's arm. The metal of her manacle gleamed against the blue linen of his tunic—a clear reminder of her position as captive rather than wife. But surely she could figure out some way to have a little privacy with Giffard while Montgomery was there.

Damien looked relieved to no longer be on such dull duty as guarding her. The others gave them a few sideways glances, but mostly ignored them.

Once they were in the bailey, Montgomery leaned

down to her and whispered into her ear, "The scenes in the miniatures depict the royal member."

She barely caught herself from choking. Why would he not let the subject rest! "I—I do not care what sort of depraved paintings you are looking for," she exclaimed, coughing to hide her reaction.

"Perhaps your sister should make you a potion for your cough."

Perhaps you should stop bringing up such horrid subjects. "'Tis the dust only," she assured him.

"Of course." He watched her closely as they walked. Too closely. She set her gaze on the castle gate and quickened her pace. "We want to make it to the cathedral before it is too late."

Montgomery's bicep felt thick and strong against her fingertips. For an instant it felt odd to be walking together rather than being dragged by the wrist from one place to the next. Still, their union was anything but normal. A confusing swirl of emotions stormed inside her.

Last night he'd held her in those arms, stroked his fingers down her belly and between the folds of her nether lips. She'd wanted him. Today she was chained and wanted to find a way to escape. Vexing.

They passed under the portcullis. Windrose was set nearly in the midst of the bustling port city and the cobblestone streets were crowded with people and buggies. Huts and shops lined both the outer castle wall and the road, broken up only by occasional trees and hedgerows.

Travelers passed, going to and from the keep. A few gave her bonds a bug-eyed gawk, then passed in a hurry. What an odd sight she must be with her beautiful dress and her iron chains. Ludicrous. But surely servants' gossip would have told the townspeople of their unusual marriage by now. Naught to do but hold her head high. She would escape soon enough, then she would have the last laugh.

"The king intends for the painter to be tried for treason and hung," he said casually as they walked.

A shot of terror streaked through her and she forced her fingers to stay relaxed and not grip his arm in a fit of tell-tale horror.

She must get rid of these two paintings in her tube as soon as possible—hopefully pass them off to Giffard. Then, she needed to destroy the other two miniatures in *The King's Mistresses* series along with all evidence that she was the artist of any erotic works.

"You look suddenly green, wife. Are you well?"

The heady fragrance of rosemary wafted in the breeze from a shrub on the wayside.

"Forgive me," she said lightly, plucking a sprig from the pungent plant and crushing it between her fingers. "As an artist, I find it disturbing that a bit of paint on canvas would be worthy of a charge of treason and death."

She prayed the simple explanation of her bizarre behavior would suffice. Her other nudes were also illegal but these were days of liberal morals and a blind eye to such things.

"The king was most displeased at the size and shape the artist gave to the royal member." Now that they were away from others' prying ears, he spoke in a normal but low tone rather than whispering as he had done earlier. Evidently, his mission for the king was a secret one. "The king likes to think of himself as a battering ram rather than a small prick."

Oh, dear stars. Male arrogance. She had not thought

of that. Until she'd seen her husband's manhood, she'd assumed a man's member was rather scrawny. In the paintings, she'd made the royal rod a limp and rather minuscule item. While she had been trying to capture the shallow and bawdy life at court, she had not been trying to mock the king's member.

Forcing herself to straighten her spine, Brenna threw down the rosemary and took a firmer grip on the wooden tube holding her paintings. "Surely not all men are as endowed as yourself and perhaps the king should not feel so insecure in his manhood."

His eyes took on a twinkle and she relaxed some. She would face this new development head on and leave the future to the fates. Unless they tore up the floor planks, no one would find *The King's Mistresses* while they were in the town. Somehow she would find a way to give the two miniatures of Montgomery and herself to Giffard while Montgomery was not looking.

"Perhaps a man simply does not like being a laughingstock," Montgomery countered, passing by a row of shop buildings. "I have experience with that of late."

She swallowed. The course of the conversation flowed too closely to their own issues. Licking her lips, she gave him an over-bright smile, and held her arm to allow the afternoon sun to glint across the wrist manacle. "Women either, my lord."

He regarded her for a second, then unfastened his cloak and swung it around her shoulders.

She blinked, surprised at his action. The garment hung to her ankles and completely covered the network of chains. It was a small mercy, but she was glad she would not have to march through town like a prisoner of the crown.

"Mayhap the king is being excessively sensitive and

he should let the past go," she said, wrapping the cloak around her body.

"'Tis not always wise to let bygones be bygones." An edge of darkness formed in Montgomery's tone, and Brenna wondered what demons lay beneath his steely demeanor.

They walked on for a bit.

Once they were down the road just a short ways, the town began crowding around them. They passed beneath a faded sign that was painted with a depiction of a shoe and another with rolls in a basket. The scent of baking bread wafted into the street. More and more people passed speaking a splattering of Welsh, English, French, and other languages she did not recognize.

Houses and shop buildings lined the road, some even leaning against the outer walls of the castle.

"The future of England is best served with justice and a fair trial for everyone," Brenna said, motioning at all the different types of people. "Punishment seems quite dire simply because the artist had the proportions wrong. Anyone could have been mistaken about the royal member."

Montgomery laughed. Laughed! "His majesty was not pleased a'tall to have become the laughingstock of the court. Whispered about in ladies' chambers and jokes made in the stews."

A man driving a cart full of hay made a wide berth around them. A woman hollered from a second story window and Brenna jumped aside just before a chamberpot full of waste came raining down into the busy street.

Brenna wrinkled her nose. There were advantages to being locked in a tower and not having to deal with so many people. And no doubt it was the safety of her chamber that had made her think she could release the miniatures of the king with no consequences.

She turned down a street and headed to the town's cathedral—a large ornate building that poked up into the skyline.

"And now the rumor that two more exist in the series has made them quite a popular source of gossip," he continued. He was looking around at the various shop buildings and carts clattering down the cobbled streets, but his arm flinched in her hand—or was that just her imagination? "The word in the stews is that the other two would be worth upwards of five thousand pounds."

Her head snapped up and she nearly tripped on a pebble. "Five thousand pounds!"

He lifted a brow at her gasp and steered her around a puddle in the road. "What do you know of these paintings, Brenna?"

Brenna willed herself to keep walking toward the cathedral, toward Brother Giffard, instead of racing straightaway back to her chamber and burning the artwork in the hearth. No doubt the king was angry beyond measure. Having the underworld of London willing to pay five thousand pounds for a portrait of a misshapen royal member would send him into fits of wanting kingly revenge. Her folly would be her ruin. She must destroy the last two afore they were discovered. Either that or sell them off as quickly as possible, take the gold and flee.

"My lady," Montgomery said, "you are looking green again. Mayhap we should stop for a tankard of ale."

"Yea, my lord. A cup of ale." 'Twas always best to quench one's thirst afore being tarred and feathered and thrown into the king's dungeon.

Chapter Seventeen

James gazed intently at Brenna, who was wringing her fingers into her new silk skirt, and tried to fathom what lay beneath her mysterious green eyes. The king had sent him a private missive wanting an update on the miniatures and thus far he had naught.

She was hiding something.

But what?

Did she know the artist?

Was she the artist?

He had searched every cavity of her tower chamber. He'd questioned her sisters and every servant in the keep. There was no evidence of illicit art—no motivation for her to paint such scenes either.

Suspecting her was untenable.

Still, he determined to get to the bottom of the erotic miniatures. The chains on her wrists and ankles gave little clanking noises as they passed down the busy street of the town's main merchant row and headed toward the cathedral.

His neck prickled with unease. Something did not feel right about this trek into town.

He stopped in the midst of the road and turned her toward him, tipping up her chin. "Brenna, did you paint the miniatures of the king?"

"Of all the horrid things!" Outrage flashed in her eyes and for an instant he thought she would try to slap him as she had in the chapel.

He snatched her wrist to prevent such a motion. "Peace, Brenna. You are not a true suspect."

"Well," she huffed. "I should think not! I was supposed to be a bloody nun until you came along and forced me to marry you."

He nearly laughed at her use of "bloody" and "nun" in the same sentence. If she was faking her outrage, she was damn good at it. Still, she was a woman who needed to be taken in hand. She'd fooled him too many times. "Careful, love, your bargain involved curbing your tongue as a respectful wife should."

She lifted her chin, but bit back any other retorts.

"Give me the wooden tube."

Her nostrils flared, but she handed him the tube. "You will find naught there."

He pried the lid off and peered inside at the painting curled within the dark space. He wiggled his fingers around to determine the subject: an angel flying off to heaven carrying a soul. Another of the birth of Christ.

Of course, even if she had painted the portraits, and he had no convincing reason to believe that she had, she would not bring *The King's Mistresses* to the cathedral.

Realizing naught but strife would be gained by continuing to question her, he handed the tube back, and headed down the lane that led to the opening of the church's grounds.

She smiled at him, her gaze veiled. Was there a hint of victory in her eyes?

It would definitely do them good to spend time with each other so she could adjust to having him as lord. This battle betwixt them was not one he could afford to lose.

The cathedral stood in front of them: a massive structure with ornate architecture. A beautiful park, contained by a high stone wall, surrounded it. Several shrubs were in bloom and the grass and trees were closely clipped and well watered.

Spread around the grounds were various other buildings: a library, several administrative buildings along with various garden sheds and the kitchens. The place was almost a village unto itself.

Brenna saw Brother Giffard across the grounds, sitting beneath a spreading oak tree to the left of the main hall where the men who lived here stayed. He wore his customary brown robes and appeared to be writing on a tablet. Her heart sped as she racked her mind to come up with some excuse to speak with him by herself.

Looking up, Giffard saw them and rose to his feet. As was his custom, he wore no shoes. His bare soles stepped lightly across the grass as he approached and she averted her eyes from the fur atop his toes.

"Brenna, my child," Giffard said, holding out his hands as he drew near. "How good of you to come. And Lord Montgomery, it is nice to meet you at last." He beamed at both of them as if he had not a care in the world or that the purpose of this visit wasn't to give him erotic miniatures and plan her escape. He motioned them toward one of the buildings near the kitchens. "Won't you come and join us for the evening meal?"

Brenna said a silent prayer of thanksgiving that Giffard was so versed in sliding easily in and out of conversations with the nobility. His shoulders were relaxed and his mannerism loose. The appearance of Montgomery with her clearly had not flustered him in the least. As they walked to the hall with Giffard chatting amicably about nothing of consequence, Montgomery visibly relaxed. Her heart rate calmed.

At the feasting hall, trestle tables lined the walls and some of the church's workers directed them to a place to eat.

Brenna grew more and more agitated as the meal wore on. Her whole purpose for coming to the cathedral had been thwarted by Montgomery's presence. For certes, Damien would have been chatting with some of the younger men by now, boasting and teasing them about their dull life at the church and she would have had a chance to slip the miniatures to Giffard. But Montgomery sat close by her side, not allowing her even a second to breathe.

At last the trenchers were cleared, the trestle tables were wiped down and Giffard grew quiet, as if he too was at a loss.

"I brought paintings to show to Bishop Humphrey," Brenna said, taking the tube from where it lay beneath her feet. She may as well finish up the charade of having her work hung here in one of the buildings so they could return to Windrose.

With luck, she could take out the religious works and not disturb the erotic ones. She fiddled with the tube's cap and the rolled-up canvas inside. Drawing out the painting of the angel carrying a soul up towards the heavens, she smoothed it out on the table before them.

"It's truly magnificent, my child," Giffard praised, nodding his tonsured head. "I have spoken to Bishop Humphrey about having some new pieces to hang here in the feasting hall. I was sorry he did not join us for the meal."

It was on the tip of her tongue to ask if he had told the bishop that the paintings were hers, but, of course, he likely had not since all of this was a ruse for her to speak with Giffard about the miniatures. And her escape, which—she stifled a sigh—seemed very far away at the moment. Montgomery's leg pressed against hers as he leaned forward and gazed at the painting.

After a time, a man wearing sleek black robes slid up next to them. He had a long, narrow face and a pinched expression as if someone had squeezed his head between two millstones.

The pious and judgemental Bishop Humphrey.

Her nemesis.

Quickly, she tucked her hands and arms into her cloak not wanting him to see the manacles or what her lot in life had become.

Sneering at the canvas, he cleared his throat. "We have no place for your art here at Windrose Cathedral, Lady Brenna. Go back to your castle and be a wife to your new husband."

Brenna stiffened, her old animosity rising thickly to the surface. Bishop Humphrey had been her nemesis for years with his insistence that women should not be painters.

"I have come here with my husband's blessing, as you can see," she said, nodding toward Montgomery who, she noted, had also stiffened.

"A word alone with you, Lord Montgomery," Bishop Humphrey said.

Ah! Brenna's heart leapt. At last she would be able to have an instant alone with Giffard.

No doubt Humphrey planned to give her husband a complete lecture on the place of women. That could take hours. She ran her finger down one of the chains; her husband needed no such lessons.

"Of course." Montgomery rose, his hand trailed toward *l'occhio del diavolo* tucked into his belt. Light from a stained glass window cast dazzling blue and green sparkles over her husband's wide shoulders. He gave Brenna a "stay-here" glance before moving off to one corner of the room with Bishop Humphrey.

"Lean toward me as if we were discussing something philosophical," she whispered at Giffard.

Quickly she uncapped the wooden artist tube again and fished out the two miniatures, using her cloak and the trestle table to hide what she was doing. She pressed it into Brother Giffard's hand.

"Hide them well," she admonished.

With a hasty slight of hand, the small canvas disappeared into his robe. No doubt a move he had perfected from years of practice.

"Only two?"

"'Tis all I could manage."

He glanced over at the bishop and Montgomery who were deep in conversation. "Have you had any luck in obtaining the key to your bonds?"

"Nay, naught. But he releases me each night for a time." She did not mention why, but her cheeks burned at the memory and, for certes, when Giffard saw the painting he would know exactly the reason.

"There is a ship leaving six weeks hence. Mayhap that will give me time to sell your work and obtain passage."

"For both me and my sisters," she insisted.

"Hmm." He drummed his fingertips on the table. "'Twill cost a great deal of gold for three noblewomen. Depends on the value of the work and if it will fetch that much."

"It's good," she muttered, turning the tube's cap over in her fingers.

His brown robe fluttered as he shrugged. "We'll see. The market can be tricky. And 'tis only two paintings."

"I can get you the other two of *The King's Mistresses*," she whispered, remembering what Montgomery had told her about the price they would fetch in London.

Giffard's eyes widened.

A hand clamped down on her shoulder and she jumped. She looked up to see Montgomery standing before her and Bishop Humphrey storming from the chamber.

Had her husband heard their discussion? Her heart raced.

"Roll your work, Brenna. We head home."

She gave one last look at Giffard who sprawled out across the bench, nonchalant as always. To look at him, one would have thought they were discussing the recipes of mince pies.

By the time they reached Windrose, exhaustion threatened to overwhelm Brenna. After the cacophony of the city, they returned to the voices of men, women, dogs, cats, pigs, boys and girls of the keep. They swirled around her like a wild storm pulling her this way and that, keeping her from her one purpose of verifying *The King's Mistresses* were safe.

Wearily, she climbed to her tower room with Damien in tow. Montgomery had left her to see to the progress on the new roof that was being built on the kitchens. She ran her finger around the manacle on her wrist, determining to do what it took to get free. The sun had set and tallow candles were lit in the hall. Their acrid smoke tinged the air.

In a few moments' time, Montgomery would join her in her room. He would release the chains as he always did. And he would bring her body to that beautiful, crashing peak where she forgot that she had been bound all the day long.

The conflicting emotions were too much. With luck, she would have a few moments to take her paintbrush to canvas and soothe the turbulence rocking in her mind.

Damien, stroking his facial hair, nodded at her as she made her way into the hallowed quiet of her chamber and closed the door behind her.

Alone in the blessed, blessed quiet.

She glanced out the window, wanting with some desperation to simply sit in the embrasure and stare out at the darkening sky.

But first, she needed to see about *The King's Mistresses*. She had told Giffard she would bring them to him, but mayhap the smarter course was to destroy them.

Hurrying to her painting desk, she scooted it outward so she could crawl behind it and pry up the loose floor plank. She knelt, reached into the opening and dug through the parchments.

The half-finished gladiator was there.

Another self-portrait.

Several others.

No paintings of the king and his mistresses.

They would be at the bottom of the pile. She rifled through them again.

Naught.

A sinking notion gurgled in her chest.

Gone!

'Twas gone!

She could neither take them to Brother Giffard nor destroy them. Nausea waved over her.

She searched again for good measure, her fingers frantic. She creased one of the parchments. A knot formed in her throat.

She replaced the floor plank and all its materials.

Straightening, she took a deep breath and pushed the desk back into its place.

Nay. She must be mistaken. Most likely, she'd placed the portraits elsewhere. Her fingers trembled. That did not seem possible. Montgomery would have already found them.

Opening and closing the two rough drawers on her table-desk, she began her search. She felt over and under the variety of items in each drawer. Quills, ink, vials of pigment.

Naught.

Had Montgomery already found them?

Nay. For certes, he would have done more than merely ask her about them if he had.

Then where? And who had taken them?

Taking a deep breath to steady herself, she restarted the search in a more systematic way, taking each item from the drawers before putting them back, then moving around the room searching every trunk and every corner.

Bloody hell. Her heart pounded as she wrapped

up the search. They must be in the bedchamber. They must.

Panic worked into her throat. She tried to think of the last time she'd seen them.

"Have you lost something, my lady?"

She lurched and whirled at the sound of her husband's voice. Devil take it! How had he entered so quietly? "What are you doing here?" she gasped.

A twinkle formed in his indigo eyes. "I sleep here . . . among other things."

Her hand flew reflexively to her throat as he closed the distance between them. She stepped back as he leaned down, his face nearly touching hers.

"Why are you so jumpy?" he asked.

"I'm not jumpy! You—you just shouldn't walk around like some sort of spy." Had he seen her push the desk back over the loose floor planks?

A nervous flutter formed in her stomach. If he found the painting of the gladiator and the half-finished one of herself, more questions would be forthcoming.

He strode to the bed and leaned against the edge of the mattress. The curtains shivered. "Come to bed, Brenna. 'Tis been a busy day."

With a breath of relief, Brenna moved toward him. She tried to tell herself that the thrill trembling in her belly was only the remnants of edginess. But the desire to melt into his arms, to forget the anxieties of the day, flowed through her as seductively as holding a new paintbrush.

His lips met hers and he reached beneath his tunic to take out the key to her bonds.

Chapter Eighteen

Days later, drawing on her memory of how Montgomery looked fully enlarged with passion, Brenna painted in the sketch of a man climbing onto a bed to kiss a sleeping woman. The chains were bound to Brenna's forearms with twine to keep them out of the colors.

She smiled at the parchment; this painting was darker, richer still than her others had been. She'd been working for hours and her brain felt a little cloudy with obsession.

She wanted to be ready when she could steal time to meet Brother Giffard again.

Against her will, her legs grew restless as she painted the man's member. It was such an interesting sight, how the flesh protruded between his legs.

So masculine.

So large and interesting.

She took a deep, satisfying breath. Copulating with Montgomery had given her artwork a new layer or realism and complexity that made her heart soar with joy.

Wetting her lips, she added a crescent-shaped scar

onto the man's left shoulder. Just like the one her husband sported.

Of a truth, her lord's body fascinated her. She tapped the side of her paintbrush on the edge of the table. It was not just his body, but the man himself.

During the days, he hired and managed workers to bring the land into good repair. New whitewash appeared on the castle's walls and new thatching on the roof. He cared for the keep in ways her father had neglected.

Every night, he removed the chains and kissed her until she felt frenzied with passion and gently made love to her. If he didn't replace the chains every morning, she might actually start to like him. She tamped down that daft thought. She needed to escape. She could not live her life trussed up like a harem slave.

But, he didn't treat her like a slave: for the past three days, a new garment had arrived every morn— something she had not had in years. She marveled at the fine workmanship and the bright colors. He listened to her concerns about the household and had implemented some of her ideas to make meals smoother. She'd seen her sisters from a distance on several occasions but had still been unable to contact them. They seemed well.

She gnawed the end of her paintbrush; surely he gave her clothing as another way of owning her—so she would not embarrass him with the rags that were her own garments.

Even so, she could not stop herself from luxuriating in the way the silk felt against her skin. The one she wore now was particularly fine—a deep green with little roses embroidered into the neckline and down the sleeves. With its long, trailing sleeves and square cut bodice, it was her favorite so far.

She wished she had been able to change garments before she began to paint, but the chains prevented that and she had to use what minutes she could steal to work on her more passionate art.

Turning her attention from the man in the painting to the background, she added shawls and a table and then, with a few brushstrokes, a broken vase appeared.

She stopped and leaned forward on her stool, scrutinizing her work; she had not intended to paint a broken vase. Frowning, she let out a small huff of frustration. Sometimes she got carried away and things seemed to just paint themselves onto the canvas, like little fragments of another time and place.

Dipping her brush into the blue tempera, she decided to change it into a lady's kerchief. Broken vases did not suit the erotic mood of the painting.

Annoyed that the unwelcome vase had stopped her concentration, she glared at it and leaned forward. The manacle around her wrist clipped her artist's palette and in slow motion, it tumbled from the table into her lap. Paint splattered her bodice and onto her new skirt.

Bloody hell! She snatched the palette, flung it onto the table and grabbed a rag.

Crimson, yellow, and blue spotted the green silk. She wiped frantically at the colors. The stain widened.

Of all the horrid things.

Lurching to her feet, she took water from a pitcher, dipped the rag in it and wiped more.

The colors darkened, became one huge smear of brown instead of several spots of individual colors.

She groaned. Not her new dress. Now her favorite one.

In her mind, she heard her father yell at her. *You clumsy cow! How dare you paint while wearing your new gown; now we'll never get rid of you!* She cringed at the memory, not wanting to feel the ache in her chest that ne'er went away. She had been fourteen, and they had been summoned for the queen's birthday celebration. She'd spent weeks working on a special miniature to give as a present. It was her first time to be presented at court, and she had wanted to make a good impression. She had hoped, romantic as it was, that the queen would like the painting, feel kindly toward her, and secure a good marital match for her. Something that would make her father proud.

She had been dressed and the portrait had been ready to go. But, as she waited for her family, she realized the holly berries in the artwork were not quite right. She hastened to fix them, to put just a finishing touch on the piece.

Brenna rubbed her temples, wanting to erase the memory and the shame.

She had spilled her palette, dumped a pot of pigment and three eggs onto her dress—ruining it. What a clumsy horrid thing to do.

Her father raged at her when he arrived. Servants watched as he picked up her painting—her only gift for the queen—and dunked it into the chamberpot.

"That's all your work will ever amount to: something fit for the dung heap! The queen doesn't want your stupid imaginations."

Then, he'd forced her to strip naked in front of the servants and shoved one of the chambermaid's garments over her head. Agony laced her chest, just as it had all those years ago when she was a girl. The dress hadn't been so bad, for perhaps working in the kitchen, but it was grossly plain and out of fashion to be seen by the court.

Brenna shuddered at the memory.

The queen had been most displeased. No marriage calls came. Her father snarled at her that she'd ruined everything. He'd given away all her clothing and never bought her another dress.

She hadn't wanted to tell her husband what it meant to her for him to buy her new garments, or how much it squeezed her heart.

Bootsteps sounded out in the hallway. Montgomery! Brenna wiped even more frantically at the big, brown spot, then abruptly stopped.

It was useless.

The dress was ruined.

Best to face him with dignity. When Montgomery took away her nice clothing as her father had done, she would be no worse off than she'd been afore he'd arrived.

She rapidly hid the erotic painting of her husband beneath the floor planks. It wasn't the best place for it to dry, but she could not take chances on it being discovered.

Then, turning toward the door, she stiffened her spine and waited with resolve for what her husband would say. He was a man who took pride in how he dressed. The very shine on his boots told her that. He would have no use for clumsiness.

She stood rigidly upright and lifted her chin when the door opened.

Montgomery entered, filling the chamber with his presence. He wore a crisp, pressed blue tunic and flawlessly polished boots. How *did* the man walk around without getting dust on his shoes? Nary a wrinkle marred his hose. Perfect. As always.

His gaze flickered over her face. "My captive wife, how good of you to be in attendance."

She clenched her jaw, waiting for him to begin his lecture.

As if oblivious of the mess she'd made, he smiled and stepped toward her.

Her legs quivered.

Leaning down, he kissed her cheek and his fingers trailed down her bodice.

"What the . . ." He stepped back, staring at the muddled paint on his fingers.

She forced down the little skip of fear her heart made. She would face this bravely, no matter how much he railed at her. She had borne the shame before, and she could bear it again.

"You've gotten paint on your dress," he said.

"I do not expect you to understand," she said stiffly. "I can have one of your servants return the others to the merchant tomorrow. Surely, they can be resold for a goodly amount."

Montgomery's brows slammed together, and he looked at her like she'd just grown a horn. "You want to return the dresses?"

Lifting her chin, she met his steely gaze. She would not let him know how good it had felt after all these years to wear nice things again. She should never have accepted the garments in the first place—it vexed her heart and was akin to betrayal of her duty to her family. It made her long for a life here instead of a nun's lot in Italy.

"Yea, that is correct."

He loomed over her, confusion clouding his face. "You want to return *all* of the dresses because you got paint on one of them?"

"You can yell at me if you wish," she continued, heedless, reckless. It felt like her heart was breaking to let go of such beautiful things. "But it will not do any good. God made me clumsy at times and clumsy I am."

Montgomery's shoulders relaxed, and he gave her a smile that could have melted Snowdonia. In sharp contrast to his perfect clothing and warrior exterior, the two overlapping teeth were cute and boyish. "You think you are uncoordinated?"

She winced, waiting for his smile to turn into a snarl. "I am."

"My dear captive wife, I am not a harsh leader to those who obey me, so listen carefully"—his fingers cupped her shoulder, and she cringed—"you are never, ever to say that about yourself again. Any woman who can paint such beautiful paintings as I have seen you do is not clumsy. Do you understand?"

Her mouth fell open. If he would have suddenly grown wings and began to fly around the chamber, she could not have been more shocked. "You–you are not angry?"

He laughed and thumbed her on the nose with the paint that was on his fingers. "'Tis only a dress, silly girl."

In that moment, her manacles were forgiven. Warmth flowed through her like wine. All the hurts between them disappeared like smoke and she felt her heart crack open. She blinked, unsure if she wanted to feel this strange tenderness. 'Twas so much more intimate than even the copulation between them had been.

Without allowing herself to dissect her purpose, she stood on tiptoes and pressed a kiss on his lips. The paint smear on her nose transferred to his cheeks, her messy nature rubbed off on his tightly controlled perfection. "La." Smiling, she rubbed it away with her finger.

His arms closed around her, enveloping her in his strength and his scent—that compelling mixture of spice and woods. Her heart sped, and she reached up wrapping her arm around him and drawing him closer, wanting more of this comfort, this feeling of having flaws and being accepted anyway.

She pulled him backward, toward the bed, eager to explore him. Always before, he had been the initiator, the one who touched her and loved her until she spun with passion. This time, she wanted to give him pleasure as he had given to her. Her sex was still overly warm, ripe with desire, from the portrait she had been painting; her fingers longed to touch the body she had just captured on canvas.

She kissed him aggressively, tasting his mouth, his neck, his ear.

A low growl escaped his throat, and a surge of female power whipped through her. She had thought, assumed, that his coupling with her had only been because he wished to obtain heirs. But here was a man focused on the present moment, not future children.

Desire spread through her, wetting her like gesso over canvas. She wanted him. All of him. Inside her.

"My lady," he murmured.

Yanking at the bottom of his tunic, she pulled it free from his belt and pushed it upward so her hands could trace across the planes and valleys of his torso. She laced her fingers through the hair of his chest.

The key to her manacles hung on a leather chain, as did the heart-shaped locket.

They tumbled onto the bed, his hands at the top of her bodice. He pulled the garment downward, trying to yank it off, but the chain and collar impaired the movement of her elbows and neck. Her arm caught, pinning her into the dress. The damn chains!

Pausing, he reached back. She thought he was retrieving the key, but instead, he plucked the knife from his belt.

"'Tis ruined already, my captive wife."

"Wha—"

A soft rent sounded as the blade sliced through fabric. Cool air caressed her skin. She shivered.

"I'll buy you more," he whispered.

Wetness leaked from her woman's core as she recalled the last memory they had together with the blade. Her nether hair, still short, was growing back, and she wondered if she should ask him to shave her again.

Sighing, she threaded her fingers into his hair, enjoying the crisp, prickly texture against her palms. His easy acceptance of the ruined dress had cracked open a portion of her heart she'd long thought was mortared closed.

She could love a man such as him. The thought gave her pause, but he leaned forward and swirled his tongue around one of her nipples before she could entertain it.

"Jaaaaames," she murmured, closing her eyes.

Raising his head, he gazed at her. His eyes glowed with blue fire. In several skilled motions, he made quick work of the dress. The hard metal was cold against her skin and the garment fell away in slices.

Anticipation grew. She licked her lips.

He gave her a pirate's grin and reached for the key to the manacles. She remained still, as she did every night when he performed this ritual of unlatching her.

But unlike other nights, she did not like the separation of their bodies. She wanted to touch him, to bring him closer. As he unlocked one of her wrists, she reached her arm toward him, wanting to slide her fingers over his skin.

He snagged her wrists, disallowing her the privilege.

She let out a frustrated whimper.

The pirate's smile grew, one corner of his mouth lifting higher than the other, as he looped the chain around the bedpost. Because of the ring through the collar that connected the wrist manacles, her other hand drew to her throat with the motion.

Confused, she tried to sit up, wriggling against the chains, and the palm wrapped around her arm.

Undeterred he snapped the manacle back around her wrist.

She gasped. "What the bloody hell are you doing? I was not going to fight you."

"I know." His gaze was hot as the fires of Hades as his eyes raked over her body. Despite her awkward position, her nipples tightened.

He feathered his hands down her body. She quivered, the sensation intense and confusing.

She rattled her bonds against the bedpost, frustrated. "There is no reason to bind me thus," she grumbled.

"No reason, save that I wish to," he whispered, running his tongue softly across her earlobe.

"Oh." She swallowed, uncertain at this new game. Ne'er before had he left her chained for their private time together. The sex between them had been a sacred time where their issues and strives melted away.

"Say my name again."

"James."

"Nay. Say it in that low, throaty voice that gives me permission to do whatever I want with you."

Heat pricked her cheeks at her own wantonness. At the way she had wanted him earlier. At the wetness that still seeped from her quent.

He ran his thumb along her collarbone. His touch burned her skin, sending shivers down her spine. She should not enjoy his possession so much, yet she did.

"James," she murmured, closing her eyes.

"Very good. Lift your legs into the air."

Blushing, she obeyed.

"Open them."

She complied, squeezing her eyes shut so she would not have to see him hovering over her. Her eyes flew open when he grasped her ankle with the same determination he had used on her wrists. The manacle clicked open. She tried to wiggle away, but he looped the chain upward, fastening it so that she was bound, legs open on the bed before him.

She felt her blush move from her face down her body, warming her. And that wicked betraying place betwixt her thighs cared not at all.

She wanted him. Still. Now. Here. This way. Anyway he wanted.

He traced one finger down her stomach and slid it between the slick folds of her secret parts.

Whimpering, she arched her back. Every move, every touch seemed heightened because of her inability to move around, as if parts of her were on fire. She wiggled her hips toward his hand, wanting his fingers on that special area where the sensations culminated.

He slid his hand aside, just out of reach of his fingers touching that one spot. She rocked further toward him, but he moved his finger down the side of her quim instead of upward where she wanted him.

"Prithee, my lord."

"Shh."

She quieted as he continued long, slow strokes touching and teasing and pressing and releasing her inner and outer lips. The sensation grew, burning, overwhelming. Liquid seeped down her hips; a pool of need.

She strained against the chains holding her arms and legs, wanting somehow to force him to touch that one place, her woman's pearl. She bucked her hips. She whimpered.

Still, he moved away, obviously in no hurry to possess her as she desired. As she needed.

She nearly screamed in frustration as his fingertips brushed her pearl then moved aside. Knowing that moving her hips to follow his hand would do her no good, she tried pressing her legs together to stave off the assault on her woman parts. But the bonds kept her legs open, an easy target for his diddling fingers.

"Please, my lord."

"Not yet."

"But I'm ready," she grumbled, her hips quivering.

He gave her a wicked grin. "That is for me to decide."

"Prithee."

In answer to her plea, he slipped his hands upward to tease her nipples in the same way he had done with the folds betwixt her legs. With a sigh, she gave herself over to the sensation, fully surrendering to his pleasure. To allowing him to lead. Wave after wave of ecstasy floated over her. Every touch burned her skin. She wanted him, longed for him.

He held her in ecstasy for what seemed like hours until she could think of naught but him. He kissed her eyelids and moved over her body.

At long last, she felt his cock at the entrance to her woman's core, enlarged, throbbing, just as it had been in her painting. She let out a whimper as he slid into her, not slowly as he had done for the past nights of lovemaking, but quick and hard and animalistic. She breathed out a small gasp of pleasure that his need met hers. Finally!

She did not want him slow or easy. She wanted hard, quick strokes.

He pumped inside her and, at last, pleasure burst like a broken dam. Moaning, she soared in the sensation, lost in emotion as he too cried out his own pleasure.

Dear heavens. It seemed she was floating, hovering over the mattress instead of lying upon it. For long moments, she was unable to move, or even to think clearly. Her body felt languid and detached from her mind.

After a time, he kissed her cheek in the most tender of gestures, then moved to unlock the manacle and collar. He tossed them onto the floor planks.

The loud clank as they landed reverberated through her brain, crashing in on the luxurious sensations that she had just experienced. How could she have enjoyed such things so freely?

She shuddered, suddenly chilled and confused. She had just been tied with the very bonds she hated and she had not hated them at all. A maddening despair welled inside her and her eyes prickled with hot tears. How could she have? How could she? Shivers started at her toes and worked their way up her body in unartful jerks.

Drawing the bedcovers over her nude form, he hugged her tightly.

Thank the saints he didn't talk, didn't try to tell her it was all right.

It wasn't all right. How could such things be all right?

She squeezed him back, snuggling into his warmth and hanging on for the sake of her sanity. Would she ever be a puppet in his hand?

As the moments passed, so did the odd, overwhelming despair and disgust with herself that she had surrendered to him so thoroughly. That she'd begged him for release and indeed would have begged for much more if he had required it of her.

He kissed the top of her head and she relaxed, wanting naught more in life than to lay right here and forget the world existed.

He rearranged their positions so that he laid on his back and her head was cradled in a comfortable little spot between his shoulder and his chest. She snuggled into his warmth and inhaled the scent of his body, content now in this new languid state.

Her hand trailed over his torso, making circles on his skin. He was so beautiful. Magnificent. A woman would ne'er tire of lying in his arms.

His eyes closed and his breathing became soft and regular, punctuated from time to time with soft snores.

Her fingers snagged on the leather cord holding the locket. Remembering how possessive he'd been with it, she wound it around one of her fingers wondering if she dared ease open the latch. Curiosity grew in her mind. Was it from an old lover? Did it contain a lock of hair? A portrait?

Licking her lips, she eased upward on one elbow. The locket rested atop his wide chest, delicate, shiny, and silver. Beckoning her with its secrets. Usually he took it off afore they copulated.

She slid her palm toward it.

Montgomery shifted, turning onto his side.

Biting back a small gasp, she jerked back.

A soft snore escaped Montgomery's throat. Relieved, she reached her hand slowly across him. Her fingers closed on the prize and she flipped it open.

She caught a glimpse of a portrait of a sleeping baby girl with delicate lace bows in her dark, curly hair.

Then Montgomery's hand clamped down on her wrist.

Chapter Nineteen

"I explained already that you were not to touch the locket." James felt his wife's pulse throb against his palm as he held her wrist. Annoyance slid through him, both for the intrusion of his privacy and for the breaking of the peace that had come between them.

"Forgive me, my lord." She wiggled her fingers.

Her bones seemed delicate as a bird's leg as they danced beneath his fingers. They had shared a passionate time together—each one giving as much as the other—and he was reluctant to smash their new-formed truce. His hand loosened, and he released her.

They laid in silence for a moment.

"Who is she, my lord?"

Irritated at her impertinence, he heaved a breath. "'Tis not your concern."

The bed ropes creaked as she sat up and traced a finger down his shoulder. Her touch reminded him of a gentle spring rain, soft and intoxicating. She kissed him on the arm. "Prithee, my lord. Do not force me out."

He growled at her.

Undeterred, she rubbed her cheek against his bicep. The gesture was so gentle, so loving, it felt foreign.

"'Twas a long time ago," he said, not wanting to examine the memories that still burned inside him. His child. The daughter he had lost. Her tiny body had gasped out its dying breath before it sagged in his palm, dead and lifeless as his wife who had just birthed her.

Guilt welled inside him.

If only he'd arrived moments sooner. If only, months earlier, he had not shown mercy to the man responsible for her death. Compassion was a weakness he could not afford. People died.

"What was her name?" Brenna whispered, sprinkling little kisses on his cheek and down his jaw.

He didn't want to tell her. He didn't want to say anything. He didn't want to open that gateway to the painful memories. He didn't want—

"Aislin." The sound of his own voice shocked him. It was more of a rasp, the sound of the past being torn open.

"Your daughter?"

"Dead."

"Oh." She did not press him further for explanation, as if understanding that he needed some privacy in his thoughts.

Instead, she hugged him tightly, as he had done her when he had unchained her after their intense coupling. She fluttered light, butterfly kisses on him that seemed to want to reach inside of him and heal the broken parts, as a mother would comfort a child.

A welling of emotion rose inside him, stinging the backs of his eyes. He'd never told anyone about the baby. Not even his brother or sister-in-law knew about her. The feelings seemed too raw, too burning, too sacred to share. Whenever he'd felt any manner of compassion toward one of the criminals he punished, he'd remembered the pain mercy had brought him.

"I was betrayed," he said at last. "I showed compassion for a man and did not kill him as he deserved. In return, he paid me back by tracking down my wife and murdering her. She was pregnant."

As if she could soak up his raw emotion like a paint spill, Brenna patted him on the chest. She did not pry, but he knew her ears were open if he wished to speak of it. The sensation of floating in a sea of comfort engulfed him, allowing him to open his mind to the harsh memories of the past.

"The baby lived for a short while." He could still smell the blood, still feel the delicate movements she'd made, still hear her gasp. His child had been strong, but too small. The birth had been too early.

"I washed her body and packed her in linens. The next day we landed in a port of a bustling city. I found an artist and forced him to paint her." A lump formed in his chest, nearly crushing him. Ne'er before had he spoken of such intimate events. "I did not want to forget the importance of returning measure for measure."

Brenna paused in her kisses and moved so that she could stare down at him. Her hair formed soft curls around her face that bounced when she cocked her head to one side. "Why did you spare *my* life, my lord?"

The fouled beheading had been an unspoken thing between them. Even now, he was not quite sure why he had stayed his hand on that day.

Reaching upward, he thumbed her cheek. "You are too lovely to slay, my captive wife. And much too interesting in bed."

A flush of good spirits spread through him as a

pretty blush pinkened her cheeks. It was much more pleasant to dwell on his beautiful wife than events of the past.

Her fingers traced down his chest and caught the silver heart.

He drew in a breath, but did not stop her.

She flicked open the locket.

"Brazen wench. I said I will not kill you so you begin already to test your boundaries," he grumbled, but it was without heat even to his own ears.

Compassion shone in her eyes as she gazed at the portrait of Aislin. "She's lovely. Her hair is thick and dark like yours."

Closing his hand around hers, James lifted and kissed Brenna on the lips. She melted against him as she had when she had been bound to the bed, only this time the emotion between them was seeped with something deeper than the sheer, hot passion they shared.

"The gossips are wrong; you didn't murder your wife," Brenna said. It wasn't a question. That she understood the unspoken burden he bore caused another lump in his throat. She touched him gently, running soothing hands over his shoulders.

James brushed his fingers over her cheek, humbled by the concern gleaming from her eyes. "I cared for her—but I was reckless and selfish. She was a peasant and our marriage was doomed from the start. We were not supposed to marry, but she became pregnant and I could not allow our child to be labeled a bastard. She was young. Pretty in an unusual way, much like you. I forced her to marry me. Forced her to go to the continent with me. She hated the ships. She hated the cold. She hated traveling. I left her in one port with friends while I completed the voyage.

She should have been safe, but she wouldn't stay." His voice broke. "A man I had released years earlier found her. He dragged her further north and held her hostage, torturing her until I arrived."

Anger curled inside him as he remembered the bastard who had held his pregnant wife, cold and naked in a dungeon, raping her at will.

He'd killed the man with his bare hands, taking joy in the act and then dragged the body through the streets and fed it to the dogs. "I should have secured her, locked her in a chamber until I finished my business and could travel home with her."

Brenna blinked, as if understanding something for the first time. "Did you chain me so that I would not escape and venture out alone?"

"'Tis dangerous times for a woman to travel without escort, Brenna. Whate'er our issues, you are my charge now."

"I thought you only wanted to humiliate me, that you hated me."

"I do not hate you, Brenna. I—" He didn't have words to complete the sentence. *Like you? Love you?*

Nay, he did not love her. He was not ready for love, not when the memory of his wife and child still burned in his chest, leaving a hole where his heart should have been. But Brenna was fascinating. Interesting.

"I have known many noble ladies, my captive wife, and for the most part they are obsessed with gossip and clothing and naught much else. I am a wealthy man, oft gone on the king's business so I assumed it would not be difficult to make an amicable match with whomever I married." He smiled at the word "amicable." Their relationship had been anything but.

He slid his arms around her, rolling her until she was

pinned beneath him on the mattress and the locket was caught between their bodies.

She gazed up at him with soft eyes, as if bringing all of him inside herself to warm the cold corners of his soul. Cherished. He felt cherished.

This woman was not like other noblewomen. She was passionate. Intense. She saw things others did not see.

Where others accused him of murder, she had looked at the locket and seen through the gossip's fodder. She wasn't interested in gossip—she was interested in art. While she seemed to love the expensive new clothing he'd bought her, she'd been even more delighted when he'd opened her painting trunk.

Her sisters and father had mistreated her, but she'd bargained for their lives. He'd embarrassed her by forcing her to walk the castle bound like a prisoner, but still, she responded to him, giving herself to their passion.

"'Twas my recklessness that killed my wife and child. I went a little insane for a time afterwards, giving myself over to all manners of passion and drink. My brother and sister-in-law saved me from myself and since that time I've lived a life of contained duty."

And right now she looked at him with such trust in her eyes that it made him feel dirty for the things he'd done to her.

If he wasn't careful, he could begin to feel for her.

Feelings are for ninnies, he heard his father begin, but Brenna's voice sliced through the taunt as if she wielded the dagger.

"Do you regret sparing my life?" she teased.

He gazed down on her, taking in the way her lids

half closed and her mouth was yielding and wet. "Not at the moment."

Her lips curved into a slight smile and her fingers threaded into his hair pulling his face closer to hers. Their mouths touched, and he felt her soften and surrender to him, a look of complete trust on her face.

It tore at his heart. Another woman had trusted him like that and he'd let her down. Brenna had plenty of reason not only to mistrust him, but to hate him, yet there was no mistaking the look in her eyes.

"Make love to me, my lord," she murmured against his lips.

He drew back, almost shocked. Not at her passion, but at her choice of words. *Make love.*

"You don't hate me either," he stated, mystified by the realization. He'd nearly beheaded her. Whipped her. Humiliated her. How could one woman contain such an amount of passion that even such deeds did not diminish it? That amount of passion both baffled and intrigued him. When he had been so passionate, he'd been reckless, selfish, and it was only by supreme containment that he'd reined himself in. Yet, her passion was neither reckless nor selfish. She gave up her freedoms for her sisters. She gave of herself to him.

He feared what going back to that sort of passion would bring to him, but, silently, he vowed to never let this one down. In an easy motion, he rocked his hips, pushing his already-hardened member inside her.

Her queynt was warm, wet, ready for him.

He kissed her eyelids. "Forgive me, Brenna, I cannot love you. I do not have a heart left."

She did not defy his claim but wrapped her legs around his waist, giving herself to him. Before, she'd been chained and could not have stopped him even if she had wanted to—which, he had been sure she didn't—but this time, she controlled her willingness. She controlled how much she lifted her legs and how much she drew him into herself.

He felt shattered by the simple act of passion. He did not deserve such.

Their lovemaking was slow and luxurious, a far cry from the frenzied pace they had set earlier that night. The locket felt warm between them, and he felt his own heart beat against it. A heart he thought incapable of ever feeling anything again.

Chapter Twenty

Brenna awoke more content and happy than she had in years, mayhap even her whole life. Enjoying the delicious soreness in her body, she stretched her arms and legs.

And realized that for the first time in weeks, she was not chained to the bed and forced to lie there until her lord and master arrived to see her dressed and fettered.

Lord. Master. Those words took on a different meaning in light of last night's passion and the sharing of words between them.

James had mastered her body in a way that she'd never thought possible. He'd been tender. He'd been fierce. She blushed remembering the wanton way she responded to him, and her heart broke thinking of the baby he'd lost.

Mayhap she could give him another baby.

She rubbed her temples. Where had that thought come from? Shaking her head, she padded over to the washbasin and splashed cold water on her face. The man was making her daft.

It was only a matter of time before he discovered

something that led him to the fact that she was the painter of *The King's Mistresses*, or until her father showed up, or any number of things that would prove this truce between them was only an illusion.

But it hadn't felt like an illusion last night. There had been warmth and a measure of care between them.

He still loved his wife. He said he could not love again because he had no heart left. A streak of jealousy shot through her. Had he ever shared passion with his wife the way he had with her?

She dressed quickly, still amazed Montgomery did not show up and snap the manacles around her arms as he had done every morning. She stretched her arms up and out and down, reveling in the feeling of freedom.

Montgomery was wrong. No matter his words, they *had* shared something special last night. He had felt it too or he would not have left her unbound this morning. Something had changed in their relationship— something she couldn't quite put her finger on.

She made her way to her painting desk and sat on the stool. Being unfettered, able to move in freedom, felt marvelous. She stretched again, just because she could.

Would he leave her thus?

The urge to paint while unbound overtook her. She reached for her mortar and pestle to begin making the tempera.

And saw the key.

It was in the middle of her cluttered painting desk atop a stack of parchment.

She picked it up, fondling the cool metal between her thumb and forefinger. Being free was one thing. Being given the key was another.

Warmth flowed through her. If their relationship

was always as it had been yester eve, their marriage would be tolerable.

Nay. Not tolerable. Wonderful!

She gazed out of the window into the bailey.

Below, her husband directed the repair of an out-building used to house hay for the winter. He'd spent gold making updates and changes to the castle. His own gold. He'd showed more concern for the keep than her father had.

Sunlight glinted off his dark hair. It had grown somewhat longer these past weeks and was not so stiff and orderly as it had been. It looked a little unkempt and reminded her of what they had done together in the bed. The reflection sent heat into her woman's core.

She watched him, enjoying the way the line of his back moved as he walked in his precise no-nonsense manner. He directed the workers with such ease of command.

He smiled at the men from time to time, and it seemed obvious that they were not working hard out of fear, but because of a genuine desire to please him.

As she had wanted to last night.

That wayward thought brought a rush of blood to her cheeks. She *had* wanted to please him last night. She'd been so far gone with lust, she would have done anything he wanted just to experience the rush of ful-fillment.

But she should not want him thus. She wanted to go to Italy, be free of the duty of a keep. And she def-initely did not want children. Right?

Turning away from the sight of her husband and the perplexing feelings he brought up, she mixed the tempera in a mortar with some leftover eggs from yesterday. They were still fresh enough for use, but she would have to head to the chicken yard later for more.

Once the colors were ready, she positioned her parchment to paint.

Her fingers itched to capture the joy of last night's coupling, but she did not dare work on another miniature for Brother Giffard in broad daylight when James could interrupt at any moment.

Free from the burden of trying to formulate something to sell, she relaxed her mind and allowed herself to paint whatever her imagination brought forth.

A man appeared on the parchment—strong, sturdy. He held a broadsword in one hand and had a fierce look on his face. The scene was passionate, compelling. At the bottom, shards of glass littered the floor along with a broken vase.

She stopped.

Another broken vase.

Bloody hell.

Swiping at the vase with a rag, she smeared the paint on the parchment. Why had this odd thing appeared twice in her artwork? The vase had only started showing up after she began coupling with Montgomery. Were they some warning against her passion? An omen for some future disaster?

Unease prickled her neck and she could not shake the premonition that it meant something important.

Irritated that her blissful mood was broken, she shoved her paintbrushes into a jar of spike lavender oil.

The door swung open. Adele limped inside, followed by Panthos and Duncan. St. Paul was missing from her entourage; perhaps he was mousing as cats were wont to do.

"Adele!" A leap of joy burst in Brenna's heart and

she raced across the room to hug her sister. It had been weeks. "I feared he would ne'er let me speak with you again!"

Smiling, Adele hugged her back. "Are you well?"

Brenna blew out a breath, not knowing how to answer. Her sister's presence brought back the guilt of enjoying her husband's touch in full force. "Montgomery is not odious, if that is what you are asking."

"He raped you."

"He—" Their relationship was too complex to explain. Brenna patted her sister's arm. "I am well. But, I have missed you terribly. Is Gwyneth all right?"

"Montgomery has set a wedding date for her. And for me as well."

"A wedding date!"

"Aye."

Concern burrowed into Brenna's mind. "He will give you a choice of husbands," she said confidently. Thus far, he had been fair in his dealings.

"The husbands have already been chosen. Neither Gwyneth nor I had any say in the matter."

"But he—" Brenna's throat clogged. Promised. She would speak with him. Surely her sister misunderstood.

Adele closed the door and glanced around. "Are you alone?"

"Yea."

"Nathan has sent word." Adele's voice lowered to a conspiratorial whisper. "He is coming with a full force of men to siege the castle."

A sinking sensation pitted in Brenna's stomach. "Siege," she repeated numbly.

"Aye. There is passage arranged for the three of us

on a ship leaving two weeks hence. We will head straight for Italy."

Italy.

Her dream.

Adele swept her hand toward the painting desk. "You will finally be able to study art on the continent as you have always desired. Why the odd look on your face, sister?"

Memories of the way James had felt betwixt her legs, slowly sliding in and out of her queynt, flooded her mind. She coughed to cover her reaction. "What will happen to Montgomery?"

Adele wrinkled her nose and waved her hand to dismiss the question. "Nathan's missive indicated 'twas imperative we get on that ship. Likely there will be a fierce battle. Will Montgomery put you in shackles again or have you won his trust?"

Picking up the key, Brenna rubbed it between her fingers, feeling the rough edges. "I–I–I do not think I will have to wear the bonds again."

"Good. You have done well. There was some indication that Papa was with Nathan, but that was unclear."

A knock sounded and both Brenna and her sister jumped.

"Mistress?"

'Twas Damien.

"My lord has asked that I escort you to the bailey."

Unease snaked up her spine. A siege. A battle. Husbands for Adele and Gwyneth. Life was winding into a tight mess of confusion.

Talking with her sister had slid away the dazzling, rainbow vision she'd had of Montgomery this morn and, even without the chains, she felt the collar heavy about her throat.

"I shall be out anon," she called to Damien. Biting her lip, she slipped the key into her bodice. She would speak to her husband about the marriage of her sisters, see if she could untangle some of the knots.

"Later we will make plans." Adele turned toward the door, clapping her hands for Panthos and Duncan to follow.

Brenna rehearsed words in her mind, trying to formulate the right way to speak to Montgomery about the plight of her sisters as she watched him across the bailey.

The sleeves of his tunic were rolled two crisp turns, revealing his beautiful thick forearms. Brenna felt herself go a little weak-kneed just looking at him. Silly, foolish girl.

He was directing the workmen, pointing at a pile of wood and marking something on a scroll with a quill. The sun blazed against a clear blue sky, but the air felt stifling. Spring was sliding into summer.

Servants and workmen scurried around the grass. Hammers rang. Dogs barked.

Montgomery's eyes blazed an uncanny blue as he turned toward her. Confusion rumbled in Brenna's stomach as lust shot through her quim.

The intensity of his gaze, the fierce possession that gleamed in his eyes spoke to a secret part of her feminine soul. She was his and she wanted to be.

But their relationship was doomed. Her brother would attack. She would be leaving for Italy, her beloved dream. She approached him, her slippers sinking into the soft earth.

Smiling, Montgomery slid an arm around her waist and kissed her fully on the lips. His generous mouth felt so right and so wrong at the same time. Even knowing their relationship was cursed, she lusted for him. Again. Now.

"You have not thanked me for removing your bonds," he murmured in her ear, nibbling slightly on her neck.

She quirked a brow. Part of her wanted to rail at him for wanting thanks for something that never should have been. But she could not afford to be trussed back up with escape so close at hand. "I–I thank you, my lord."

He kissed her again. "And you are welcome. But if you ever conspire escape or think of not holding to our bargain, you will be placed back in them. Perhaps for life."

His words sobered her. Dread formed in her stomach. "You promised to give Gwyneth and Adele a choice of husbands," she said without preamble, as if the thought would burn a hole in her tongue if not released. Silently, she prayed Adele had been mistaken, but her heart felt heavy in her chest.

He set her slightly away, a dark unsearchable look coming over his perfect features. The boyish smile disappeared and only the hardened leader remained. "It was not possible."

Anger curled inside her, a deep agonizing hurt that she had believed his promise and had started to think their marriage had a chance of becoming real. "That was not our bargain!"

"Our bargain did not include your father's escape either, so some changes must be compensated for."

"We already discussed that!"

"Peace, Brenna. The king wished to see your sisters properly wed, so properly wed they will be."

"'Tis unfair!"

He straightened, his precise, perfectly ordered persona slamming into place. "I am your husband and you will abide by my rule."

She glared at him, frustrated helplessness coming over her. Men's war. Always women were pawns in men's war. Ne'er were they free to live, to travel, to paint, to make their own way as men were.

He grazed his knuckles across her cheek. Shivers ran through her in spite of her anger and frustration.

"Your sisters will be cared for. You must trust my judgment."

"Trust your judgment?" She wanted to slap him.

"Aye, as you did last night."

"That was—" Turning her face aside, she gazed out at the castle lawn. The grass was brown and worn with bare patches of dirt showing through: trampled because of the busy activity around the keep. Trampled as her heart had been. The lawn was brown and worn with bare patches of dirt showing through. "—Different."

"Different? How so?" Even though she was not looking at him, she felt his gaze boring into her, hot, intense, as if he could brand her with his eyes.

"We were—" Heat prickled her cheeks. He'd bound her in an open position to the bedpost and cut off her gown with a knife. She hadn't just trusted him. She'd enjoyed it. She'd been a full, contributing member to the passion between them. "Devil take it! That was about copulation! This is about my sisters' lives," she hissed.

"My captive wife"—he lifted her face back to his so she was forced to gaze into his glowing eyes—"if I won't harm you, why would I harm those you love? The king insisted hasty unions—there was no time for courtship. If I did not choose, Edward would have. I know the men who will marry your sisters. They are good men."

A part of her wanted to trust him and she hated that part of herself. Silly, foolish girl. "It's not right," she said.

"Gwyneth is not in a state of mind to choose wisely. 'Tis better for her that I make the choice."

"Men ever think they know what is best for women."

"The man chosen for Adele is a woodsman who loves animals."

"She has no wish to marry at all."

"She will accept it, just as you accepted me." Curling his fingers around the nape of Brenna's neck, he drew her close and kissed her again as if to prove the surety of his words.

She stiffened herself to resist, but his lips crashed on hers, stealing all her resolve. She melted against him, caught up in his spell as helpless as she had been last night.

Stupid, wanton ninny.

Guilt coursed through her. How could she have so little care for her family?

When he released her, it was on the edge of her tongue to tell him of the siege. Mayhap if she did, peace could be accomplished by talking instead of fighting.

But if he broke this promise, what would keep him from breaking the other one toward her brother?

Glancing down at the key tucked into her bodice, she reminded herself that it had only been hours since she'd been free to walk about unfettered. He was not a man who parleyed with his enemies, real or conceived.

If she told him of the plan, she would for certes find herself locked up again and her sisters as well.

And, even then, she knew she would be unable to resist the sweet, insistent call of his body.

Perhaps she could talk to Nathan herself, get him to see the futility of the siege.

A workman interrupted them, drawing her husband aside to ask his opinion about repairs to the cistern.

"I have a surprise for you," Montgomery said to Brenna when he was finished talking with the man.

"A surprise?" Her heart sank. The last "surprise" he'd given her involved four manacles and a collar.

"Why so pale, my captive wife?" He handed his quill and scroll off to a man in a feathered hat, placed her hand in the crook of his arm.

"I do not like surprises," she said.

He led her across the bailey and out the castle's gate. "You will like this one."

Chapter Twenty-One

By the time they reached the town, the afternoon sun painted the land in brilliant colors. Brenna's dread dissipated a little more with each pace down the cobbled road. Her husband's steps were as orderly and precise as ever, but there seemed to be an ease in his stride that bespoke good tidings.

In her heart she knew she should bring the conversation back to the issues with her family so she could perhaps glean some insight on what to do. But she was reluctant to break this peace, and guiltily she enjoyed this new game they played.

"A hint of where we are heading," she pleaded with a laugh, slightly frustrated with his mysterious glances and complete refusal to discuss the surprise.

"Nay. Trust me." His shoulders were relaxed beneath his perfectly cared-for tunic. 'Twas clear that he had something mischievous on his mind and anticipation, even a little excitement, grew inside her.

Exasperated at his lack of answer, she blew out a breath. She had asked six times already.

He answered with looks that waffled from stern to boyish, but he would not tell her their destination.

They turned down one cobblestone path, then an alleyway, then through a tavern. It seemed he was deliberately trying to confuse her sense of direction.

Frustrating, vexing man.

He grinned as if thoroughly amused with himself. His cute overlapping teeth showed, as did the dimple on his chin. His eyes sparkled, blue and gleaming, reminding her of the ocean. A woman could become lost at sea in his gaze.

She should pinch herself, wake up from this foolish time spent, from the games they played that made her think they might have a life together.

She would be leaving in a fortnight. There could be naught but war between them.

"Best it be a grand surprise for all this trouble," she said with mock fierceness.

"You will like it." He led her down yet another side street. "Now stop hounding me, captive wife," he continued, "or I'll place the scold's bridle on you and lead you there that way." His tone was light and the threat without heat.

She laughed, feeling free as a child. She had completely lost her bearings and was forced to follow helplessly along after him. "I'm going to ruin my new dress!" she admonished.

"All the better so I can cut it off of you later." He tugged her further down the cobbled street.

She did not want to fall into the trap of enjoying his presence, and yet, she already had. His teasing manner seemed to melt places in her heart that had long been frozen. Brenna wondered about the ease that had come between them. It was dangerous. More dangerous than the tension had been.

They went through a row of shrubs and then around a building and over a fence.

"You are lost," she accused as they headed down another alleyway and finally came to a dead end at a stone wall that reached above her head.

"Of course not. I never get lost."

"Never lost?" She smirked at the wall. The stones were old and worn with moss growing in their midst. A rotted apple core covered with ants lay at the base and a few weeds grew from cracks in the cobblestone.

James ran his fingers along the chinks between the rocks as if looking for something. She enjoyed the flex of his buttocks, the way the muscles of his thighs tightened against his hose.

"I have an innate sense of direction," he bragged. "Always had. Probably why I love to sail so much, to feel the wind on my face."

A vision of him, barefoot with the wind rippling through his tunic cut into her brain. His hose would be torn, ragged from days at sea and his clothing would be wrinkled with wear. Such a far cry from the precise stiffness in the man before her now. How did someone so in love with sailing, so passionate in bed, come to adopt such a rigid persona? Did it have to do with his baby and the silver locket he wore?

It struck her that there was so much she did not know about this man she was married to. "You *love* to sail?"

Turning, he gave her a quick kiss on the cheek. "My brother gave me a ship. Even now, I itch to return to the sea."

"Oh." She cocked her head to one side, unsure why

his announcement flabbergasted her. She knew he was a privateer and had his own ship. But, except for rare glances she caught when he was betwixt her legs, his head thrown back in passion, he always seemed so ordered. Precise. Exacting.

Life at sea did not suit that sort of controlled existence. Waves rolled, ships pitched; the ocean could not be ironed with the same meticulousness as the maids bestowed on his tunics.

Would he be freer out on the open water? Would he smile more—show off that pirate's grin of his?

"Why do you like to travel?" she asked, curious to know more.

He helped her over the wall and they found themselves in the midst of a garden. "Because I am free to just be alive, to adventure and explore."

Her heart quickened at that admission. They were not so different from each other as she had thought. "'Tis the same reason I paint," she admitted, glancing around at the various clipped shrubs. "Where are we?"

Peonies, marigolds, lilies, and cowslip were planted in lush beds. Their brilliant colors reminded her of her artist palette. Rosemary grew in spiny scrubs, their pale blue flowers delicate as a veil. Trees crowded the sky so she had no idea where she was in relation with the rest of the town.

"Just a short walk from here," he said, not really answering her question. He took her hand and led her to a worn path. "I told you I knew where I was."

"So you did," she said, unsure if he was bluffing or no. His steps seemed confident.

They walked for a moment and Brenna admired the chirping of birds and the buzz of bees. The rich aroma of earth and leaves scented the air. It seemed that all of nature was alive here. Flowers and trees were as carefully tended as the bristles on her paint-brushes. The lawn was clipped into a lush, green carpet and every scrub was neatly trimmed.

She did not know such a place existed in the town.

She paused, admiring a bed of foxglove. "'Tis won-drous. Is this garden the surprise?"

Squeezing her hand, he kissed her temple. "Nay, but nearby. You will see soon enough."

Curiosity beckoned her, waving through her mind in intense curves, and she followed her husband, con-tent now to allow him to lead her wherever he wished. Just as she had when she was chained to the bedpost with her legs spread apart.

"Tell me of your travels. Of the ship and the ocean."

He smiled, the look in his eyes becoming hazy and far away. "The wind bites your skin, stinging with the spray from the salt. The ship rocks, soothing you to peace and lulling you to sleep at night."

"It sounds like a fairy's world," Brenna said, en-thralled. Despite her intense dreams of reaching Italy, she had never traveled further than London. "I would like to go to Italy," she said dreamily, then caught her-self. He must not know of her desires to be in Italy.

"Ah. Italy. Italy smells of wondrous spices—garlic, scallions, onions, and other savory treats. 'Tis a spe-cial place with loud, unique people and a bustling supply of artists." He plucked a flower and gave it to her then ducked around a low row of hedges and stared up at the backside of a building. "Here we are."

The cathedral. Or rather the outbuildings and ad-ministrative offices of it.

"'Tis the sanctuary." Astonished, she gazed upward at the turrets. She'd never guessed they were on church property, yet it all made sense now—the beautiful lawn, the peaceful gardens. They had come from some odd direction and she had been so spellbound by their day together, she'd been a little lost.

"What are we doing here?"

"Shh." Pushing open the side door, James led her inside. The wide expanse of the eating hall loomed out, open and overwhelming in its proportions. The room was quiet and empty of people. Trestle tables stacked along the walls awaiting the next meal.

She stepped inside, then stopped, her jaw falling slack.

The walls held two of her paintings—the largest pieces of her collection. One depicted the Virgin Mary holding Baby Jesus and the other was a rendition of Saint Peter walking on water, the other disciples watching from the boat.

Stunned, Brenna stared at the portraits. Her breath caught in her throat and she could not speak. Looking at her artwork here was almost like seeing them for the first time. As if the pieces belonged to a stranger rather than being painted by her own hand.

She had tried so many times to have her work displayed, but Bishop Humphrey had always thwarted her plans.

"How?" she mouthed, when she had finally caught her breath.

James smiled, running a finger down her shoulder. "You are pleased?"

She cleared her throat. Pleased? She could scarcely believe her eyes. 'Twas as if she had stepped through some mystical doorway and her dream had come true. "I am astonished."

The lazy trace of his finger flowed from her shoulder

to her wrist. He took her hand, bringing her knuckles to his lips. "My lady, there is no reason you cannot both paint and be a wife. You are a fabulous artist and deserve to have your work displayed in a place of esteem. Methinks that over time, the church will see fit to move your paintings from the eating hall to the cathedral itself."

She threw her arms around him and kissed him wildly, recklessly, heedless that they were on church property and their families would soon be going to battle. Ne'er in her life had someone honored her artwork in such a manner. Her heart soared.

Laughing, he embraced her fully, meeting her kiss. "The nunnery does not suit you at all, my lady."

For a moment, only the two of them existed and she gave herself over to complete abandon. Giddiness bubbled in her heart and she wanted to dance up and down like an overexcited child.

He wrapped his arms around her until her body was bent slightly backward and she felt she would tip over.

Their lips met with desperation, their arms and legs wound around each other like starved lovers. Heat flowed through her queynt and she surrendered to his touch.

This time between them would not last—indeed, it could not—too many events had been set into motion. She must tell him about her brother. About their plans. Get him and Nathan to reach an agreement.

Loud, shuffling footsteps sounded behind them.

They broke apart.

Brenna blushed to the tips of her toes as she realized Bishop Humphrey walked toward them, his face even more pinched than usual. A set of rosary beads draped from his thin fingers like slime on a bog branch.

Clearing his throat, he gave them both a glare of disapproval. The scent of incense surrounded him like a cloud of condemnation.

She lifted her chin, inwardly cringing and wanting to hide in one of the many alcoves of the hallway.

James grinned, clearly both unintimidated and unabashed. "Good day, good bishop. I hope the repairs to your cathedral are going as planned."

"We"—Humphrey made a sour face, wringing his pale fingers in the cloth of his robe—"thank you for your generous donation to our cause."

Ah. So that was it. Montgomery had bribed them into hanging her paintings.

"And how did the men and ladies of the congregation like my lovely wife's work?"

The bishop's pinched face tightened. "Lord Stanmoore has made an offer on the first painting," he grumbled. "The gold will be useful should you decide to sell the work."

Pride burst in Brenna's heart. She wanted to let out a whoop of hooray. She *knew* others would like her work, if only she was given the opportunity.

"No problems that they were painted by a woman?" James pressed.

Brenna nearly snickered at her husband's audacity. Humphrey's ears were already red and glowing and it seemed rude to drag the scene out further but she enjoyed his embarrassment and wanted to gloat at his discomfiture.

If she had been allowed to show her paintings years ago, likely she could have been accepted into a convent for the use of her skill instead of having to marry.

"You will allow us to sell them and split the profits, Lord Montgomery?" Humphrey clicked his ringed fingers on his rosary beads.

It must have pained him to have to ask and Brenna could not contain her glee.

"Nay," she started. "I do not wi—"

Montgomery squeezed her arm, cutting off her words. "Aye, for certes we can reach an acceptable bargain," he told the bishop. "I will return on the morrow to discuss the matter."

Brenna seethed, wanting to yank her arm from her husband's grip. She did not want to sell anything to help Bishop Humphrey, not after the years of issues between them.

Furthermore, it irritated her that her business dealings were no longer her choice to make, but her husband's. How unfair the lot of women.

She opened her mouth to speak, wanting to demand they take her paintings down from the walls.

"We must leave. I will return later." James gave her a warning look, turned abruptly and steered her to the exit. "Say naught," he gritted out in a low voice as they passed the trestles.

Annoyance steamed through her, but she bit her tongue, choking back her words. She scurried to keep up with his long paces as they quit the building, leaving Bishop Humphrey staring gape-mouthed at them.

Inside, she fumed.

As soon as they were away from the building and out of earshot, Montgomery hauled her close to him, pulling her upward so she had to stand on tiptoe. Her brows drew together in a scowl as she realized he was angry too. He loomed over her. "You will not dishonor me by arguing with me in front of that man."

"How dare you agree to sell my paintings without my consent," she shot back hotly.

"As your husband, 'tis my right."

"As the artist, 'tis *my* right to decide where my work should be sold. And I do not like that man!"

Of a sudden, his shoulders relaxed. He reached up and smoothed down a curl that had worked its way out of her cap. "Peace, Brenna. I do not like him either, but there are more important issues than him if you become known as an artist. Selling a few paintings for the church will help. Lord Stanmoore has many grand feasts to show off their estates and home. Your work is of an excellent quality and likely you could become well-known not just here, but all over the continent should he wish to commission more of your paintings. This is a bustling merchant town and many foreigners visit the cathedral here."

Conflicting emotions whirled through Brenna as she began to understand James's goal and all it meant to her. She had been thinking of only a tiny market, of the victory of having her artwork shown on church property. He was thinking of the world.

"I am a merchant and have been trading goods for many years, Brenna. You can trust my judgment in this matter."

No one had ever showed true support for her artwork. His belief in her felt like a punch in the stomach.

"My brother is coming," she blurted out, then wanted to kick herself. How could she sell her family out so easily? Guilt ran through her.

"Your brother?"

"Yea. He is bringing men to attack and siege the keep a fortnight hence."

James seemed to visibly withdraw from her.

Placing a hand on his chest, she leaned toward him, willing him to understand.

"You planned this," he accused.

"I did not! I only just learned—"

"Master Montgomery! Master Montgomery!" A street urchin wearing ragged clothing came running up to them. "The keep is on fire! Hasten!"

Chapter Twenty-Two

Dread coursed through Brenna in long, deep waves as James grasped her hand in a tight grip and began running back toward Windrose to check the extent of the fire.

He dashed through the village streets, around puddles and through stores. His boots rang on the cobblestones.

The worrisome thought that her father had returned flittered in and out of her mind as she gasped for breath, trying to stay up with her husband. She wanted to scream, to deny the possibility.

They scrambled onto the main road. Only a half-mile to the keep now.

A tall plume of black smoke rose into the evening sky, mingling with the clouds. It came from the north tower—her chamber. The scent of ash hung in the air.

"Blast that we did not take the horses!" James cursed, running faster.

Her heart pounded in time with their footsteps. She stumbled, unable to keep up with her husband's stride. Without stopping, he yanked her into his arms and, still sprinting, carried her toward Windrose.

She bounced against him, clinging to his neck. Her added weight did not seem to bother him. He sped up, racing now for the keep.

The acrid smell of smoke burned her lungs, and she saw flames shooting from her window. Servants had begun to line up in a formation to haul buckets of water from the well to the tower.

Dear heavens.

Her paintings.

Her work.

Her supplies.

All of her life's passions had been in that tower.

The icy tendrils of panic flooded her limbs. They ran under the portcullis and she fought James's hold on her. He released her, setting her onto her feet.

Heedless of her safety, she ran for the tower's steps.

Montgomery snagged her wrist, wheeling her around. "Nay, wife. 'Tis dangerous."

"My paintings!"

"Can be re-done. This world has paints aplenty but only one you."

She screamed at him, crumpling nearly in two, but he held her back. She wanted to rescue her work, to salvage what she could from the consuming, hungry fire.

"Nay! Nay! Nay!" She fought blindly against him.

Montgomery hugged her, his strong arms both binding and comforting.

Bile rose in her throat as she watched the tower burn. Orange and blue lights shot into the night sky. The new roof caught aflame, as did the woodpile. Heat radiated into the air.

Brenna's panicked cries turned to sobs of despair as the orange and red tongues of fire licked up more and more of the keep, more and more of her tower.

She buried her face in James's tunic and squeezed her eyes shut, wishing she could cut off the sight.

But she could smell the ash, hear the crackle, and feel the heat. The fire was consuming her paintings, burning her life's work. And it felt as if it burned off little pieces of her soul.

Her dreams lifted into the air like so much smoke. Tears stung her eyes, flowing freely down her cheeks.

"Brenna," Montgomery rasped, pulling her out of her stupor. He held her slightly away from him by the upper arms. "Listen, wife. I have to direct the men to save what we can of the keep."

She nodded jerkily, wanting to protest, to cling to him and beg him to stay with her. But she knew he had duties, responsibilities.

'Twas selfish to think of only her own work when the entirety of the keep was at stake.

"Go to the bucket line and help them with water. The activity will keep your mind occupied more than standing here watching the burn."

She clenched her jaw to keep herself from screaming, but she knew he was right. Through tears, she gazed at him, fixating on his face. Sparks from the fire were reflected in his eyes and she felt herself tremble.

"You will be all right. But we must work, not stand around goggling."

The firm authority in his voice reached her frantic brain and for once in her life she was glad, grateful even, for his controlled, masterful demeanor. Swallowing, she latched onto his command like a drowning soul would reach for a lifeline. She forced her legs to move toward the bucket line and take a place among the workers.

Taking a bucket, she passed it to the person in front

of her, concentrating on the task and the solid weight in her hands rather than the nebulous agony of her loss.

The night fled on, the fire burning higher and higher into the sky. Brenna worked, and kept on working even when her arms and shoulders screamed in agony. Bucket after bucket passed through the line in a rhythmic flow like a giant undulating snake.

Townsmen joined them. Father Peter raised his hands to pray for rain. Adele lifted her staff and began her own chant. Gwyneth stood on the edges wringing her hands.

Embers from the tower's roof fell onto other sections of the keep. Smaller fires started. Servants ran to throw dirt and water on them to keep the flames from spreading. The fire's glow flickered over the worn grass.

Brenna passed more buckets. Sweat rolled down her temples.

And then, sometime after dawn's light began to climb the horizon, God heard their pleas. A soft sprinkle trickled down from the sky, adding heaven's effort to those of the exhausted workers.

Rain! Blessed, blessed rain.

Fatigued servants danced, their spirits lifted as water sizzled against fire.

The morning dragged on, but the battle for the keep turned. Father Peter began nodding his head and giving thanks. Adele lowered her staff; Gwyneth was nowhere to be seen.

The sky opened. Harder rain fell in a sheeting deluge until, at last, the flame was extinguished.

Workers began to leave, heeding their bodies' exhausted cry for rest.

The stench of desolation surrounded them: burned

wood and damp earth. Soot covered the area where the tower had been. The roof was gone and only the blackened stone wall remained.

Panting, Brenna collapsed to the ground, sitting with her knees drawn to her chest and her head on them. Rain fell on her face and hair, pouring down in unheeded waves. Her back ached. Her limbs felt heavy and numb. Her sodden skirt clung to her thighs.

After the frantic hurly-burly of the fire with the clatter and shouts of workers, the silence was disconcerting. Bewildering, even.

Gone.

All her artwork was gone. Her paintings destroyed. Sickness settled in her belly and she hugged her knees. Everything of worth that she owned was in that tower. Her brushes. Her drawings. Her paint pigments. Even the gold she'd saved for her trip to Italy. It would take years to recover the loss. And some things were irreplaceable: the large board she'd painted of the birth of Jesus, the one of Noah and the flood, the one of the Archangel Gabriel fighting Lucifer.

The only paintings she had left were the two James had taken to the cathedral.

Nausea overtook her and she squeezed her arms as if she could somehow hug the heartache out of her body. Hot tears mixed with the cold rain.

"A woman! Master Montgomery, come!" Ogier the woodcutter called to James from the burned-out entrance of the tower.

Brenna watched her husband pace across the keep's ground. His tunic, usually so precise, clung in wet ripples to his muscular body. But even his beautiful form could not keep her from the despair she felt. A fierce wave of gratitude spun through her that he had taken those two paintings to the cathedral. At least she had those pieces to prove that she was an artist.

A tall man wrapped fully in a cloak sank beside her on the ground. His cloak spread out into the mud. He turned his face allowing her a glimpse inside his hood. Thick dark hair, rich brown eyes and a sharp jawline showed in the shadows.

Nathan! Her brother.

Her eyes widened and her breath caught in her throat. She had not seen him in two years and a leap of joy skipped into her heart.

"Shh," he admonished, "Montgomery cannot catch me here." He smiled slightly then ducked his head, enveloping his face in shadow.

Heart pounding, she stared straight ahead at the charred tower.

Nathan took her hand and started to rise. "Come, now. We must go."

Understanding dawned on her, and she wanted to scream with outrage. "You set the tower on fire," she accused. More tears flowed down her cheeks.

"It had to be done."

Red fury clouded her vision and she nearly hurled herself at him. "Adele said you were coming in a fortnight. I could have gotten my things."

Taking her arm, he lifted her to her feet. "There was no time. There is no time now. Come."

Her legs shook; the exhaustion and depth of her emotions made her feel confused and weak.

"Put this on." He produced a spare cloak from beneath his own and thrust it around her shoulders. "Hasten!"

"Lady Brenna is dead in the tower!" a servant called out across the bailey.

Coldness ran through Brenna's limbs and she shrank back from her brother. A burned tower. A dead woman. Madness was upon them. She dug her heels into the rain-soaked earth, resisting Nathan's pull on her arm. "You murdered someone!"

"Nay, sister. A corpse freshly dug, fully charred beyond recognition. Hasten! Afore Montgomery discovers the truth."

She stumbled along as he wrapped his arm around her shoulder and half-carried, half-dragged her over the muddy lawn.

No one paid them any attention. Many from the town had gathered to help with the fire and they blended easily with the crowd of dirty, worn workers. Some went into the tower to see the charred corpse while others wandered wearily back to their homes. Servants lounged in doorways, too exhausted from the night's work to pay heed to two travelers walking from the keep.

Her heart seemed to bleed with each step away from Windrose. It was on the tip of her tongue to cry out, to protest. Nathan must have gathered as much, for he placed his palm against her mouth and stifled her cry.

"There is naught here for you but heartache, Brenna."

Heartache? Like the heartache of losing her paintings.

"If he catches us, we will both be thrown into the dungeon." Nathan kept walking, pushing her up through the gate and onto the road. "Father wanted to attack, but this way I can save all three of you while minimizing the damage to the keep. 'Twas only one tower that burned."

One tower.

Her tower.

Exhausted, Brenna went, stumbling along beside him. But her heart protested—she wanted to stay here with her husband, with the man who forced stodgy old churchmen to hang her paintings not with her brother who burned them like so much garbage.

"My paintin—"

"Foolish girl!" he said, pushing her along. "Castles and lives are at stake. There is no time to mourn canvas!"

He was right, of course. But that did not stop the ache in her chest or ease the hollowness in her stomach. "Adele? Gwyneth?"

"Are awaiting us at the ship. We sail for Italy tonight."

In a hot, stinging wash of realization, Brenna knew she would ne'er see her husband again. Ne'er feel his lips on hers. Or his hard member against her soft core.

She stopped, sliding her slippers along the cobbled road as Nathan urged her forward. "I can't go. You go without me."

Her brother's arm tightened around her and he dragged her forward. "Adele said you might protest, that Montgomery is a devil who has cast a spell on you."

"He's no sorcer—" She shuddered. Mayhap he was a sorcerer. She certainly had been enthralled by him. Even now, she wanted the comfort of his arms and their strength around her. She wanted to sink into his embrace, knowing he was in charge and well-capable of handling her churning emotions. As he had when she was bound for his pleasure, open and vulnerable and starving for his touch.

"I will not go," she said firmly.

Nathan growled, forcing her forward, shoving her now. "Heed me, sister, Gwyneth has given *The King's Mistresses* o'er to the king's men and they know you are the painter. While you think you may be doing your wicked artwork in private, your secret is no longer concealed."

"Nay," she gasped.

"Whatever relationship you had before, Montgomery will not want you now, and you will spend the rest of your days in a nunnery repenting the evilness of your deeds."

Her body jerked as if he'd slapped her. Nathan held her upright, dragging her with him. The cobblestones ate into the soles of her slippers and her sodden skirt bound her legs, making it hard to walk.

"How could you?" she rasped.

"'Tis for your good. Now hasten ere they catch up before we make it to the port."

She wanted to scream. She wanted to wail. But all the screams in the world would do her no good if Montgomery knew of *The King's Mistresses*.

All was lost.

She felt she was in a bog where every step sank her further into the muck. If she stayed, admitted she was still alive, she would be burned at the stake. But to go? How could she face a desolate life without Montgomery's arms to hold her deep in the night?

They passed hedgerows and other travelers. The sun lifted into the sky, but there was no warmth to be had. A waiting carriage took them further through the town, past the cathedral, toward the docks.

The ship loomed ahead of them. Waiting. Waiting. Ready to sail.

At this safe distance, she chanced throwing back her hood and looking toward Windrose Castle, which rose above the huts and buildings of the town. From here she could not see the burned tower.

As if it had not happened at all.

Her heart ached.

She sniffed the air, wanting to smell the ash and the scent of her pain. Wind rose from the sea, its briny aroma drowning out the smoke.

Would Montgomery mourn her? Would he ache inside as she did that their time was over? Or would he hate her? She had no pretty words from him. No declarations of love, or even of care.

He had told her that he had no heart left for love.

But he had liked her artwork, liked her passion. Liked the intimate times they had shared. He had believed in her paintings enough to force Bishop Humphrey to hang them in the cathedral.

She sniffed. Even that would be gone once he realized she was the painter of *The King's Mistresses* and that he had been helping a traitor. Her heart sank with the realization.

Montgomery was a man of honor. A man of duty. A man who did what was necessary for his king.

Nathan hustled her up the ramp of the ship and called the captain.

Wind stung her cheeks and ripped tears from her eyes as the ship pulled slowly out of the dock. The smell of sea salt cut into her senses.

Italy lay ahead.

Italy.

Her dream.

Her chance at a new life. Her chance to be captain of her own destiny, a woman of independence.

'Twas what she had always wanted.

With a sob, she laid her head on the ship's rail and wept.

Chapter Twenty-Three

James coughed from the lingering smoke as he made his way toward the blackened tower to rescue anything of value from the charred remains. Rain dripped off of him in sheets. Heaviness of heart settled in his chest as he saw the extent of destruction, of the burned thatching and scorched windows. Likely there would be naught left of Brenna's artwork.

"A woman—Lady Brenna! Master Montgomery, come!" Ogier the woodcutter called to James from the burned-out entrance of the tower.

Fear stung his underarms, colder even than the rain. He lurched into a dead run, racing into the tower and up the narrow steps that were slick with rain and soot. Had Brenna gone inside the tower after all?

Two other workers were already in Brenna's chamber, huddled over the bed. Her canvases and boards were little more than ashes and charred remains and sickness over the destruction rumbled in his stomach. Part of the floor had collapsed and charred boards stuck up in the way. He picked his way around the ashen remains.

"Master," one of the servants said and stepped away

from what had been the bed, a look of distress clouding his face.

A woman's body, charred as black as the paintings lay crumpled on the bed. Her features were unrecognizable as was the color of her dress.

"'Tis Lady Brenna, my lord."

Bile rose in his throat and tears stung his eyes. Not Brenna. Not his Brenna.

"Nay, 'tis not possible," he rasped. He'd seen her just outside, had he not?

Her hand, a burned stump, clutched a scrap of parchment. His chest felt as though it would burst with pain.

With a shudder, he fell to his knees before her. It had been years since he had truly prayed. His life had been about seeking retribution for the sins of others, his own sins he had ignored. But, at this moment, he wanted to pray in a deep mournful soul groaning. *Please let it not be her.*

He'd known the depth of her pain, of how she wanted to rescue her artwork. He should have chained her.

With a moan, he wrenched her hand open to see what the dead woman was clutching.

A painting: an erotic miniature of a naked man mounting a bed to couple with a woman.

He stared at it, blinking to clear his eyes.

A crescent-shaped scar was painted on the man's arm exactly like the one on his own bicep leaving no doubt that the painting was of himself.

Zwounds. Brenna was dead.

Why had he not stayed with her? Why had he not re-chained her so she would have been unable to go for her paintings?

Feeling sick, he crumpled the painting in his fist.

The pain in his heart was briefly eclipsed by the realization that Brenna was the painter of *The King's Mistresses*.

He'd suspected. In his heart he'd known. She'd been too passionate in bed, too open to her own body and senses for a virgin. Tears fell from his eyes and dripped off his chin.

He sank his forehead against the blacked charred body of his wife, angry and hurt and disconcerted. His shoulders quaked as waves of pain banded around his body. He clenched and unclenched his fists around the crumpled painting, unsure what he would have done if he would have discovered it while she yet lived. It would have been his duty to take her to the king, but her absence made a hollow space in his heart.

"There is your man! There is the painter of *The King's Mistresses*! The very man who was sent to find the artist." Brother Giffard entered the chamber, followed by a host of ruffians. His finger shook as he pointed it at James.

"Grab him, men!" A man with a short, dark beard called, "In the name of Edward the king."

James leapt to his feet. "Wha—"

The men closed in around him before he had time to collect himself. One ripped the miniature from his fist.

Ogier shrank away as did the other peasants, suspicious always of the dealing of nobles.

"Here's proof, Captain," the man said, unfolding the miniature and handing the naked portrait over to the leader.

"I did not paint that." James stared from one man to the next in astonishment. They were scarcely more than a band of thugs, likely not even soldiers from the king's army but rogue mercenaries sent on a secret mission. What they were accusing him of was ridiculous. "I cannot paint."

Giffard shrank backward out of the room as the men closed in around James. The monk's robe swept along the ashy floor and his bare soles were black with soot.

"Giffard! You dog! Tell them I'm not the painter!" James called, remembering Brenna's affiliation with the monk. No doubt that had been her true purpose in going to the cathedral that day.

The monk did not turn around and the king's group of ruffians blocked James from following him.

Betrayal ripped through him.

"We are to escort you to London," the captain explained as his men drew a myriad of swords, knives, and other weapons. The sharp points gleamed.

James glowered at them, fury rising inside his chest. He indicated the corpse and took a deep breath. There were too many to fight them all at once. The lingering smoke burned his lungs. "My wife has just died and I must bury her."

The men exchanged a look, but did not lower their weapons.

Dark beard bristling, the leader pulled himself up to full height. "There is no time."

"But—"

With a hand signal, the men closed in around James.

James's skin itched from the abundance of lice that crawled in the hay of the small prison cell the king had thrown him into. He had not been taken to London to explain anything. Instead, he was here, held in this secluded catacomb, under the charge of painting the *The King's Mistresses*.

Of all the bedlamite things.

He was paying penance for Brenna's deeds—something he would tell the king if he could gain audience, but Edward had not given him a trial when he'd sent his band of thugs and had him thrown into this dungeon.

Festered sores puckered on his skin. The fetid stench of mold, rat piss, and decay hung heavy in his nostrils. He winced as even the kiss of air burned the many scratches and bruises his torturers had given him. But none of them hurt as much as the ache inside his chest.

He'd let Brenna off her chain for one day. One damn day.

Anger ripped through him in agonizing waves, tearing at his heart. He had begun to care for her. Began to love her. Her passion. Her stubbornness. Her sense of being alive. He had begun to think they could make a future together. A real future.

She had denied that she had painted those miniatures, and like a lovesick fool, he had believed her.

For certes, Godric and Gabriel searched for him, but the place he'd been taken was so isolated, so secluded, the chances of finding him were slim.

James ran his finger along the worn iron bars, searching again for chinks or some softness in the metal so that he might free himself. Rust flaked off in chunks, its metallic smell irritating his nostrils.

He was forgotten. Left to rot. Thirst burned in his throat with a deep, aching need. It hurt to swallow. Hurt to breathe.

For an instant he was seven years old again and his father had locked him in the cupboard beneath the stairs because of his incompetence. Because he had been dallying with the idea of adventure instead of taking care of important matters.

He gritted his teeth. Brenna had given him a reason to believe in adventure again. In passion. He had longed to take her to Italy.

He sat back on the rotted hay, holding his head in his hands as memories of their time together whirled through his mind. She'd touched a part of his soul that he'd thought dead—that part of him that longed for the open ocean, for laughter and for the pleasure of a woman's thighs around his hips.

He wanted to hate her. Truly, he did. But he could not. Not even knowing that their passion had been a one-sided ruse to find a way to escape.

Mayhap he could hate her if she was still alive. But, she was dead.

His last memory of her was of a body that had been charred beyond recognition. Its blackened face had gaped up at him with soulless eyes. Even as he raged against her betrayal, his heart ached with loss. Against his command, she'd gone into the tower to rescue her paintings.

How could one hate a dead woman?

Pain ripped through him, and he wanted to tear at his ragged tunic, allow the coldness of the cell to seep into his heart and shut off the hot passion she had planted inside him.

Brenna.

His Brenna.

His beautiful, impossible, passionate, rebellious Brenna.

She'd clung to him, crying over her paintings, over her artwork—he should have stayed with her longer, snapped chains on her to keep her from going back into the tower. Instead, he'd sent her to the bucket line, believing that her fiery soul needed labor and activity to keep from collapsing.

And—she'd obeyed him.

She'd obeyed him! For the first time ever without argument, it had seemed. He'd seen the sweet surrender in her eyes to trust his leadership.

She'd gone. He'd seen her passing buckets. While other noblewomen might stand aside as passive observers of circumstance, she had fought for the survival of her tower. For hours, as he passed this way and that, he had seen her, sweating, grunting, hauling bucket after bucket the same as the other workers. He'd been called here and there to direct men, but she was always in the line each time he returned.

The corpse had been thoroughly consumed. Black. Unrecognizable.

An impossibility unless she'd been inside the tower at the height of the blaze.

She had not gone inside the tower.

She was not dead.

The thought streaked through his brain so hard, James unfurled his body and nearly knocked his head on the hard iron bars imprisoning him. Agony shot through his legs at the movement.

She'd betrayed him. She'd planted that corpse in the tower, its fingers curled around the miniature of him and her, and had Brother Giffard accuse him of the paintings. It was the only explanation. And then she'd left. Likely for her beloved Italy.

Fury caused a red haze to form in front of his eyes.

Betrayed.

Again.

He forced himself to focus on the discovery of

Brenna being alive. New strength flowed through his limbs—fueled by the strength of hatred and revenge.

The storm of his emotions struck him like a stinging splash of saltwater into the wounds on his soul. He was used to holding himself in control so his own passions would not overwhelm him, but this seemed overpowering. Somehow, she had masterminded the tower burning in a ruse to escape. She'd faked her death and turned over the paintings to the king to see him taken and imprisoned. And then thumbed her nose at him by curling the corpse's fingers around an erotic painting of the two of them.

How?

Had she been in contact with her father all along?

Ignoring his body's pain, he rose and began an exploration of the cell again. Somewhere out in the world, *she* was there. Still alive. He would find her.

He would take her to the king and force her to confess all. Gain his tattered honor back. And his lands.

Toward the edge of the cell, where the bars touched the crumbling wall, his fingers touched wetness. Tiny drops of moisture flowed down one corner of the prison, dripping from a crack in the ceiling.

Raw need for vengeance forced him to his knees, to stick out his tongue and lap the moisture from the bars. He nearly choked on the taste of thick iron and decay. But, the water cooled his throat and gave him strength.

He worked his fingers along the rough edges. The bar he had licked was worn from the water, a tiny bit softer than the others. More pliable.

Wrapping his hand around it, he pulled. It creaked, groaning in its socket like an old man.

Taking a step back, James sucked in a deep breath and gathered every ounce of strength he could fathom. On his best days, a bar such as this would be nigh impossible. He was exhausted, thirsty and weak from eating only the thin gruel his torturers gave him and whatever rats he could catch.

He focused his mind on Brenna. On her betrayal. On the passion they shared. Agony and fatigue subsided as his heart beat a steady rhythm like a war drum.

He wrapped his palm around the metal again and braced his foot against one of the other bars and yanked. His muscles burned, cramped, pulled. The bar began to bend. He gritted his teeth, encouraged by the slight curve, and doubled his efforts. Sweat beaded on his temples and ran down his cheek, stinging the scrapes and bruises.

His heart thumped with exertion as every fiber of his being worked, strained, against the ancient metal. He could not let go now. Muscle against iron.

She'd made him into a fool one too many times. That thought pierced his brain, lending more strength to his effort.

With a groan, the bar bent loose and popped from its socket. A loud crack rent the air.

Panting, he pulled the iron aside and, thoroughly spent, fell to the dungeon floor. His muscles quivered and jerked as they recovered from the exertion.

Blackness tinged the edge of his vision and light sparkled against his eyelids. Through sheer strength of will, he rose, determined to find Brenna.

He would have his revenge.

Brenna mindlessly painted another halo on some damned forgotten saint. She sat in a stiff-backed chair in the midst of her stark studio at the convent of La Signora del Lago located in a sleepy village off the coast of Italy. Her eyes felt glassy and, despite the warmth of the Mediterranean sun, her fingers were frozen and stiff. Still, she moved the brush across canvas, trying to numb the raw ache in her chest.

This morning she'd had a novice to help her mix the colors. This afternoon, she'd had tutors. The abbess had excused her from prayers so she could finish the portrait in time for the archbishop's visit at the end of next week. Mother Isabella had been more than kind to her, she'd accepted her into the bosom of the abbey as if she were an indulged daughter. She had brushes galore and expensive canvas instead of boards and parchment.

Everything she'd ever wanted: Time. Tutors. Paint. Brushes. Helpers. Canvas.

But her work came out flat and dull, the colors muddy and lifeless.

She didn't want to paint halos and saints. She wanted to paint—

A sharp pain banded her chest. She took a breath, inhaling the scent of spike lavender oil. Nay, she could not think of him.

Thrusting the brush into the blue pigment, she swabbed forcefully at the canvas, wanting to force the portrait to life and her emotions to death, to never again think of the husband she'd left behind.

A broken vase appeared.

Bloody hell!

Irritated, she threw her paintbrush onto the table. She thought she would stop inadvertently painting broken vases as soon as she had gotten away from Montgomery. But whenever her mind wandered even for an instant, another one appeared—as if conjured by the fey.

What did they mean? Why did they appear? Questions. Questions. She'd tried to fathom it out, but no answers came.

Three broken vases had been painted yesterday.

Four others the day before.

And countless numbers in the weeks she had been here at the abbey.

The blue color seemed familiar, as if she should know what it meant. Her temple throbbed and she rubbed it, her hand grazing over the scar that marred her cheek.

"Signora?" One of the novices, a timid girl named Alma appeared at the door of the studio. She had a sweet moon-shaped face and eyebrows so pale they disappeared into her skin. "Be ye well?"

"Yea, Alma." Not bothering to correct the painting, Brenna rinsed her brushes and folded her rags. She would paint no more today. Mayhap a walk in the sunshine would enlighten her soul.

"You are unhappy."

"Nay, not unhappy. Only—" Numb. As dead to the world as that lifeless body her brother had planted in the tower. As dead as her paintings.

"But you have everything here, paint and tutors and—"

"Clean these for me, Alma." Indicating the pots of paint scattered on the table, Brenna cut the girl off sharply.

Blinking, the novice bobbed a curtsy. "Si, signora."

Gathering her shawl, Brenna walked out of the chamber and followed a path that led into the abbey's vineyard. She would apologize for her testiness later. For now she wanted to be alone.

Birds chirped. Bees buzzed. Globes of grapes hung heavily from the vines.

But all of it seemed gray and drab. Not even the bright Italian sunshine could make up for the darkness that haunted her soul.

The passion of that broken vase had swiped her numbness away, and she felt peevish, incomplete, unwhole.

She missed James. Wanted him. Longed to lie with him and feel his manhood inside her, his muscular arms around her body. Reaching down, she rubbed her belly. Her flux was late and her stomach seemed a little swollen. She had told no one, but inside she felt a rumbling, a changing.

The thought of pregnancy sent an icy chill trickling through her veins. This past while, she had blocked the growing sensations in the womb, just as she had blocked the growing emotions in her mind. Was she breeding?

Her stomach rumbled and she turned her thoughts away from the prospect.

Where was he? Did he miss her too?

Feeling lost and disconcerted, she wandered farther through the rows of vines until she reached a back path that led out of the abbey's holy grounds. Her fingers touched the iron handle. She would walk to the sleepy nearby village, allow the exercise to banish him from her mind. The abbey was secluded and quiet and the road safe in these parts even for a woman alone. Later she would return and paint.

With quick steps, Alma slid behind Brenna and laid her arm on her shoulder.

Impertinent wench!

Brenna turned, opening her mouth to order her

back to the painting chamber, to clean the brushes before the paint crusted and ruined the bristles.

Instead, her mouth dropped open.

Not Alma.

Her father was there, dressed in a splendid surcoat and hose. The Italian sun had darkened his skin and bleached his hair. He would have been handsome except anger shone in his eyes.

"Nathan told me that you had sheltered here, disobedient wench that you are," he spat out.

Ache formed in her chest. Why did her father hate her so that every discussion between them was ripe with strife?

"I know you never wanted me to be a nun," she said softly.

"You will not be content at the abbey." He drew himself up to full height as a diabolical gleam formed in his eyes.

She touched her belly again, concern over the possibility of breeding nibbling at her mind.

"But you cannot leave," he continued. "I came to tell you that your husband has broken free from his dungeon cell and it is unsafe for you to leave the abbey."

"Dungeon?" Her heart stopped beating for a moment, then began again in a fast, thrumming rhythm.

"Aye." He shook his fist in the air in victory. "I heard he was tortured, his bones broken, his pretty face bruised and battered."

The vineyard swam in front of her eyes as if she'd drunk the grape's wine already. "M—Montgomery is not in a dungeon."

The gleam in her father's gaze brightened. He plucked one of the fat three-fingered leaves and shredded it. "Bah. Stupid chit."

She took her father's arm, fear pounding through her veins. This was not right, could not be right. "What are you talking about? My husband is at Windrose."

Her father laughed. "Your *husband*"—he spoke the word as if it were a curse—"has been found to be a traitor. Nathan has been restored to our lands."

Her knees buckled and she had to grab one of the vine's posts for support. "W–what? H–how?"

"Montgomery was accused of painting a set of revolting portraits entitled *The King's Mistresses*."

Her jaw dropped open and a flood of guilt coursed through her veins. "Nay!"

Her father sneered at her. "Gwyneth took the miniatures from your room and turned them in for the reward. It was not difficult to build suspicion in the mind of the king."

Brenna could scarcely catch her breath.

Victory gleamed in her father's eyes. "Leave here and it is certain death for you. Montgomery will be looking for you."

"He thinks I am dead."

"Mayhap. But a woman of your ugliness is not so easily forgotten. Your scar makes you memorable. Word may leak out."

Straightening, she stared at her father, the old anger and pain leaking into her numbed heart. "Why did you come to warn me if you hate me so much?"

She could have sworn a deep hurt crossed over his face before it was covered once again by cruelty and fury. "Because you deserve this fate. Just as your mother did." He turned on his heel and walked away.

Chapter Twenty-Four

Brenna glowered at her father's back, torn between wanting to beg him for information and wanting to crugal him over the head with the nearest limb. How heinous that she had ever even tried to win his love or go along with any of his plans against Montgomery.

Her father's heart was black as the devil's. His boots crushed the sprigs of grass as he walked away from her. He was mad, driven to insanity by his own rage. If she ever had any doubt about that before, it was wiped away.

She blew out a breath, aching with the realization that she had chosen her family over James. A family that had carelessly burned her paintings.

Every discussion with her father ended with her emotions in turmoil and feeling as downtrodden as the lawn he walked on. Why, of all her siblings, was she singled out for his spite?

Just forget him. You can paint away the pain, she chided herself.

Only—her paintings brought her no pleasure anymore. She could not replace the ones she had lost.

There was only numbness when she lifted brush to canvas. Pain laced her heart, too deep to deny.

Her mind whirled as she thought over her father's words: Montgomery branded a traitor, thrown into a dungeon. Why was she not told? Did they think of her as a complete puppet?

Squeezing her eyes against the sting of tears, she determined to go directly to Mother Isabella to see what she knew of the matter. Mayhap she could bring some light to this confusion. The abbess always had welcoming arms and a generous heart for hurting souls. During her first weeks here, she had shown such great love that Brenna thought she might be able to heal the loss she felt from leaving James. But— what if Mother Isabella was in on the deception.

Blind to the beautiful serenity of the abbey's courtyard with its flowing vineyard, Brenna wandered across the grounds, and made her way down the hallway of the sleeping quarters to the abbess's chamber.

She raised her hand to knock and heard voices within. Someone talking with Mother Isabella. A man. Her father.

Frowning, she leaned closer and set her ear against the wood.

"Montgomery is missing," her father said. "We need the baby to ferret him out."

Baby?

An icy streak slid up Brenna's spine. There were no babies here in the abbey except—she gazed down at her rounding stomach—hers.

The full weight of breeding sank into her like a stone on water. Starting at her toes, a shudder ran up her legs and spine and ended with a quake across her shoulders.

Somehow she had ignored the sensations growing

inside her womb—numbed them out as she had all her other feelings these past weeks. Her breasts were more tender than usual. Her stomach was thickening. Every time those things had bothered her, she'd fled to the studio and numbed her thoughts with dull painting.

But ignoring them did not make them go away. She had had no flux since before she had been married.

She had experienced some queasiness, but it did not come in the mornings, so she had discounted it as unhappiness, on her longing for Montgomery.

Leaning against the door, she closed her eyes and let the feelings wash over her.

Zwounds. A baby inside her. Montgomery's child.

A pregnancy would explain what her father was really doing here at the abbey. Reaching down, she cradled her belly as she racked her brain, trying to decide what she should do next. Another shudder ran across her shoulders and her mind swirled like paint being rinsed from a bucket.

A part of her wanted to find her husband, to throw herself on his mercy. A part of her wanted to run further way—from both her father and Montgomery.

"I cannot give you the babe," the abbess said.

Her father snorted and Brenna could see the sneer on his face as clearly in her mind as if the wooden door was not between them. "You can. And you will. You had no trouble giving me Brenna to protect your own place."

A gasp welled in Brenna's throat, and she stuffed the side of her index finger in her mouth to quell it. Confused, she peered through the crack between the door and its frame, trying to fathom out what they meant. She could make out her father's torso and legs and a portion of the abbess's habit.

"Prithee," the abbess pleaded. "I was young. Too young."

Horror began to trickle into Brenna's mind and the world seemed strange and dreamlike as if evil spirits had whisked away all that she knew was real.

"Bah!" her father said. "You tossed me aside like a piece of offal, then came running back for help when you found yourself pregnant. Brenna has been naught but trouble, but I raised her, just as I promised."

Brenna's legs felt liquid and unsteady. Her heart thrummed and she wanted to cover her ears and not hear what else her father would say. But she could not turn away.

"You cannot have the babe," Mother Isabella insisted. "I will not give away another child."

Her world turned upside down and sickness churned in her stomach. Her father and the abbess? It wasn't possible, couldn't be possible. Her mother was dead, drained of life from the grinding pace of being caretaker to a busy household—not living here in Italy as an abbess.

But, it would explain the strange animosity her father seemed to have for her alone.

From the crack in the door, she saw her father take a vase from a nearby table. A blue vase. His large hand closed around it. With a violent fling, he hurled it into the hearth.

The shattering sound moved through Brenna as if she'd been shot in the eye with a dollop of paint. A sharp pain sliced through her cheek, through the scar that marred her face. Her hand snapped to touch her skin. No blood was there, but her face burned with pain.

Her body began to tremble as an unchecked memory flooded through her mind. Her father. A broken face. The scar on her cheek.

Devil take it!

He and the abbess had argued on that day all those years ago. He'd thrown a vase.

Disconcerted, she blinked a few times and the pain receded to a dull throb.

Surely it was not possible for her to remember such an event. She would have been only a babe, a small child still crawling around on the floor. Mayhap she was imagining things.

But all the paintings, the broken vases?

Confusion swelled in her mind.

Inside her heart she knew, and did not know how she knew, that what she had been painting were memories of her own past. Her cheek pulsed as if caught by the memory, as if the scar was a witness to the truth.

She closed her eyes, wanting to straighten and run back to her cell, wanting to deny it all. Sweat beaded on her hairline and ran down her temples.

"I won't let you harm Brenna's babe," the abbess said, her voice brittle.

Brenna clutched her stomach, wanting to rock the child within her in a way she had never been rocked. She bit her lip to keep her teeth from chattering.

There was a silence. Through the slit in the door, Brenna saw her father, tall and angry with his fists balled and a sneer on his lips.

Her heart skipped frantically in her chest. It felt as if the world she knew was being savaged by hungry wolves. The skin on her cheek ached as she pressed her ear as close as she could. Should she open the door? Confront them? Run away?

"Then," her father continued, "'tis time your superiors know the truth. Do you think they will allow you to keep your place as Mother Abbess after they learn you had a dalliance with a man outside matrimony, became pregnant, had a child and shirked your responsibility to that child? Do you think they will allow Brenna to remain sheltered in the abbey when they learn she is the bastard of that union and that the king of England wants to behead her for her paintings?"

Cramps tightened Brenna's womb. Her knees quivered and her head spun. She tried to take a deep breath but seemed unable to suck air into her lungs. She had to figure out what to do.

"Don't be a fool!" her father continued. "Give me the babe. I will ferret out Montgomery from where he has run from his prison and then sell the babe to a wealthy family in need of a child."

Sell her baby? Brenna held onto the door to keep from sliding to the floor. He wanted to *sell* her baby? Anger began to eclipse her confusion, pushing through the thick sea of paralysis. Never would she allow such a thing. Children should be loved. Cherished. Held. All the things she had never experienced.

Hot tears stung the back of her eyes, but she blinked them away. She needed to *think*, not become a crumbling mess of emotions.

Montgomery's command came back to her, strengthening her. His calm assertive voice slid across her brain: *You will be all right. But we must work, not stand around goggling.*

This time she was able to pull a draw of air into her aching lungs and fill her chest.

"I will contact you when the babe comes," the abbess whispered, sounding defeated.

Nay. Nay, they would not. The clouds in her brain cleared with that thought. Whate'er happened, they would not sell her baby.

Reeling, Brenna lifted the hem of her kirtle and hurried down the hall to her small chamber, her mind racing with what she must do.

She had to leave! Now! Afore the babe got any larger. Afore she was tangled further into their webs and schemes. Once she had chosen to remain part of her father's plans. She would not make that mistake again.

In a rush, she fluttered around her room, gathering the few goods she would need for her journey. She considered the paintbrushes, so long her passion, and realized her life was dull without Montgomery. She missed him. His perfect body and handsome face.

Only—her father said his face was broken and his body bruised. All the emotions of the day consumed her in a torrent, and she had to hold herself upright by leaning against the wall. She forced herself to suck in huge gulps of air. She needed to stop so she could think straight and formulate a plan. Sweat still dripped down her temples, making her feel both hot and cold at the same time.

She needed money. She needed a destination. She needed to get her babe to safety and she needed to somehow make things right with the king to clear her husband's good name.

If the abbess or her father knew she wanted to leave, likely they would hold her hostage here. If James found her before she had a chance to make it right with the king, her lot would be no better.

Squeezing her eyes, she prayed for guidance. Would God even hear her prayer? Surely for the sake of the innocent child growing inside her, He would hear her cry.

Please, God, please.

Godric. Meiriona. The names came fast into her mind, giving her a sense of hope.

She would ask them for refuge and also for their help in dealing with the fickle Royal character.

With a breath of thanksgiving, she opened her eyes and glanced around the chamber to determine what to take. Her paintings could be sold or bartered for passage. She would wait until nightfall then steal her paintings from their frames and roll them into her wooden tube. She would take a few painting supplies in case she could find work along her journey.

As she prepared, an intense feeling of rightness came over her. Courage flowed into her limbs. For weeks she had been numb, passionless, but now purpose burned through her, clarifying what needed to be done. Her body stopped shivering and the sensations of hot and cold cleared to normal.

The old thrill of rebellion slid through her and she suddenly had the urge to paint again—the first real feeling in over three months. The nunnery was quiet and boring, the countryside dull and painting only religious scenes dulled her brain.

Mayhap she had been unable to paint life, because she was no longer living it.

After night fell, she worked stealthily in the candle glow packing for the journey. She stole a knife, cheese, and bread from the kitchens.

At last, she took her meager supplies and her wooden tube and sat on her cot, waiting for dawn's first light and thinking through her plans. Until she was able to secure a guard, she would only travel by day.

This was a peaceful area, but once she reached the coasts and a larger city, she dared not travel alone. She would find a safe, clean, well-lit tavern and ask for recommendations for hiring a companion for the journey.

With luck, she could find a family traveling the same direction and blend in with them. There were many cottages and huts on her way into the village. She would steal boy's clothing from a clothesline.

When the sun began to pinken the sky, she stood and looked around at her tiny cell one last time. Here was safety; outside was certain death.

Her life was already forfeit when she reached the king, but she had to clear her husband's name before she died and give her babe a safe home. No matter Montgomery's feeling about her, no matter if he hated her, he was a man of honor and he would not hate his child.

Her stomach sloshed, and she took several deep breaths to quiet her queasiness.

Moving like a shadow, she made her way to the outer wall of the abbey. The gate was barred for the night with heavy iron. Finding some crates, she stacked them for a makeshift ladder. As she looked over the wall at her unknown future, her heart raced, but she steeled her mind.

She scrambled over the wall and landed softly on her feet. She steadied herself against the outer wall and took a deep breath as she gazed out at the countryside.

Luck was with her: only a few steps down the road a boy's tunic and breeches hung on a line.

Crossing herself, she offered a prayer of thanksgiving. Surely, 'twas a sign of God's blessing.

At that moment, a large hand reached from behind a tree and latched around her upper arm. The fingers were blunt and dirty. She screamed, but her cry was cut off as a second hand slapped her hard across the mouth.

Her captor dragged her into the woods.

Chapter Twenty-Five

Heart pounding, Brenna struggled as muscular arms surrounded her like steel bands and cut off her air. Bile rose in her throat.

Her captor dragged her further and further into the trees, away from the abbey, away from the little huts, away from the safety of the road. Branches scraped her face. Her shoes fell away and mud squished between her toes.

She fought harder, kicking and biting. Nay! Nay!

"One word and I'll slit your throat," a hard voice whispered as a knife appeared and cold metal was placed against her neck.

Terror shot down her limbs as if streaks of lightning had invaded her body. Eyes wide, she stared down at the blade. It was a short dagger with a gilded handle, a small pommel and a single ruby in its hilt. Too delicate for this man's brute hands. *L'occhio del diavolo.*

James.

She stopped fighting, surrendering to his arms as she had done for so many nights. And her wicked, stupid, mindless woman's core cared not a whit that the knife was held to her throat in rage instead of for pleasure. Her body only remembered the slicing off of her clothing for fiery lovemaking and the scraping of hair from her slit for passion. Warm, creamy wetness flowed from her queynt in an artless, aching need.

"James," she mumbled against his palm, her heart soaring that she had found him, that she could confess at last and they could begin their relationship again.

His hand loosened when she did not scream. "Do not call me that."

"My lord," she tried again.

"Nor that." He yanked her roughly through the trees. "'Tis 'master' I'll hear from your lips and that while you are on your knees begging me for mercy."

All erotic need disappeared at his words, at the blackness of his tone. The chime of bells, more distant now, signified the calling of the nuns to morning mass. But they would not miss her—she was always in the studio with the paints during this time, indulged by the woman whom she had just discovered had given birth to her.

Fear tightened her chest, crushing the breath from her lungs and causing her legs to not move properly. She slipped and slid, his hold and fast pace made walking awkward. Her bare feet sank in the mud and issued sucking noises as he headed across the countryside.

Memory flashes of how he'd dragged her down the chapel's aisle coursed through her, as biting as the remembrance of her father and the blue vase.

"Cease dragging me," she mumbled against his palm.

The knife pricked her skin. "Shush, dear wife, mine. And quit fighting me. You cannot hope to win."

"I'm not fighting you, dolt; I'm trying to keep up!" The vehemence in her tone must have shocked him because he loosened his hold slightly.

Turning, she saw his face. Half-healed purple bruises marked his cheek, and three deep scratches made an uneven "w" across his forehead and temple.

Mercy. Without thinking, she reached to touch him, an ache forming in her chest. This was her fault.

He slapped her hand away, fury snapping in his eyes. Even though the blow had not been fierce, the movement cut into her as if he'd plunged the blade into her heart.

She'd never seen him so cold, not even when he'd stood over her with a whip in his hand. Then, he had been intent on securing the safety of the keep. Now, he looked like he could kill her without flinching. Without remorse. As if the civility had snapped inside him and only the beast remained. Full of hate and dark passions.

His hair was wild about his head—long and uncombed. In no way or fashion was he tightly contained as he had been before. Guilt rose in her throat that she was the cause of such change in him.

"I—I'm sorry," she whispered. Her heart felt leaden in her chest. "I know you are angry with me, but—"

"Nay, I am not angry," he said mildly; the icy hatred in his eyes belied his words. The mottled purple bruise on his cheek shifted in color. "I am furious."

Bile rose in her throat as she realized exactly how unpredictable this situation was. He led her into an olive grove. Her teeth chattered, and she glanced around wondering if she should try to run. If she did, he would only catch her.

"I–I was leaving to clear your na—" she stammered.

"Silence!" he roared. "Ere I cut your lying tongue from your mouth." The red mote glowed in his left eye.

Cringing, she wrapped her arms around her stomach, praying for guidance on how best to protect the child within her. Should she confess her pregnancy? Was his anger at her so deep that he would harm the babe?

"Do not fight me or I will knock you unconscious and carry you on my shoulder."

He was like a wounded animal, half-crazed in fury. His hands clenched and unclenched.

Gathering her courage, she gazed up at him. Once she had thought of him as only a beast, but he had proved otherwise. He was honorable, more honorable than she had been. The whole purpose of this journey was because she believed in his honor. She would not waver from that now, no matter how insane he acted. Surely the husband she had known was still inside him.

He might slit her throat, but he was not the sort of man who would beat her for the pleasure in it.

"Just hear me ou–"

Her words were cut off as he ripped a strip of fabric from the neckline of her kirtle and stuffed it unceremoniously into her mouth. "I told you already to keep silent."

She gagged against the cloth and tried to push it out with her tongue.

"Cease."

She obeyed, glowering at him. Why did the man have

to be so vexing? So irritating. She had escaped from the abbey for his honor and he was acting like an ogre.

"Listen to me!" she yelled against the gag, but the words were too garbled to be understood.

He tied the gag into her mouth with another strip torn from her kirtle. The bands bit tightly into the corners of her mouth. One strand of hair pulled, feeling like a sharp bee sting.

Annoyed, she snarled at him. Mayhap she'd spent too many nights lonely, painting him in her mind as a hero to be pined over rather than the man he was.

With a long-suffering sigh, she followed him as he latched onto her upper arm and headed through the woods.

Surely he would calm down in time and allow her to explain.

"Welcome to the voyage to hell," James drolled as he pushed Brenna up the ramp to his waiting ship, a long vessel with three large sails and two smaller ones. She whimpered against the gag as he shoved her before him across the deck and down the steps to his cabin. With quick strokes he untied the gag.

"Jame—"

He closed the door on her, locked her inside and went back to the main deck so he could not hear her beat on the door. He did not want to listen to any pleas for mercy. She was his prisoner and he was taking her to London to face the king's wrath. Period.

His crew ran flawlessly around hoisting sails and pulling up the anchor. They set sail in record time.

He inhaled the soothing scent of salt spray as he leaned over the rail of the ship contemplating the confusing feelings Brenna brought up. He wished he could banish her from his mind, but even now his thoughts lingered with her and his body burned with desire to claim her.

The blasted wench had fallen asleep against his chest as they rode for the docks and his waiting ship. A trickle of drool had ran down her chin from the side of the gag, but all the same, she'd relaxed against his torso. If she would have fought him, he would have known what to do, but he had no answer for her simple act of trust.

Staring out into the brilliant waters he steeled himself against those thoughts. She was a betraying bitch. And that was that. There was no room for softness toward her in his life.

He stroked the hilt of *l'occhio del diavolo*. The devil's eye dagger was an apt name—their marriage seemed to be cursed with ill-fated luck. He propped one bare foot against the lowest rail and looked out across the ocean toward the bright blue sky.

Gentle waves licked up the side of the vessel as the ship sailed toward England. The vivid blue waters stretched out miles ahead of them as the rugged coastline of Italy disappeared into the distance. The sun beat down, hot and relentless. The wind ripped his tunic. His bruises were mostly healed and pained him little.

On the ocean, he felt alive.

He was glad to be sailing toward home, toward England and toward regaining his honor.

At that moment, Brenna lurched up beside him, pushing him slightly aside. She looked green and shaky. Hanging onto the ship's rail, she bent in two.

He grabbed for her, irritated she'd escaped from

the locked cabin where he'd left her. Vexing wench. Did she ne'er learn when 'twas time to surrender?

She shook her head as he pulled her away from the railing.

Her cheeks puffed out and, with a gagging sound, she vomited all over him.

Blast.

Seasickness.

No escape at all.

With a look of disgust, James observed his ruined tunic.

"S–s–sorry," she said, with a little sniffle. "I was headed for the railing."

She looked so vulnerable his heart gave a little twinge. Seasickness was a nasty illness that he would not wish on even his worst enemies.

He stifled the urge to comfort her by telling her that it would pass after a day or two. But, of all things, he would not feel sorry for the betraying bitch. That path led to death. And dishonor.

"How did you get out of the cabin? The door was locked."

Reaching up, she plucked a hairpin from her hair and handed it to him. "I studied how to pick locks while I was at the convent. I'll not be locked in chains again or locked in my room."

He took the pin and eyed her suspiciously. "Why are you divulging your secrets to me?"

"I do not want to escape from you. I want you to trust me when I tell you I was leaving the abbey to find you."

Lies, lies. More lies.

Snarling at her, he latched her arm, turned on his heel and headed to the cabin to wash. "If you have learned all about locks, then you will have to spend every moment by my side."

"James, I came to find you—I *want* to be by your side."

What utter hogwash! "Silence," he growled. If he allowed one inkling of pity to overcome his heart, he would be unable to take her to London so she could face the king's wrath.

"Please, James!"

"I told you not to call me that. You must listen. I swear I knew naught of your imprisonment. I am so sorry for these scars. Ne'er would I have marred such perfection or hurt you this way—or in any way."

The lying little hoyden. He stopped and glared at her. If he didn't need her alive to go before the king, he'd be sorely tempted to toss her overboard. "One more word and you'll spend the remainder of the journey gagged, understand?"

"Bu—"

He lifted a brow as if to ask if she planned to finish the word. He had no patience for her schemes.

With a sullen look, she nodded and fell silent.

Brenna both seethed and worried as she fell into step beside her husband. Why was he being such a dunderhead? If only they could discuss the matter so she could explain that her mission was the same as his—to see the king and regain his honor.

Every time she looked at his face, at the scar that made a huge "w" across what had been perfect features, another stone of guilt sank into her heart. She'd scarred his face the same way her father had scarred her own. Such evil.

Once they reached the cabin, he ripped off his tunic and washed himself. She rinsed out her mouth and scrubbed her teeth with the edge of her finger. Now that the sickness was gone, she felt hearty again. Rubbing her belly, she wondered what she should do. The pregnancy brought on these strange waves of nausea—not necessarily in the mornings as she had been told. 'Twas no wonder she had not fully acknowledged she was breeding.

The silence grated on her nerves. Should she blurt out that she was pregnant? Would he gag her if she told him? Would he be angry? Be happy?

She watched him warily.

Perhaps she could seduce him. Perhaps if she could get him to make love to her, some of his pent-up anger would lessen and then they could talk. Then she could explain.

Tentatively, she approached him and touched his bicep. The muscle felt firm and warm beneath her fingers, reminding her of all the many nights she'd spent in his arms. She drew a little circle on it, a sign of her interest.

He whirled toward her, his lips drawn into a snarl. Water dripped from his torso where he had sponged himself. "Playing the whore will get you naught. You disgust me."

The harshness of his tone bit into her. She gasped and withdrew her hand as if it burned. "I just tho—"

"I told you to remain silent."

Placing her hand over her mouth, she stared at this stranger she was married to. Her heart ached. The purple bruise on his cheek darkened and she wondered how much the injury still pained him. But there was no way to ask. Clearly he was still attached to his fury.

He turned away as if the very sight of her revolted him. His back was laced with red whelps that undulated in a macabre dance as he bent and drew a fresh tunic out of a trunk.

A quarry of guilt sank into her chest. "I'm so sorry," she mouthed to his scarred back. He didn't turn around to see and she did not dare speak the words aloud.

Tears wet her eyes and trickled down her cheeks as he drew the tunic over his body. Those stripes should have been hers—she was the painter, not he.

The pain he had suffered must have been enormous to cause welts so large. What animals would have done such to him? A wave of sheer hatred for her father and all his schemes passed through her. She had been naught but a pawn—he did not even care for his own grandchild—would have sold it off like a mule.

Slowly, she sank into a chair, wanting to sink her head into her hands and weep unabashed.

For the next three days, James did not speak with Brenna at all except to bark orders at her to get dressed or to follow him up to the main deck or to the galley. The voyage back to England would take several weeks and he refused to become entangled with her lies. Already he could feel himself weaken toward her.

He kept her by his side at all times, not trusting that she would not escape even if he locked her in his cabin or bound her again. If she jumped over the railing to avoid her fate, he would never be able to clear his name. He disallowed her to speak with any of his crewman lest she beguile them with her womanly arts the way she had enthralled him.

Because he had come straightaway from the dungeon, he had no chains to fetter her. Their close proximity stretched the edges of his sanity. Her scent teased his nostrils and every time she moved he was reminded of how she'd felt beneath him in the bed.

Amazingly, she did not complain or appear to be even thinking of escape. In fact, she seemed eager to follow him around. But he knew better. Likely her docility was a new ruse to entice him to ease up on his restriction that she stay in his sight at all times.

Always, he could feel her gaze on him, as if she wanted to tell him something—more of her lies, most likely. She'd even offered herself to him, and, curse his cock, he'd responded. He'd told her she disgusted him, but the truth was he wanted her more than ever. She did not disgust him, he disgusted himself with his rampant, unchecked desire to bury himself inside her. To take her to some faraway place and keep her as his love slave. He loathed the thought of returning her to the king as was his God-given duty. He'd ranged from fully erect to semi-hard ever since he first touched her.

"Stay here," he commanded, leaving her by the railing so he could speak to his captain about the course of the journey and the direction of the winds.

She nodded and gazed over the rail at the sea, a look of contemplation on her features, a line furrowed betwixt her brows. The wind plastered her dress to her form, revealing the sweet curve of her buttocks and the arch of her lower back. She wore no veil or hat and her hair whipped around her. It was longer now, just past her shoulders. The copper curls danced and glowed, forming ringlets of fire around her head.

Heat flowed to his groin. Silently, he cursed his wayward member which throbbed with desire.

It had been too long since he had been with a woman. Surely that was the only reason she affected him so.

He tried to turn his gaze away, to concentrate on what his captain was saying, but Brenna lifted her face into the air. With her eyes closed, she arched slightly backward. The sheer wantonness of the movement, coupled with the days of watching her, smelling her, touching her, called to him like a siren's song.

More heat pushed through his veins. He wanted her like a drunkard wanted wine. A desire so heady he could smell it, taste it.

He took leave of the ship's captain and stepped forward to take her. To claim her.

He stopped, forcing himself to regain his control. He could not allow her to push him over the edge. Giving in to her would lead to being a fugitive all his life, running from the king's men and remaining landless and wild, whipped about in the wind like a sail. He might even take up preying on weaker sea vessels for the joy of the battle. There was no end to his dark passions once they were uncapped—had he not proven that already after the years when his child and wife had been murdered?

Brenna finished her stretch and, using the rail for leverage, curved her back the other direction like a lazy cat.

His mouth went dry as her dress clung tightly to her buttocks and thighs. *Take her. She deserves no mercy from you.*

He sucked in a breath inhaling the briny air.

She's your wife. Your property.

Until they landed, and he turned her over to the king, her body belonged to him.

Desire crashed through him in storm waves.

There was no reason to deny himself. No reason not to sate his lust on her. To use her as she had used him.

Hell, she'd offered herself just days ago; if she had no qualms about tupping, why should he?

That nefarious thought formed, he moved toward her to drag her down to his cabin. He was on fire for her.

The wind must have hidden his footsteps because she did not turn until he was nigh upon her. He touched her shoulder and she let out a small gasp and whirled sharply.

"Ja—"

He set his fingers against her lips. "Shush. I have not given you leave to speak."

Brenna closed her mouth and stared at her husband, wishing he would soften just a little so they might come to some understanding. Even if he took her to the king and she was tortured and beheaded, she wanted him to know that she'd had no part in his imprisonment—that she had not given *The King's Mistresses* over so that he would be accused and tortured.

"I want to *fuck* you," he said, looming over her.

His words burned a hole right through her heart, igniting her indignation. No discussion and then *this*. She'd heard the word once and knew its meaning, but it seemed so crude. So cold.

He seemed so cold.

Blasted man.

But her body, betraying wanton that it was, cared not a whit that he acted the coarse barbarian. Cream flowed freely from her woman's core and desire swirled through her veins.

"You are mine." He ran his hand from her shoulder to the tip of her breast in a claiming gesture, heedless of the others that were on the deck. The ship rocked gently with the sea waves and birds cried out overhead.

She raised her chin, unhappy with how he was acting and wanting to slap his hand away and deny his words. But there was more than her pride at stake. She needed to discuss the baby, the king, their relationship and so much more.

"We need to talk," she said.

"We talk afterwards." His fingers diddled her nipple through the fabric of her tunic. "Not now."

Her breast tingled where he touched her and she wished she could deny her desire for him.

It was another bargain. Another unsavory agreement. Sex for conversation. What a horrid role she was cast to play.

Still, she was in no position to turn him down. It had been her one desire for three straight days that they converse.

Swiving him was certainly no sacrifice. Her body craved his touch. Her quyent felt empty without his member to fill her.

The wind whipped at his tunic, flaunting the width of his shoulders. "Well?"

"Fine. But you must hear me out after."

He shrugged as if to say it would make no difference at all. An ache formed in her chest, but she tamped it down. He was wrong. He had to be. It would make a difference.

She expected him to offer his arm, or take her hand, or at the very least, latch his big fingers around her wrist and drag her in his wake.

Instead, he turned on his heel and stalked toward his cabin, obviously expecting her to follow like a bitch in heat.

The coldness of the movement set a hollow pain in her heart. And a tremble of anxiety about what would soon occur. For an instant, she gazed out at the sea and the clouds swelling on the horizon. A dark cloud hung to one side—an impending storm? Birds flew overhead.

As soon as she took her clothes off, he would see the slight swelling of her stomach, the evidence of the baby growing inside. Dresses hid her growing width, but naked, she would be utterly exposed. What would he say? What would he do? Would the moment of reckoning prove his true honorable nature or would he remain aloof and uncaring?

Trepidation caused her legs to tremble. Gritting her teeth and determining to win him over, she left the ship's railing and trailed after him. Like a bitch in heat.

Chapter Twenty-Six

"Flip your skirt and bend over," James snarled, not even wanting to wait for her to undress. His cock throbbed and he wanted to bury it inside her with a raw, aching need.

For months, he'd thought of nothing but her. For the past few days, his resolve to be distant toward her had been drained, sucked away by the nearness of her presence. Her scent nearly drove him daft—gesso and paint and something uniquely feminine.

He had disciplined himself, not allowing himself to feel the desire that pulsed through his body, but now, unleashed, it consumed him, as hot as the fire that had consumed the tower.

As soon as he touched her, all his anger, frustration, passion, and need for revenge seemed to culminate right into the member standing fully erect betwixt his legs.

Trembling slightly, she sucked in a breath, and he wondered if she would lose her nerve for the deed.

Instead, she scrunched her dress over her hips and scrambled onto the bed.

He growled at the sight of her naked flesh, at her rounded stomach and sweet, heavy breasts. Need thrummed through him in a painful ache. "Nay, not that way. On your knees. I will take you from behind." He had wanted to do it that way when they had been together before, but he'd been so concerned with soothing her anxiety, making sure she had enjoyed their coupling that it had seemed awkward. There had been no time to introduce her to his position.

She licked her lips, whether from anxiety or from desire, he could not tell. Obediently, she flipped onto her stomach and raised up on all fours. The round globes of her buttocks jutted into the air.

Holy heavens. The woman was a vixen.

He unloosed the ties of his breeches and shoved them down around his thighs. Not bothering to undress further or concern himself with her pleasure, he sank one knee on the bed, grasped her hips and thrust himself into her warm core. The mattress squeaked. So did Brenna.

He paused, her small cry halting his single-minded purpose to dive directly into her and pump until he was spent.

She twisted to look at him. Her eyes were dilated and he could see the pulse thrumming in her throat.

"Did I hurt you?"

A bewildered, but not pain-stricken look graced her face. "Nay," she whispered, "'twas a surprise is all, my lord. You are very large and fit very deeply inside me."

His blood fired. Reaching forward, he cupped her breasts and tweaked her nipples. She moaned and her eyes fluttered shut. He pinched the pert tips slightly harder, not wanting gentle lovemaking, but something raw and violent.

She cried out in a moan of pleasure/pain and squirmed to take him deeper.

Her sheath contracted around his member, echoing his need for something fierce and wild.

A storm of pleasure, of rightness that he was buried inside her—inside Brenna, his wife—spun through him in a crashing wave.

There was so much passion between them, so many open emotions. Closing his eyes, he allowed himself to become awash in sensation. She wiggled her hips, rocking back and forth, sliding himself in and out of her velvety warmth. The globes of her buttocks jiggled in a uniquely feminine display.

Giving in to his need, he climbed fully onto the bed, pumping with reckless abandon. Little whimpers and grunts issued from her throat, driving his need to an even higher pitch.

Moaning, she pressed her face into the mattress, lifting her hips. Still moving in and out of her, he twisted her body slightly so that he could slide one knee beneath her and enter her even deeper.

She gave a little mewl as her pelvic mound came into contact with the dancing muscles of his thigh. Rotating her hips, she ground herself into his leg.

They rocked back and forth, the position heightening his pleasure. She whimpered, and the sound sent him over the edge.

With a growl, he shot hot semen inside her.

He remained there for a short time, allowing the waves of afterglow to wash over him, then withdrew and rolled beside her on the bed. Wrapping his arm around her body, he spooned her from behind.

She whimpered. He knew she had not reached the same pleasure as he had.

With a slow stroke, he trailed his finger down her body so that he could friggle her to climax. His palm skimmed over her stomach.

And stopped.

He had noticed her belly was rounded, but had somehow been blind to how *much* more rounded it had become. It felt firm to his touch. As if a child grew inside her. Suddenly, the glow of her skin, the seasickness, the amount of food she ate, the quickened growth of her hair made perfect sense.

A baby.

His baby.

"You are breeding!" He rose up on one elbow, his hand still clutched around her stomach.

"Yes," she whispered.

"Why didn't you tell me?" he roared, angry at this new trickery. This new betrayal cut him through a heart he no longer thought he possessed. How dare she keep something so important to herself! What if he had harmed her?

She rolled in his arm and gazed up at him, her eyes wet with tears. "You would not let me."

Fury shot through him. "But, I suppose, you planned to," he said sarcastically. How dare she let him tup her so fiercely! "I could have hurt you!"

"You would not hurt me," she whispered, and again he was taken aback by her trust. She shook him. "James, you must believe me when I tell you that I was leaving the abbey to find you."

He sucked in a deep breath, looking at her suspiciously. The innocence on her face contrasted sharply with everything he knew about her. With all the things he had suffered.

He frowned, torn between belief and denial, unsure

what to do with her or how this complication changed his plans. He couldn't very well take her to the king to be beheaded while she carried his child.

"The child is mine?"

She looked like she would toss a pillow into his face. "How dare you even ask!"

Her indignation pleased him. He paused, unsure what to say. "How long have you known?"

"A few days." With a sob, Brenna closed her eyes and buried her face in his chest. "The same time I learned you had been imprisoned for my crimes. J–James, you have to believe me. I had naught to do with it. Trust me! You've asked for my trust and received it in the past. I–I was coming back to you and to the king to confess the truth."

Against his better judgment, he hugged her tightly against his body. God's blood, but she felt good in his arms. A foolish part of himself wanted to believe her.

A loud knock sounded on the locked cabin door. "Master! Master! A British ship with king's soldiers approaches. They are demanding to board us and insist on your surrender."

With a lurch, James hitched up his breeches, tied them and grabbed his sword as he raced for the door. He frowned at Brenna, her betrayal once again piercing his heart. No wonder she had wanted to tup him; she needed him distracted so that the king's soldiers could overtake his ship. The bloody wench.

Brenna scrambled off the bed, but he exited and locked the cabin before she could follow.

"Wait!" Brenna called, pounding on the locked door, a lurch of fear climbing into her throat. Her heart beat like the wings of a thousand bees. How dare he lock her in here while the king's men attacked?

She rattled the door, desperate to get out and somehow make this right. Whirling, she raced to the desk to find some instrument she could use to pick the door's lock. James had taken all her hairpins.

She rummaged around until she found a trunk filled with navigational tools. A quadrant, an hourglass, several ropes, a journal, a quill and several other items were neatly stored within the box.

Taking a few smaller instruments, she poked them into the lock, praying her new skills would prove true. Jiggling the mechanism this way and that, she fiddled with it for what seemed like hours.

Finally, the latch sprang open with a soft click.

Relief nearly made her weak. She crossed herself— a habit she'd gotten into while in the abbey—and slid the door open to peer into the hall. She needed to find the king's man in charge, and confess her crime. She could have them take her to the king instead of James.

From above deck, she could hear men shouting and stomping.

She inched down the deserted hallway to the stairwell that led above deck, wishing that she had *l'occhio del diavolo* or some other weapon to defend herself.

"Surrender Montgomery or prepare to die!" she heard a loud voice call. A cannon blasted, rocking the ship.

Her heart thumped wildly, beating a furious tattoo and she quickened her pace. She could not let them take James, not when she'd just found him again.

"Brenna!" a familiar voice called from down the hall. "Thank the stars I found you."

She looked up and saw her brother sliding toward her carrying a sword. He looked harried, his dark hair sticking up. His tall body looked whipcord strong and he had a determined expression on his face. "Nathan!"

"Come with me. I will take you to safety."

Anxiety flowed over her. 'Twas a repeat of what had happened that night when she had left Windrose. She stiffened her spine, refusing to be sucked into his plans again.

"What are you doing here?" she demanded. "Did you stage the attack?"

"Nay, Father did. He is in alignment with the British Naval fleets."

Her lips tightened. Of course. Her father was set on all of this.

A loud crash sounded above them, followed by a battle cry.

She cringed.

Nathan grasped her arm. "Come on. I have a waiting boat, separate from the one Father is on. Father is"—a dark look came over his features and he furrowed his brow—"not well."

She wrenched her arm away from him. "Nay. I'm going to the deck to confess my crime and have them take me to the king instead of my husband."

"Do not be daft, sister. You'll be killed."

"I cannot run away from my responsibilities, Nathan." Her voice held an accusatory note. Nathan had taken off to Italy and left them along with their father for too many years. "Step aside."

"I cannot let you do something so foolish." He blocked her path. He was as tall as Montgomery but not nearly as wide.

She thumped her brother hard on the chest. "Listen

to me, there are things afloat here bigger than you. You are no longer a child, Nathan. Face the truth."

"He'll take our lands if we tell the truth."

She frowned at him. "Lands that would be safe had you lived up to your own obligations," she accused.

He ran his knuckles down her cheek in a soothing manner. "I know I have done wrong by leaving you so long with Father, but in the end you were able to be with Mother Isabella in the abbey as you always wanted."

At that moment, Montgomery's hulking body appeared in the stairwell leading down to the cabin. Anger clouded over his features, bringing the plains and valleys of his face into sharp relief.

"You bloody little whore," he snarled. "To think, I did not even question that the babe was mine."

She whirled. "James!"

Raising his sword, James paced straight for Nathan. Nathan drew his own sword.

The blades flashed little flickers of light across the wooden walls of the hull.

"Nay, my lord," she cried, "he's not my lover, he's my brother!"

A wicked gleam formed in her husband's eyes and he raised the sword even higher. "Even better."

Fear trembled through Brenna. Straightening to her full height, she raised one hand to ward off Nathan and the other to stay her husband. "Stop it! Both of you! There is a better way to end this."

"I know exactly how to end this," James said, the mote in his eye glowing red as he stepped forward.

"Cease!" Brenna roared. The ship rocked beneath them.

Nathan unfastened his cape and threw it to the

floor planks like a gauntlet. He crouched into a fighting stance.

Turning her back to her brother, she squared off on Montgomery. "Prithee! You swore you would talk to me!"

Glaring at Nathan, James eased forward. "'Tis too late for talk."

She shook her finger at him. "I paid the price for your conversation and 'tis conversation we will have."

His gaze flicked back to hers and he gave her a look that told her he thought she might be an escaped patient from St. Mary's. "Careful, wife."

Frustration and anxiety tightened in her gut. "Mayhap you have forgotten the bargain, but I have not. My body still burns for you."

Whirling around, Brenna glared at her brother, who was lowered into a fighting stance with his sword ready. His dark brown hair hung in waves about his shoulders. "This arrogant fool is my husband and your rightful overlord. You will not harm a hair of his head or you'll have comeuppance from me."

"Aside, wife," James commanded. "This is men's business."

Spinning back around, she narrowed her eyes at him. "And that"—she pointed at Nathan—"is my irresponsible, pig-headed brother. And *you* will not harm a hair of his head."

The two men glared at each other, both of them rising to their full heights and preening like peacocks.

She huffed out an exasperated breath. "I definitely remember that in our first bargain you agreed to parlay with my brother."

Nathan sneered. "I have no reason to talk to this man. Let his blood run red beneath my feet."

Scowling, Brenna stomped to her brother and slapped him hard across the face. Her palm stung.

James laughed.

Nathan stepped back, his eyes fierce, his hands balled into fists.

"You touch her and you are dead," James ground out. "I'll take pleasure in feeding the pieces of your body to the sharks."

A flicker of understanding ignited in her brother's eyes. "You *love* her," he accused.

Another cannon blast shook the hull and pieces of the ceiling rained down on them.

"Call the men off!" she demanded her brother. "You can end this right now, Nathan!"

"Aye, Nathan," Montgomery mocked in a falsetto singsong voice, "call it all off like the little coward you are."

"You!" Brenna pointed her finger at James, closed the distance between them and poked him squarely in the chest. "Cease! Now!"

A cannon shot rang out, causing more dust and splinters of wood to flow down the walls and ceiling. A panting man came barreling down the stairs. Blood stained his tunic.

"Master! The main sail has been hit and men under the British flag are boarding the ship."

At that moment, soldiers stomped down the steps. They carried swords and crossbows and wore a motley of different uniform pieces. One lugged a hand-cannon, nearly staggering under its weight.

"I've found him!" a crossbowman called to the others, motioning them further down into the already cramped hull.

James whirled on them.

"Take him!"

They rushed at James.

"Get back, Brenna!" James commanded, pushing her behind him and facing off the herd of armed men rushing down the steps.

Brenna screamed as she was pushed aside, crowded by bodies. James fought, his sword swinging this way and that. But there were too many. They flowed down into the hallway like a flood, shoving her and Nathan to one side and surrounding Montgomery. Swirling arms and legs, seemingly disconnected from their bodies, crowded the hull. The scents of sweat and battle burned rancid in her nostrils. Loud shouting, clashing swords and hard thunks filled the air.

Montgomery fell.

"James!" she screamed as he was pushed to the floor and shackled.

He grunted as one of the men he had cut kicked him in the side. *L'occhio del diavolo* skittered across the floor planking toward her. "Get back, Brenna! Take the knife and use it if any of these dogs attacks you!"

"Cease!" she screamed at the men. Picking up the dagger, she tried to push her way past the soldiers to get to her husband. "You don't want him! It's me you want!"

None of the men even turned around. Their sweaty bodies formed a wall around James.

Tears stung her eyes as she realized that even though he believed she'd betrayed him, he had tossed her his weapon so that she could defend herself if she needed to. "Cease! I'm the painter!"

Nathan slid beside her, sheathing his own sword. "They are soldiers on a mission. They know naught about *The King's Mistresses* or the reasons he is being taken. They follow orders and that is all."

A feeling of helplessness flowed through Brenna. "Do something!" she screamed at her brother.

"The king wanted him alive," said one who appeared to be the commander. "Haul him to his feet and make haste to London."

"Nay! You can't take him. He's done naught wrong!" She grabbed the commander by the arm.

He gave Brenna a cursory glance and tugged down his tunic. "That is for the king to determine. Sorry for the disturbance, my lady. To the ship, men."

"Then take me with you!" she gasped. "Take me so I can explain to the king."

"No women on board my ship," the commander said, motioning the soldiers forward. The crew gave her little consideration as they made their way past her and headed up the stairs. The dim light of the ship's hull flickered across their faces and seaworn clothing.

Brenna gazed wildly at her brother. "Nathan, you must stop them!"

Nathan shrugged. "He wanted to feed me to the sharks."

Dragging Montgomery roughly behind them, two of the soldiers hauled him up the stairs. His legs bounced lifelessly against the steps making a loud thump with each step.

Brenna grasped the wall to hold herself upright as she tried to determine what she should do. Fighting the men physically would do her no good. She had to follow their ship and somehow convince the king of her husband's innocence in this matter.

Trembling, she climbed the stairs after the soldiers and watched with a fearful heart as they loaded James onto the British Naval ship. Nathan followed the men, his cape pulled close around his tall body. From the deck, her father glared at her, his expression smug.

She turned away.

"I'm sorry, miss," James's ship captain said when she approached. His bristly beard fluttered in the mild ocean breeze and he looked genuinely downtrodden. "There were too many of them."

She nodded numbly. "We have to rescue him."

"We don't have enough men for that, miss. We'll have to get his brother's fleet first." The captain scratched his head and looked out at the British Naval ship, which was already getting smaller as it headed away. "Don't even understand what this is about. Master James always had good relationships with the crown. He even acted as a privateer from time to time. They called him The Enforcer."

She blew out a breath, looking out over the waves lapping against the two ships. The sun cast red and orange shadows on the water. It would do her no good to confess her crime to the captain. "Just follow them to London and find me a courier to reach Brother Giffard; he's a traveling monk who spends a lot of time at court. I have to gain private audience with the king."

The captain gave her a little dip. "As wife to Master James, we are here at your command." Turning, he shrugged and made his way to the stern of the ship. "Ne'er did understand them blue bloods," he muttered.

Brenna gripped the rail with white knuckles, unsure she understood herself.

Chapter Twenty-Seven

Brenna's belly was round and full as she sank into a low curtsy before the man sitting in a heavily gilded throne upon the dais. The babe kicked inside her, pounding on her bladder and sending shooting pains down her back, but she remained in her bowed position. Several months had passed before Brother Giffard was able to set up an audience with King Edward. She had only one chance.

The king's private chambers sparkled with yards and yards of cloth of gold fabric and she could see fanciful designs woven into the carpet. 'Twas obvious that the room had been built to intimidate as well as impress—likely the king had many of these secret meetings. She wondered vaguely how many Giffard had set up as he had done for her.

The king seemed to leave her in the curtsy for a long time. Another intimidation tactic. There was no need; she was already intimidated nearly out of her mind. 'Twas a near repeat of the time when she was a girl and had been taken to be presented before the queen. That had been a disaster.

Her heart thrummed and her knees shook; the babe inside her seemed agitated too—beating so strongly with its fists that she had to resist all urges to clutch her stomach. She feared she would pee on the rug.

"Rise."

She did so, shakily, blinking at the man sitting before her and wishing her stomach would stop jumping so much. He was a tall, beautiful man with dark shoulder length hair and a relaxed mannerism. 'Twas obvious from his clothing he had more than a streak of vanity. No wonder he had been so angry at her paintings.

She shuddered. Life and death were in her next words. For herself. For her husband. For the baby she carried. The fact that he sat on a gilded throne in a private chamber spoke volumes. Her mouth felt dry as a desert.

"Brother Giffard said you wished to speak with us concerning your husband," the king said regally.

For a heart stopping moment, she decided her plan had been daft. She had been painting like a madwoman on the ship as they sailed to London. Hidden in folds of her skirt, an extremely flattering portrait of the king was tucked away—painted and repainted until it was flawless. At the time it had seemed the perfect appeasement gift for the royal pride.

Now . . .

She opened her mouth to speak, but only a squeak came out.

Not knowing what else to do, she took her small gift, wrapped in exquisite fabric, from the fold of her skirt, sank to her knees, lowered her head into a position of fealty and held her arms up to the king. She had one chance to save her husband; she prayed it would be enough.

"I am here to beg for my husband's life and plead for his forgiveness by the crown. This crime was my fault alone." Her voice shook.

The king drummed his fingers on his throne. He did not reach for her gift, causing another wave of trepidation to pass over her. A sharp pain shot through her womb and she stifled a gasp. "What do you know of your husband's crime?"

She did not dare look up. The royal character had already been bruised. "I know he is innocent."

"And do you know *what* he is innocent of?"

At that, she did look up, gazing into the handsome, proud face of the king. Her heart skipped as she realized she *had* gotten the painting correct.

Surely, surely he would forgive them all when she explained the other pictures had been painted when she was only a girl and too naive to know better. Vain men always were in need of an artist—she could pledge herself to his service as a painter and spend the remainder of her life making up for her mistake.

"I know he has been accused of painting a series of miniatures entitled *The King's Mistresses*—I am the artist."

The king looked taken aback. "You are a woman."

"So I have oft cursed," she said, more boldly now, determined to stay the course. A sharp pain shot through her womb and she stifled a gasp. "I beg of you to take my gift."

His velvet robe whisked into the air like a bird's wing as he swept his hand out, indicating the room. "If you think to bribe us with jewels, we have plenty."

"Nay, my liege. 'Tis something more personal. Something I made myself." Her heart pounded at the boldness of her words. What if the painting was not enough?

Feeling like a child who has made some special craft to appease an angry parent, she held her breath as the king reached forward. If he hated the portrait, she had no doubt it would mean beheading.

He unwrapped the gift with excruciating slowness. His fingers were encrusted with shimmering jewels that glittered with the movement of his hand. Another token of his vanity.

She sank her teeth into her lower lip as the last corner of fabric was pulled away.

He scrutinized the portrait, a frown furrowed on his brow. Silence permeated the room.

Doom fell on her heart. He hated it. Closing her eyes, she prayed for a quick death. "I—" she started, but it came out as a strangled choke. "I–I was only fourteen—"

"Fourteen?"

She licked her dry lips. "A reckless and stupid girl when I painted the others. I had no idea what a man looked like beneath his codpiece. I meant no harm, I swear it."

More silence. Too much silence. Would he send the guards in right away? Would she be tortured before she was killed? What about the baby? Her heart seemed to be somewhere around her throat and she could not seem to catch a full breath. Still, she pressed recklessly on. "I–I h–had hoped the n–new portrait would appease your w–wrath t–toward my husband. He was not the painter, was never the painter. He didn't even know about the paintings. 'Twas my fault alone."

Still silence. Zwounds. Her neck may have well been stretched over the chopping block. Unchecked shudders began to run through her limbs and her womb convulsed.

"Prithee, my liege," she whispered, shuffling from

one knee to the other. Heat stung the backs of her eyes. "I was but a girl. But even if there is no pardon for me, I beg of you to release my husband. He is an honorable man and has lived his life in your service. The man who accused him of painting such works is the one who is truly guilty of treason."

"And who might that be?"

She sucked in a deep breath. "My father."

"You expect us to believe that you would turn in your father to save the man you were forced to marry?" He stroked his chin. "We have heard that your husband kept you in bonds."

Swallowing, she stiffened her spine. "Yes, my liege. Our marriage did not start out so amicable, but he is an honorable man."

"Rise," the king said after another long pause.

Unsure what to make of this new development, Brenna wobbled to her feet, her knees knocking. Her fingers, always so steady to do her artwork, quivered.

The king tucked the miniature into his robe. "'Tis good work, my lady. The quality of your paintings is much improved."

Her breath whooshed from her lungs and Brenna nearly fell back to the floor in relief. He was accepting her painting.

"Your love for your husband saves you," he said. "And your skill as well. 'Twould be the court's loss for you not to be the artist in residence."

Her heart gave a little leap. "But my husband?"

"Will be restored."

This time she did sink to the floor again. "Thank you, sire. Oh, thank you."

He cleared his throat and held his hand out for her

to kiss his ring. "There will, of course, be fines associated with this pardon."

She nearly smiled at his cleverness in digging into their coffers. "Of course."

Reaching over his head, he pulled a bell cord and immediately the door opened and a servant stepped inside with a low bow.

"Tell the captain to bring Montgomery to my private chambers," the king said.

Closing her eyes, she crossed herself, grateful she would see her husband safe again.

"Inform them to bathe him first and give him a fresh set of garments. Fetch this woman's canvas and painting supplies. As the new court artist, she will be doing a rendition of the royal personhood here in the private quarters."

The servant gaped at her, made another low bow and scurried out. The glittering room seemed to close in around her. The babe kicked again, a sharp pain in her right side.

Her hands shook with nerves as she realized what was expected of her. The miniature had been done over several weeks time, painting and repainting until she'd gotten it perfect.

This portrait would have to be done right the first time. Her stomach cramped, doubling her over in pain. She clutched her rounded belly. Smaller pains of the same nature had been happening for days. Nerves from anticipating this meeting with the king.

"Lady Montgomery?" the king said.

She gave a shuddered wince as another cramp banded her middle and then a flood of fluid ran down her leg onto the royal carpets. "Bloody hell!"

The king's eyes widened. "Merciful heavens, woman," he muttered, pulling the bell cord again.

Heat flooded her cheeks and she wanted to sink like a worm into the ground. "Zwounds. The babe," she panted, clutching her belly. Why did every engagement with royalty end in disaster for her?

Servants rushed in. "Call for a midwife," he commanded, "and help this woman to a birthing chamber."

Maids crowded around her, hurrying her from the king's presence. Brenna bit back a scream as another pain shot up her belly. She began panting, trying to hold back the pain.

"Just hurry along, miss. Ol' Bertha's had lots of babies, no need to fear," said the plump maid holding onto her arm. "Even if the midwife don't make it, Ol' Bertha knows what to do."

Chapter Twenty-Eight

James seethed as he paced around the small bare room waiting endlessly for the royal summons. Manacles linked by chains surrounded his wrists and ankles. They made angry clanks as he walked back and forth. Back and forth.

He had been called from his prison cell, bathed, and clothed hours ago. But here he was, still waiting, wondering what this conference would bring—he must make Edward, that royal coxcomb, understand his innocence.

The church bells rang, marking another section of the day gone. Wasted. Waiting. Still waiting. Not even a chair to sit on. The room felt as though its very walls closed in on him. The bonds chafed his limbs. He fought the urge to pound a hole into the nearby wall to release his frustration at the unfairness of his treatment. He was innocent, by God!

With a deep breath, he ran a hand over the back of his neck and massaged his tight shoulder. His bloody betraying wife had gotten to him. He wanted to kick himself for not watching the horizon more carefully

for approaching ships. She'd smuggled her brother
on board! The little wench.

A startling pain pierced his heart at the thought—
love, he realized. How could he both love and hate a
woman so much? She was very, very bad for him. As
bad as the wine had been all those years ago.

Counting his steps, he paced across the room again.
The chains weighted down his legs, hobbling his
stride and he felt defenseless and frustrated and a
little scared about what his fate would be. Is that how
Brenna had felt for all those weeks when he'd left her
bound? Regret surged inside him. Her running away
had been his own fault—there were other ways he
could have assured she would not leave besides keeping her chained night and day. He should have built
a relationship with her, tried to get to know her. Perhaps then, she would not have betrayed him and left.

Had she had their baby yet? It had been months
since he last saw her on the ship.

A door opened, interrupting his thoughts.

A plump woman wearing a starched muffin cap and
a wrinkled apron stepped inside. She carried a wad of
silks. "Your son, my lord," she said, handing him the
bundle.

"My . . . son?" Confused, he took the package, its
weight nearly nothing in his arms. The chains clanked.

The most beautiful being he had ever seen stared
up at him with crisscrossed eyes. The baby had a red,
wrinkly face with a scattering of dusky curls on its scalp.

His heart lurched. They had brought him from the
prison to give him a child? Was this another of Edward's
mind tricks to break him? Did they mean to take him
back to his cell with a babe and no way to feed it?
Horror shuddered through him as he imagined having

to watch the infant cry and starve as he tried witlessly to comfort it. The chains felt more oppressive than even before, and he arranged the silks so that the babe's skin would be protected from the iron.

"What means this?" he demanded.

"'Tis your babe. Follow me." Motioning him, the woman turned and walked down the hall. She did not even give a cursory glance at his bonds. Was it a common occurrence to nobles to be bound thus in the palace?

Clutching the child to his chest, he frowned after her. Was this really his? Carefully, he began unwrapping the swaddling, wanting to see its body, to determine if by some birthmark or mole that it was indeed his son.

The woman turned and walked back to him. "Stop that, my lord. This way," she demanded, indicating for him to follow.

A fierce wave of protection swam through him along with the urge to run. He would take the babe and sail to the ends of the earth to protect it. One child of his had died already. This one would live.

He eyed the maid suspiciously. "What trickery is this?"

Placing a hand on her ample hip, she tilted her head to one side. "No trickery, my lord. Your wife awaits."

"My wife?"

"Aye, she just birthed the lad." The maid looked at him like he'd lost his mind. He was not uncertain that he had not.

"Why is she in London?"

The maid muttered something under her breath that sounded like a curse against the nobility. "Come along now," she demanded.

Shoulders hunched with uncertainty, James followed

her. He carefully scanned the ornate hallways for exits and escape routes as they walked. The chains hobbled his process.

A short while later, they entered a bright bedchamber with rich tapestries on the walls and a mountain of sopping wet linens in the midst of an Oriental carpet: a palace bedroom turned birthing chamber. Steam roiled from a large pot in the hearth.

Brenna lay on the bed, seemingly asleep. Her ringlets clouded around her head in a mist of out-of-control frizz.

Out-of-control.

Exactly the way he felt whenever he was around her. Why was she here in London? To betray him again?

He clutched the babe tightly, looking around at the windows to determine if he could make it from the king's palace before being caught by the guards. Not bloody likely considering the bonds.

One of the servants shook Brenna. "My lady, your husband has arrived."

She stirred, opening one eye slowly. "James. Oh, merciful heavens. Thank God Almighty."

She looked small and weak amongst the bedcovers, and he was reminded of how she had been that day he had returned from hunting her father. Would she rise and rail at him as she had then?

"What are you doing here?" he demanded, holding fiercely to his newborn son as he tried to put together all the pieces and understand what was going on.

"We can explain that, Lord Montgomery." King Edward flurried into the room, his enormous royal robe fluttering around him.

Fury coursed through James at the sight of the man who had thrown him into a dungeon without so much as a hearing, but he sank to one knee. Mayhap if he did not have the babe, he could afford to clutch his anger, but his position here was too precarious and he had a life asides his own to think of.

Godric and Meiriona followed the king into the chamber. On her hip, his sister-in-law carried a small child with large blue eyes and fluffy red hair. What a sight she made—while other noblewomen left their children with nannies all the daylong whilst at court, Meiriona would have none of that. She looked a little frazzled, but happy.

Edward extended his hand for James to kiss his royal ring.

"My liege," James said, warily. Was Brenna now in cohorts with the king to see him humiliated? Shifting the babe into one arm, he kissed the king's ring.

"Let me see my nephew!" Godric boomed, heedless as always of social convention. His wild presence seemed out of place in the palace.

James spared a glance at Edward, who gave him a little nod to indicate he had leave to rise. He stood.

Pride swelled in his heart as he pulled back a corner of the swaddling cloth to show off his son to his brother. A lump formed in his throat as Godric reached his scarred hand to gently graze the babe's cheek. The boy opened his eyes and looked cross-eyedly up at them.

"Be ye gentle," the maid admonished, eyeing the two large men suspiciously. Her gaze lingered over Godric's whitened scars and James's new red one.

"Aye, be gentle with my nephew," Godric mocked James. "I don't want him all scarred up and ugly like you."

James glanced from his brother to his wife. All three of them sported scars on their faces now, proof of the perilous events they had lived through. Sunlight shimmered through the windows, showing dust motes dancing through the air.

"Well, I just think ye should be careful," the maid interjected, hovering nearby. "We didn't borne the babe to have a clumsy oaf drop him."

"Oh, for heaven's sake"—Meiriona paced forward, bouncing the red-haired fairy child on her hip— "we've got three at home. I think my husband and brother-in-law know how to hold a baby."

The maid backed away from the men, muttering as she gathered the pile of rags and went out the door.

The king cleared his throat. "Your lady wife has explained much."

"My . . . wife?" Baffled, James gazed from the king to Brenna and back again.

"She turned herself in to rescue your sorry hide," Godric interjected. "Not that you deserve it after leaving her locked in chains for weeks on end."

"We believe in your honor and will have your pledge for fealty and see you restored to your lands," proclaimed Edward. "And you may have your wife back also, provided there are some amends made."

Humph. Edward was shrewd as always. James could practically feel his coffers being lightened. He forced himself to smile tightly instead of raging about the poor treatment he'd been given. Raging at the king was *not* the way to regain his lands or his honor. "I thank you for your generosity, my liege."

"That is, of course, if you choose to redeem her," the king continued.

James let out a breath. At last the flow of power turn back in his direction. At last he would be able to see her get her comeuppance!

"But she did just birth you a son and come to London to proclaim your innocence, so mayhap you might feel inclined to be lenient to her as we have been," the king continued.

Suddenly James understood why he'd been given the babe before being called into the same room with Brenna. Edward, that wily devil, was protecting the guilty. The king knew James was not guilty and was giving him a choice on what to do with Brenna—to take her back or to let her rot in debtor's prison.

Edward waved his hand in a magnanimous gesture. "There is also the matter of your bonds." He reached inside his royal robe and withdrew a key. "Lady Brenna, we entrust you with this." He handed her the key. "Now come, Lord Godric, Lady Meiriona, let us leave these two to work out their own bargains."

Godric clapped James on the shoulder. "You need to speak with your wife. Let me take the babe for a bit. You'll have years and years with him."

James glanced at Brenna who was sitting up in bed and transferred his son to Godric's arms. He was not at all sure what he should do with her, if he should pay her fine or no. If he did not leave her in debtor's prison, mayhap he should send her back to a nunnery.

His brother smiled, crinkles forming around his blue eyes. "Aye, boy," Godric crooned, gently stroking the baby across its tiny hand, "come with me and I'll tell you all about how hideously silly your father is."

Meiriona shifted the child she carried to punch him on the arm. "Cease."

Godric gave her a lopsided grin as they crossed the Oriental carpet. He shifted the babe to one arm and ducked beneath the doorframe, following the king and his wife into the hall.

When everyone had left, James and Brenna stared at each other for a moment, an awkward silence filling the chamber. How odd to be standing here in chains before her while her fate lay in his hands. Another of Edward's mind games.

Her gaze was bright and clear as she looked at him, and he felt himself being sucked into her emerald eyes. Treacherous territory. "I love you," she whispered.

Foolishly, he wanted to believe her, but there was too much bad blood between them for him to fall for silly love words. "I would like to believe you—"

"Then believe me, James! You must!" Brenna took a breath, plucked a metal object sitting on the table beside the bed and proffered it to him flat in her palm.

L'occhio del diavolo.

"I brought this for you," she said softly.

He stared at the blade, at the memories of passion it possessed—the stabbing, the shaving, the ripping off of her clothing and holding it to her throat when he'd recaptured her. So many things had happened between them.

His fingers grazed hers when he took the blade, sending a fission of heat running through his veins. "Why are you giving this to me?"

"I know as presents go, it is not much of one, but—" Swallowing, she slid her chemise down her shoulders and leaned her head back exposing her throat. It was a simple act of complete surrender. She had stabbed him; he had been tortured and thrown into the king's dungeon because of her artwork. But they had also shared times of consuming passion and laughter and a deep connection. Clear and simple, she was offering herself to him, no holds barred. He could keep her or kill her, his choice. Kill her and take the key to his manacles or keep her and take the key to her heart.

Mistrust and suspicion ran high, but the symbolic act touched a cord deep inside his heart, meaning more to him than all her apologies had. It blasted through his defenses the same way that she had done when she'd fallen asleep in his arms while she was captive and gagged. He had an answer for her anger, but none for her trust.

Sweeping back the bed curtains, he sank down beside her on the mattress.

With a slow, deliberate motion, he traced the flat edge of *l'occhio del diavolo* down the curve of her neck. He could demand that she give him the key to the manacles.

Clearly trusting him, she did not flinch or even blink as the dagger approached the tender skin of her throat. He tucked it into her bodice, nestling the blade betwixt her breasts as it had been on that fateful day when they had married.

He would not force the key from her hand. If she wanted him as husband, she must unlock him willingly.

She smiled at him, telling him without words that she understood the gesture—that despite the unresolved matters, he trusted her too. Their relationship had come full circle. Her green gaze reminded him of wet emeralds. He hugged her, wanting to hold her forever and never let go.

The bed curtains swung around them. "Brenna, I do not understand how you were able to convince the king to remove me from prison."

Blinking, she traced her hand across the edge of the sheet. "I appealed to his vanity and repainted his portrait."

"You brought a portrait to Edward?"

"Yea. To replace the others."

A streak of jealousy went through him at the thought. "Was the king naked in these pictures?"

She laughed. "Well. Somewhat naked. He was wearing the royal robe. But I corrected the proportions of his manhood to make him the envy of the court rather than the laughingstock."

James frowned, not liking the direction of this conversation at all. He stared at the hilt of *l'occhio del diavolo,* lusciously nestled between her breasts, and vowed silently to kill any man who was alone and naked with his wife. Even the king. "You will not be painting other men's members."

She sat up, arranging the pillows beneath her to a more comfortable position. "Already trying to dictate my artwork, I see."

"Brenna—" he warned.

Taking his face between both of her hands, she kissed him. "I did *not* paint the king's member on the king."

"Nay?"

"Nay."

"You did not see the crowning glory? Then how—"

"I painted yours."

James gave a bark of laughter that caused the bedropes to creak. The king's head and his, er, other head.

"It seemed a suitable punishment for the weeks His Royal Vainness kept you locked in a dungeon."

Her wicked sense of humor pleased him. In fact, much about this woman pleased him. Her humor. Her scent. Her passion. Her willingness to trust him enough to come to London for him.

"My lord, I was terrified to think what might happen

to you. This is all my fault. I should never have left with my brother."

"Nay, you should not have," he agreed. "You are mine."

She eyed the spider web of chains coyly. "The way I see it, *you* are *mine*. All mine."

James took a deep breath. "Brenna, we must discuss this. I had thought when I married that my wife would stay at Montgomery Castle and I would scarcely see her—that it would be an amicable life for two strangers who were not in love but forced to be together. I was selfish in the past to make a wife go with me.

"But I do not want to leave you at Montgomery Castle. My business takes me on long voyages. I have been cooped up too long and had too much of this life on land. I want to feel the sting of salt spray and taste the sea brine. I want to show our son the waves and water and many lands of this world." He ran a finger down her collarbone. "If you do not wish to go with me, 'tis best you call the king's guards, clutch the key firmly and leave me chained, because, so help me, wife, if you are anywhere I can get to you, I will re-capture you and take you with me. You were all I could think of for the months we've been apart."

Her eyes shimmered. "I want to go with you. My art-work suffered terribly and I could scarcely paint any-thing worthwhile when I was existing in that dull and listless life in the abbey."

"So, that's the true reason you came for me—because our passion inspires you and so you could paint better?"

"Of course no—" she started sharply, then stopped, apparently realizing that he was teasing her. "I love you, my lord. I believe we can create a life together. One better than each of us ever had alone. After experiencing the beauty of the sea, even Italy is too small for me. I have proven I can paint, and paint well, on a ship."

Her words thrilled him. He spread gentle kisses across her cheek, reveling in the way she shivered at his touch. "You will follow me?"

"Yea, my lord, gladly. When I met you, I was locked in my chamber and you set me free."

He hugged her, enjoying the unique gesso and tempera scent of her skin. A comfortable silence filled the chamber for a moment as they held each other.

"I have much to tell you about my past," she whispered. "I have discovered confusing and horrid things about my childhood and about my family."

"We will work it out together. We have a lifetime to talk through unresolved matters. There is naught in your past that means anything to me—only the future."

When she still made no motion to use the key, he raised his hand, letting the chain dangle down between them. "Unlock me, wife, 'tis time to begin this future together."

"Not so hasty, my lord," she said, her voice taking on a coy tone. "A bargain first."

"I will pay your fines, if that is what concerns you."

"Nay, the bargain I am thinking of does not involve the king at all."

He grinned at her, understanding her game. Their relationship had always been a series of bargains. Some of them most . . . pleasurable. "And what is it that my lady wants?"

"Hmmm," she said. "Mayhap I will have to think on this."

He nuzzled her neck. "Do not think too long or, despite

my resolve to give you a choice, I will ravish you and take the key without your consent."

She laughed and kissed him, running her fingers through his hair. "That sounds very interesting, my lord."

"I love you, Brenna. You will always be my captive wife."

Love shone brightly in her eyes. "And you will not set me free?"

"Never."

About the Author

Award-winning author Jessica Trapp believes a dynamic romance is one where two opposing characters are transformed into two people who share love and passion. Despite reading gobs of romance and science fiction instead of studying for biochemistry exams, she is a registered pharmacist. She now lives in Houston, Texas, with a husband, a son, two parents, one dog, several goldfish, and a lot of chaos. Most of the family is as passionate about books as she is. When she's not reading or writing, she dances, putters in the garden, plays chess, drinks copious amounts of hot tea, and dreams about running away from home so she can live in her van as a beach bum and work on her diabolical plan to be elected evil queen of the galaxy. For excerpts of her novels, contests and more, please visit her at *www.jessicatrapp.com*.